To my son, Merlin

Old God's Time

'Few can write like Sebastian Barry, there is a real thrill as each sentence unfolds. *Old God's Time* is a portrait of a good man facing the failings of his past. It is wonderfully alive because Barry is so attuned to the human condition, to the poetry in ordinary lives. Full of love and grief and heartache, this is an unforgettable novel from one of our finest writers.' **Douglas Stuart**

'The cocoon of language with which [Barry] creates Tom's world has a magical effect, gathering the reader up willingly and, if not exactly softening the blow of the terrible things that Tom has witnessed, then at least giving them richness and depth. That's the thing about Barry at his best – he makes you believe.' *Irish Times*

'A profound, important book . . . gorgeously crafted: rich, serpentine, deceptive, original, expansive, moving . . . Dark novels sometimes burn brightest; *Old God's Time*, harrowing and spectacular, burns brighter than most.' **Kevin Power**, *Irish Independent*

'This book still stays with me. I think about it now and it affects me. It's a beautiful, important book.' **Laura Whitmore**, BBC Two 'Between the Covers'

'There is a kind of writing so rare and accomplished that it seems to erase the very nuts and bolts of its own construction. Reading it can produce an experience that feels close to miraculous . . . I don't expect to read anything as moving for many years.' **Melissa Harrison**, *Guardian*

'A tribute to enduring love and its ability to light up the dark.' *Observer*

'Barry turns human frailty into an art form . . . The story weaves, with supreme artistry, back and forth over Tom's life . . . a masterpiece.' *Sunday Independent*

'Remarkable . . . Nobody can sing of pain and grief with such power, such glory even, as Sebastian Barry.' *The Herald*

'Masterful . . . a bravura performance.' *Sunday Business Post*

'Combining verbal exuberance and narrative intricacy, Barry reimagines the hauntings of Irish history.' *New Yorker*

'What distinguishes Barry's work is his exquisite use of language . . . Grief is threaded through this story but alongside it is stitched great strength and endurance. As Tom's story reaches a conclusion and the horrors recede like the lights of the pier behind him, it is the love at the heart of the novel that remains.' *RTE Guide*

'A book of aching and sorrow written with an ear to the poetry of common words from the master of the form. I didn't want it to end, I very much wanted it to end. I was worried and exhilarated in equal measure. I loved it.' **Kit De Waal**

'Beautifully wrought.' *Daily Mirror*

'Enthralling . . . best of all are the passages when Tom indulges old memories of love, deeply felt and so perfectly evoked they elicited involuntary audible sighs from this reviewer. This is fine, fine writing, with a heart as big as the Ritz.' *Big Issue*

'Barry is a master stylist and his prose is a constant delight . . . *Old God's Time* is above all a testament to love's healing potential.' *New Books Magazine*

'So captivating . . . it will live long in the minds of its readers.' *Independent*

'You should be reading Sebastian Barry. [He] has a special understanding of the human heart.' *The Atlantic*

by the same author

fiction
The Whereabouts of Eneas McNulty
Annie Dunne
A Long Long Way
The Secret Scripture
On Canaan's Side
The Temporary Gentleman
Days Without End
A Thousand Moons

plays
Boss Grady's Boys
Prayers of Sherkin
White Woman Street
The Only True History of Lizzie Finn
The Steward of Christendom
Our Lady of Sligo
Hinterland
Fred and Jane
Whistling Psyche
The Pride of Parnell Street
Dallas Sweetman
Tales of Ballycumber
Andersen's English
On Blueberry Hill

poetry
The Water-Colourist
Fanny Hawke Goes to the Mainland Forever
The Pinkening Boy

essays
The Lives of the Saints

Old God's Time

SEBASTIAN BARRY

faber

First published in 2023
by Faber & Faber Limited
The Bindery, 51 Hatton Garden
London EC1N 8HN

Typeset by Faber & Faber Limited
Printed in England by CPI Group (UK) Ltd, Croydon, CR0 4YY

This paperback edition published in 2024

All rights reserved
© Sebastian Barry, 2023

The right of Sebastian Barry to be identified as author
of this work has been asserted in accordance with Section 77
of the Copyright, Designs and Patents Act 1988

*This is a work of fiction. All of the characters, organisations,
and events portrayed in this novel are either products of the
author's imagination or are used fictitiously.*

*This book is sold subject to the condition that it shall not, by way of trade or
otherwise, be lent, resold, hired out or otherwise circulated without the publisher's prior consent in any form of binding or cover other than that in which
it is published and without a similar condition including this condition being
imposed on the subsequent purchaser*

A CIP record for this book
is available from the British Library

ISBN 978–0–571–33279–3

Printed and bound in the UK on FSC® certified paper in line with our continuing
commitment to ethical business practices, sustainability and the environment.
For further information see faber.co.uk/environmental-policy

Will the unicorn be willing to serve thee?
Book of Job

Chapter One

Sometime in the sixties old Mr Tomelty had put up an incongruous lean-to addition to his Victorian castle. It was a granny flat of modest size but with some nice touches befitting a putative relative. The carpentry at least was excellent and one wall was encased in something called 'beauty board', its veneer capturing light and mutating it into soft brown darknesses.

This premises, with its little echoing bedroom, its tiny entrance hall, a few hundred books still in their boxes and his two old gun cases from his army days, was where Tom Kettle had in his own words 'washed up'. The books remembering, if sometimes these days he did not, his old interests. The history of Palestine, of Malaya, old Irish legends, discarded gods, a dozen random matters that at one time or another he had stuck his inquisitive nose into. The stirring sound of the sea below the picture window had been the initial allure but everything about the place pleased him – the mock-Gothic architecture, including the pointless castellation on the roofline, the square of hedges in the garden that provided a windbreak and a suntrap, the broken granite jetties on the shoreline, the island skulking in the near distance, even the crumbling sewerage pipes sticking out into the water. The placid tidal pools reminded him of the easily fascinated child he once had been, sixty years ago, the distant calling of today's children playing in their invisible gardens giving a sort of vaguely tormenting counterpoint. Vague torment was his forte, he thought. The sheeting rain, the sheeting sunlight, the poor heroes of fishermen trying to bring their rowing boats back against the ferocious current into the little cut-stone harbour, as neat and nice as anything in New Ross where he had worked as a very young policeman – it all seemed delightful to him. Even now in winter when winter was only interested in its own unfriendly harshness.

He loved to sit in his sun-faded wicker chair in the dead centre of his living room, feet pointed towards the affecting murmurs of the sea, smoking his cigarillos. Watching the cormorants on the flourish of black rocks to the left of the island. His neighbour in the cottage next door had set up a gun-rest on his balcony and sometimes in the evenings would shoot at the cormorants and the seagulls as they stood there on the rocks innocently, thinking themselves far from human concerns. A few falling like fairground ducks. As peaceably, as quietly, as you can do such a thing. He had not been to the island but in the summer he had witnessed the parties of people going out to it in the rowing boats. The boatmen leaning into the oars, the current ravishing the keels. He had not been, he did not wish to go, he was quite content just to gaze out. Just to do that. To him this was the whole point of retirement, of existence – to be stationary, happy and useless.

That untroubled February afternoon a knocking on the door disturbed him in his nest. In all the nine months he had lived there, not a soul had bothered him aside from the postman, and on one peculiar occasion Mr Tomelty himself, in his gardener's weeds, asking for a cup of sugar, which Tom had not been able to provide. He never took sugar because he had a touch of diabetes. Otherwise, he had had his kingdom and his thoughts to himself. Although why did he say that, when his daughter had been out to see him a dozen times? But Winnie could never be said to disturb him, and anyway it was his duty to entertain her. His son never came, not so far, not because he didn't wish to, but because he lived and worked in New Mexico, out near the Arizona border. He was a locum on one of the pueblos.

Mr Tomelty had portioned out his property into segments: Tom's place, and the Drawing Room Flat, and indeed the Turret Flat, currently – suddenly – occupied by a young mother and her child, who had arrived in the dark midwinter before Christmas, in a rare snowfall. No doubt Mr Tomelty was an efficient landlord. He was certainly wealthy, owning this property, Queenstown Castle, and also an imposing hotel on the seafront in Dunleary, called The Tomelty Arms, an aristocratic sort of name. But his usual guise, at least in Tom's experience, was that of an age-bent gardener, passing along the path under the picture window with a creaking wheelbarrow, like a figure in a fairy tale. All summer and autumn old Mr Tomelty had looked for weeds and found them and ferried them off to his swelling dunghill. Only winter had interrupted his task.

The knocking came mercilessly again. Now, for good measure, the doorbell. Then again. Tom pulled his bulky, solid form up from the chair, promptly enough, as if answering some instinct of duty – or perhaps merely humanity. But it was also an obscure bother to him. Yes, he had grown to love this interesting inactivity and privacy – perhaps too much, he thought, and duty still lurked in him. The shaky imperative of forty years in the police, despite everything.

Through the glass door he could see the outlines of two men, possibly in dark suits – but it was hard to tell as the big rhododendron behind them lent them an inky halo, and the daylight was losing its grip on things anyway. These were the few weeks of the rhododendron's heartfelt blooming, despite the wind and the cold and the rain. Tom recognised the shifting-about that the figures were engaged in, even through the frosted glass. People not sure of their welcome. Mormons maybe.

His front door didn't sit well on its hinges and the lower edge scraped dramatically. There was a regrettable fan-shaped mark on the tiles. He opened it, it released its tiny screech, and to his surprise two young detectives from his old division stood there. He was puzzled, and a little alarmed, but he knew them immediately. Not quite by name, but nearly. How could he not? They were kitted out in that unmistakable civilian mufti that clearly announced they were not civilians. They had the poorly shaven faces of men who rose early and there was an air about them that whether he liked it or not drew him right back to his own early days policing, the unlikely innocence of it.

'How are you doing, Mr Kettle?' said the one on the right, a nice big lump of a young man with a brushstroke for a moustache, a touch Hitlerian if the truth were known. 'I hope you won't mind us coming out – disturbing you?'

'I don't mind, I don't mind, you're not, you're not,' said

Tom, doing his best to conceal the lie. 'You're welcome. Is everything alright?' Many times he had brought unwelcome news himself to people in their houses – to people in their private minds, in their dreamlike privacy, to which he had added only troubles, inevitably. The hopeful, worried faces, the gobsmacked listening, sometimes the terrible crying. 'Are you coming in?'

They were. Inside the door they said their names – the wide man was Wilson and the other was O'Casey – which right enough he seemed to half-remember, and they exchanged pleasantries about the awful weather and how snug his quarters were – 'very cosy,' Wilson said – and then he set about making them tea in his galley kitchen. Indeed it might as well have been on a boat. He asked Wilson to turn on the overhead light and after gazing about a few moments Wilson located the switch and obeyed. The meagre bulb was only forty watts, he must do something about that. He was going to apologise for the books still being in boxes but he said nothing. Then the two young fellas sat themselves down on invitation and they fired the professional bonhomies back and forth through the bead curtains with the happy ease of men in a dangerous profession. Policing always had its salt of danger, like the sea itself. They were fairly at ease with him, but also respectful, as befitted his former rank, and maybe also the loss of it.

Even as they talked Tom felt obliged to whatever gods ruled that fake castle to gaze out occasionally on the copper-dark sea just now getting scrubbed over bit by bit by worse darkness. It was four in the afternoon and night was creeping in to take everything away till only the weak lights of the lamps on Coliemore Harbour would bounce themselves a few yards out onto the water, speckling the darkling waves. The Muglins beacon beyond the island would soon spark to life and even further out, deeper than he knew, away off on the horizon, the Kish Lighthouse herself would begin to show her heavy light, laboriously sweeping the heaving deeps. He thought of the fish in there, lurking about like corner boys. Were there porpoises this time of year? Conger eels coiling in the darkness. Pollock with their leaden bodies and indifference to being caught, like failed criminals.

Soon the pot and the three cups were set on an old Indian side table that Tom had won in a long-ago golf tournament. The really good players, Jimmy Benson and what was that fella's name, McCutcheon, had been off sick from the flu that was going around at that time, so his meagre talents had carried the day. He always smiled when he thought of that but he didn't smile just now. The nickel tray improved to silver in the light.

He was mildly troubled that he had no sugar to offer them.

He turned the wicker chair about so he could face them and, summoning again his old friendly self which he wasn't sure he still possessed, he lowered himself onto the creaking reeds and smiled broadly. He felt a little lock in his smile before it reached the full width of older days. Full welcome, full enthusiasm, full energy, seemed risky to him somehow.

'We got the heads-up from the chief that you might be able to help us with something,' said the second man,

O'Casey, as if just for contrast a long thin person, with that severe leanness that probably made all his clothes look too big on him, to the despair of his wife, if he had one. Tom at this point was just letting the tea steep in the pot a few moments and his head was moving from side to side. When his friend Inspector Butt had come from Bombay in the seventies to try to probe the strangenesses of Irish policing – no guns, Ramesh could not get over that – he had witnessed that enchanting head movement, and mysteriously adopted it. It went with the table.

'Well, sure,' he said, 'I'm always here to help, I told Fleming that.' Indeed he had, regrettably, told Detective Superintendent Fleming that, as he went out the door on the last day in Harcourt Street, with a burning headache after the send-off the night before – not from drinking, because he was a teetotaller, but from only reaching his bed in the small hours. Tom's wife June's 'mother', the dreadful Mrs Carr, had scandalised them both when they were a young couple with kids by insisting those selfsame kids, Joe and Winnie, were in bed by six, until they were all of ten years old. Mrs Carr was a termagant but she had been right about that. Sleep was the mother of health.

'It's something that's come up and he thought, the chief thought, it might be useful to hear your thoughts on it,' said the detective, 'and, you know.'

'Oh yes?' said Tom, not uninterested, but all the same with a strange surge of reluctance and even dread – deep, deep down. 'Do you know, lads, the truth is I have no thoughts – I'm trying to have none, anyhow.'

They both laughed.

'We get that,' said O'Casey. 'The chief said you might say something like that.'

'How is the chief?' said Tom, striking out for a neutral line of talk.

'Jaysus, in the pink. You can't kill him.'

'No.'

This was possibly a reference to the brush with double pneumonia the chief had endured after being trussed up all night in a Wicklow field by two hoodlums. They had found the poor man more dead than alive. Which just about described the same hoodlums when they were finished with them at the station, God forgive them.

Now he poured the tea and delicately offered them the cups, his large hands determined not to spill any. He fancied Wilson was looking for his sugar lumps but it was not to be, it was not to be.

'You've come out a long way, a long journey, yes, I do understand. But,' he said. He was going to add something, but found no words in his mouth. It was time they left him alone, is what he wanted to say. Retired men could be let go safely – let the new ones put their minds to the work. All his working life he had dealt with villains. After a few decades of that your faith in human nature is in the ground. It's a premature burial, pre-dating your own. But he wanted to be a believer again, in something. He wanted to live in his wealth of minutes, the ones he had left anyhow. He wanted a blessed, a quiet time. He wanted—

Outside the window a gull dropped the full height of the frame, a sudden white thing in the corner of his eye, free-falling so abruptly it made him jump. Of course at this time of year the sea wind usually rose up after sundown and lashed away at the walls of the house, catching even gulls off guard. It was so bizarrely white, lit only by the light in the room, so out of control, like a suicide or an executed thing, that it threw him for a moment. But neither Wilson nor O'Casey seemed to have seen it, though they were square-on more or less to the window. All they saw was Tom looking startled. Tom could see Wilson instinctively recalibrating, deciding to change tack. Not come at this head-on like a mad little bull. That was his training in the old depot at the Phoenix Park kicking in. Don't spook the witness. But Tom wasn't a witness, was he?

Wilson leaned back into his chair and sipped three times from his cup. Tom thought he probably didn't like the tea. Not stewed long enough for a copper. Not cold or dead enough. Nor sweet enough.

'Do you know,' Wilson said, 'you're very cosy out here.'

'Aye,' said Tom, still with a trace of the fright in his voice. 'You said.'

Wilson seemed to make a bid for intimacy. Have a shot at it. Probably thinks I've gone gaga, Tom thought. Little to do except peel the plastic off cheese singles. O'Casey drank his tea down in one swift gulp, like a cowboy drinking whiskey.

'Do you know,' said Wilson, 'when my mother died – we were only smallies, my sister and me – my da wanted to move out here. Houses were cheap in the village, but there was no hospital nearby. The nearest thing was Loughlinstown, and my da, you know, he was a night nurse, so . . .'

'Janey,' said O'Casey, with the sincerity only allowable in a friend, 'sorry to hear about your ma.'

'No, no, it's alright,' Wilson said, expansively, generously. 'I was eleven. My sister, she was only five. It was shit for her.'

Whatever Wilson had hoped to achieve by these intimacies was somewhat stymied by the melancholy that dropped down across his features, as if, despite his resilience at eleven, he was now feeling the sorrow of it, maybe even for the first time. None of the three spoke. There was something much more pitch about the black of the window. Tom thought of tar melting in tar barrels, roadmenders. The lovely acrid stink of it. He would have drawn the curtains, he thought, if he had had curtains. It was what people did in films. He got up and went over to his little table and turned on the lamp there instead. It was a small brown job with a button on the weighted bottom for switching on and off. He had carried that lamp through half a dozen houses. When Joe was a mere baby and finding sleep hard to reach, Tom used to lie on the spare bed with the baby on his chest, and Joe loved to press that very button, over and over, on and off, because he liked the click. Tom used to unplug it in preparation, he didn't want a disco. It was nice to have the long, warm baby – he was very long even at a year – on top of him, the two of them getting drowsier and drowsier. Sometimes June had to come in and wake him, and lay Joe back in the cot. It seemed like a long time ago, but even now the fluid click gave him pleasure. Ridiculous. He loved his few possessions, he did. He more or less laughed, not a full laugh, a sort of dampened chuckle, because even as he was amused at himself he thought of what Wilson had said. Wilson had left his dead mother floating there in the room, and the old difficulties felt by his sister. He wondered what the sister looked like. It was another stupid thought. He was sixty-six. He wasn't looking to get hitched. Hadn't he married a lovely girl. No one could take that from her. She was dark like Judy Garland. That was all done. But policemen, working long hours and routinely dazed after six o'clock, good only for a few male pints in the evening, used to keep a lookout for the pretty sisters of their colleagues, just on the mad chance. As if privy to Tom's thoughts, Wilson said:

'My mother was a great beauty.' He said this with an even voice, no longer inflected by sorrow. He had recovered quickly.

'You didn't move house, then?' said O'Casey.

'No, no, we stayed in Monkstown, so we did. We stayed in Monkstown.'

Wilson didn't expand on whether this was a wise or a foolish decision. Tom nearly asked him if his father was still alive, but stopped himself. Why did he want to know that? He didn't. He supposed the sister must be married by now. He hoped she was alright. For heaven's sake, why? He knew nothing about her. Her mother had been beautiful, and died. He supposed the sister too might be a beauty. Chances were. He seemed to see the mother in his mind's eye, in a light summer dress, tanned, but insubstantial, like a ghost. Well, she was a ghost now. He hawked up some phlegm that abruptly wanted to choke him, as if punishing him for his wretched thoughts. He laughed, and they laughed. Then nothing again for a bit. Tom didn't know what to do. Should he offer to cook them some tea? Welsh rabbit, gents? No, hardly. Or should he? There might be a few rashers at the back of the fridge. He had a chicken hash from Tuesday, he was 99 per cent sure.

Maybe they would tell him now why they had come. It could be a thousand things. A long list of iniquities. He went back to his chair, and automatically lifted his cup to his lips, and found the tea was cold. Ah yes. He nodded at Wilson, as if cogitating the information that had been released to them. He was cogitating it. To lose your mother. It kills you, and then you have to live on. Wilson's face was beaming, as if on the cusp of wisdom, of further comment that would elucidate everything and free his listeners. Tom peered at him with that erased look he had learned, so that the person observed was barely aware of being watched so closely. As a working detective, he had always kept an ear out for the chance remark. During a long interrogation, when the suspect would be tired and maybe starting to feel defeated, to feel the little fists of his guilt pummelling at his head or heart as may be, there might be sudden remarks made, or casual remarks, or seeming non sequiturs, that could be bizarrely useful, all told. Little portals, trapdoors even, to the gradually more attractive exit of a confession. Attractive to the criminal. Even though a confession would only be the start of his troubles. Oh yes. You wanted to get the conviction so badly it hurt you, like a series of little heart attacks.

But Wilson kept his silence. He burned with it, like a modest candle.

'Sure Monkstown's just as nice,' said O'Casey.

'My wife's mother died young too,' said Tom, reflectively. 'As, as, did my own – I think.' He was embarrassed suddenly, because in truth he had no idea, he just suspected, or even hoped, in a way. 'Yes, yes, it's so hard.'

'Ah, Jaysus, yes,' said Wilson. 'Anyway, Mr Kettle—'

'Tom,' said Tom.

The three dead mothers, possibly only two, floated around for a few moments between them.

'Tom. Look it, I have the reports in my pocket,' he said, and shoved his right hand into his coat and retrieved a long envelope, which was surprisingly grubby, considering it was an official document. He stared at the dirty brown paper a while, as if pausing to talk only to himself. Tom saw the lips moving, like a person in church mouthing the responses. Wilson shifted on his hard chair, as if readying himself for the assault, gathering himself, and for the moment failing. O'Casey, skinny, sedate, with his left leg more or less thrown out from his body, the shoe twisted at what seemed a painful angle, looked very self-conscious, as if suffering now on behalf of his colleague. It was in these little moments Tom could spot he was somewhat junior to Wilson, though it could not have been by much.

'I am almost ashamed to show you these reports,' Wilson said. 'I am ashamed. I think it is a dirty business.'

Oh yes, Tom's heart goes down now. Into his slippers. He is aware now of his slippers. Perhaps he might have put on his shoes before he opened the door – it had not occurred to him. He must look a bit defunct presenting himself thus. What was the state of his trousers? He glanced down and he saw the old brown jobs he favoured and in truth they might have done with a go around the machine in the launderette. The old checked shirt, the waistcoat with some evidence, some traces, of the suppers of the last few weeks. He had had his hair trimmed at the barber's, though, that was something, and he always shaved religiously in the morning. It was his custom to sing 'Tipperary' while he did so, and above all things he valued custom, as long as it was his own, and reasonably Irish.

Wilson took the reports out of their troubled envelope and offered them to Tom. He stared at the rumpled sheaf, recognising all too well the very colour of the paper, the typed-out parts, and the printed parts, and the long gospel of whatever they incorporated executed in a sober black ink. Paperwork, the policeman's penance. He had no desire, not even a smidgen of it, to take the documents. He felt the great rudeness of his hesitation. They were only boys. Well, Wilson might be forty. A grizzled face, really, with a little scar above the left eye. A childhood wound maybe. We all have our childhood wounds, thought Tom.

Wilson shook the papers in his fist, ever so slightly. An encouragement to Tom to take the blessed yokes. 'The thing is, we can do something about it now – the game is up for these boyos.'

Tom Kettle's desire to get them away out was exhausting him. He didn't dislike them, not at all. He heard the night wind mustering, mustering itself against the seaward wall. He hoped to God there wouldn't be rain now. These boys didn't have an umbrella between them. Maybe they had driven out from town in a discreet car? Please God, let that be so. Were they too junior for a concession like that? More likely they had taken the train from Westland Row to Dalkey station and trekked the couple of miles to the castle. Tempted maybe by the allure of a pint in the Dalkey Island Hotel as they passed? It was late to be out on business like this. Was it even an official matter? Were they out on their own account, taking a chance? But they had said that Fleming had asked them. Didn't they have homes to go to? Maybe Fleming wanted it kept off the official notes. Two blatant policemen in their dark civvies. Noting the good houses all along the way. Disturbed by this mysterious wealth. Suspecting crimes! Stamping along between the posh walls, along the neat, narrow road. Talking away, or trodding on in silence. Did they know how privileged they were to be young? No need. And no one ever knows that, at the time. That thought brought another feeling. By Christ, he was on the cusp of sudden tears. This was all private to him, he hoped. The feeling seemed to drop through him fluidly, like an otter into a stream. A sort of sympathy for them, these hard, young, certain men, with their priorities in order, no doubt. Right and wrong. Catch the villains. Oh, get convictions at all costs. Go home to their wives and their babies. Life never ending. Everything in order. And nothing, nothing. Bleak destinations. No, no, that was his own stupidity. He had loved her well enough, as much as he was able. Who would be a policeman's wife? But oh, the queer sorrow of it – the lovely lightness of these young men, in their betraying suits. No, but he wanted them gone, he wanted his bit of ease back. Nine months, like a pregnancy. Never so happy. Oh, Jesus, he yearned for it now – for these two boyos to rise to their feet, and with a few last pleasantries and even cajolements regain Mr Tomelty's fussed-over gravel outside, and be quietly gone.

'I'm not even sure 'twas an offence, in your day,' said O'Casey, with an air of wide expertise, a scholar of the statute books, a chapter-and-verse man. Ask me anything, his expression seemed to say, on the statute books. Go on. Tom's odd tears backed off because now he was entranced. Intelligence was so attractive, just in itself. The light of understanding. He so wanted to laugh loudly, but he would never do that, he couldn't. He seemed to remember a little story about Wilson, it was drifting back to him, something about beating a suspect to the edge of death. Worse than the chief's assailants, much worse. Wasn't he sent up then to the border counties to head up a special unit? He must be back now. Wilson. Or did he imagine that? Too long on his own? 'I daresay it wasn't.'

'What wasn't?' said Tom, reluctantly.

'We know that you had a right old time with the priests in the sixties. I mean, in those days—'

O'Casey had been intending to press on, but Tom stopped him immediately.

'Ah no, Jesus, no, lads, not the fecking priests, no.' And he got up with surprising grace and agility. 'No, no,' he said.

There must have been a touch of comedy in it, because O'Casey couldn't help laughing. But he managed to convert it fairly smoothly into speech, and anyway Tom Kettle wasn't a man to take offence so easily. He knew there was almost always comedy stuck in the breast of human affairs, quivering like a knife.

'We know – well, we were told, we got all the gen from Fleming, we surely did, and Janey, Janey, Mr Kettle – but of course now things are not the same. You know?'

'I don't think even God Himself...' said Tom, reluctantly, in a 'queer small voice', as O'Casey opined later. 'The absolute suffering. There was no one to help me.'

Now, he hadn't meant to say that. What did he even mean? No one to help *him*. No, he hadn't meant to say 'me', he'd meant to say 'them'. Jesus, go home, boys. You are bringing me back to I don't know where. The wretchedness of things. The filthy dark, the violence. Priests' hands. The silence. That's just Tom Kettle, don't mind him, feels everything too much. Murder, you could murder, you could strike, you could stab, shoot, maim, cut, because of that silence. Better to do it, murder, kill. He felt it now. Burning. The fullest humiliation of it felt afresh. Still present and correct, after all the years.

Now he stood there and he was trembling. Was he having a stroke now? Wilson and O'Casey both had their mouths open, looking up at him. He nearly laughed again. He didn't want a stroke but at the same time he might welcome the inconvenience of it, if it might drive these men away. What was he saying? Oh, wretched night. Sure enough he heard the huge wind blasting about outside. It had no doubt ruffled the roosting places of the cormorants, out there on the cold, black rocks. He loved those cormorants, he thought. That murderer next door. With his Remington sniper rifle, if he was not mistaken, not like the old Lee-Enfield he himself had been given in Malaya to kill unsuspecting souls at a great distance. Like death meted out by the very gods. And yet, he was a nice man, a cellist. He would let loose at the Bach all hours. For God's sake. No doubt the wind had had a frolic on the island for itself, had made its roistering way across the waters, and now was throwing buckets, water tanks, reservoirs, of salty rain at the battlements. Good Christ. It was a veritable storm. Was there no mercy?

'I'll make us Welsh rabbit,' Tom said, joylessly.

Chapter Two

Well, there was nothing else for it. Just as the Welsh rabbit was mooted, with a surprising degree of appreciation – 'That'd be fucking delicious,' Wilson said, 'excusing my French' – the storm added to its wretched fervour in an attempt to turn the coast of Dalkey into the foot of Cape Horn. Wilson didn't say anything about it directly, but the storm was in the room, sound-wise. He was staring, with the wide, moist eyes of a mere child. Not staring *at* anything, just staring. Like the storm frightened him. Tom suddenly felt fatherly towards him. Senior officer. He felt he was obliged – and he was, of course he was, though he might well regret it – to accommodate them for the night.

As he melted the Welsh rabbit he was content that neither of the boys came to assist him. The grill was a mystery unto itself. Like a damp, evil grotto. He was always meaning to get down on his knees and get at it with a cloth and a lash of soap, but maybe the horrors were best left alone, after all this time. Years ago he might have thoughtlessly lifted a bit of the grease with a knife and spread it on his bread, but never now, as he had no wish to awaken another ulcer. Let sleeping ulcers lie, without grease to stir them into life. The lack of oven cleaning was just one of those original sins that bothered him as an undercurrent to his passages through the kitchen. He felt he owed it to Mr Tomelty somehow, but that wasn't a clear thought. And Winnie might give him an awful stare about such things into the bargain. Including 'the state of the jacks', as she put it. 'Could you not keep a bottle of bleach handy?' she would say, in her hopeless, loving tone. But well he knew how little the pollock, the eels and the sand dabs would appreciate bleach, and wasn't every bit of moisture he produced in the flat going down the pipes and under the garden and straight out into the murderous waters at the back? It was bad enough that they had to swim through everything else. Turds and whatnot, God knew. When Winnie swam off the little concrete jetty, the rare time, she called it 'going through the motions'. Oh she was witty, she was clever. College. Law degree. His pride. She flamed through the first year, her mother died, she emptied out somehow, she pushed on emptily, she graduated, dressed in her finery, in her grief. It was as if she needed nothing then because she had nothing. Nothing but himself and Joseph, and the same Joseph soon to be far away. The only thing she ever mentioned after that was a husband, as in, she did not have one. Perhaps that was a small thing.

Wilson ate his rabbit with the trust of a man who had never looked into the grill. O'Casey approached it more circumspectly. His instincts were more honed, Tom thought, watching him, with a feeling bordering on fondness. Even commiseration. The younger man sniffed it delicately, smiling so as to give no offence to the chef.

'Arra,' he said, 'not so bad, Mr Kettle . . .'

He whitened a little, but set into it manfully.

Winnie had never risen to an actual compliment about his cooking because truth to tell it wasn't cooking. Sustenance, survival, at best. He wondered briefly would they have been as kind about the lump of cold hash in the weeping pot – winter was condensing, interestingly, from a scientific point of view, on its outer aluminium walls. Praise always roused in him an inconvenient sense of ambition for further heights. Even praise laced with irony. Ridiculous. The Welsh rabbit was a childish dish, although in his own youth Easi-Singles had not yet been invented, much less the anaemic shovel-blades of bread which the yellow squares had obediently melted on. It was a very uncheeselike yellow, God's truth. Not so long ago he had penetrated bravely into the National Gallery. He was of the opinion that retired men should try and broaden their minds, so calcified by narrow work and general shrinkage. Anyway, he had the Free Travel Pass and it seemed churlish not to use it now and then. So in he scooted just the odd time to town, forsaking his solitude, in search of amplitude, of healing even, on the 8 bus. He had wandered about the labyrinth of sombre paintings, through the deserted marble halls, awed, diminished and silenced – he had to point himself discreetly into an alcove to belch, after a beef sandwich in Bewley's – and eventually came by chance on a tiny picture. You came on everything good by chance. He liked it for its modesty among the bigger efforts. Like a human soul should be in the world, among elephants, galaxies. A miniature 'rural scene'. *Pissarro*, said the label. And he stared at it, feeling a sudden furious gratitude, his mind entered by thoughts of France and the French countryside, where he had never been, wondering what the curious molten yellow of a little square wheat field reminded him of – he was back down on Merrion Square before it hit him. Easi-Singles. He had considered his mind duly broadened.

Oh, then on to his real favourite, the Natural History Museum further up the square. The ribs and bones of the Great Irish elk that roamed no more in Ireland, the blue whale suspended above in its own great corset of bones, the ironwork of the stairs and upper galleries like the vast skeleton of an even bigger whale, all about and above him, a whale inside a whale then, making of him a double Jonah – oh blessed, sacred place.

O'Casey, confessing to an ulcer himself, rose immediately after finishing the Welsh rabbit and stood at the beauty board, leaning against it in alarm – you could see it buckling slightly – his face turned away as if in disgrace, like a punished scholar. His right hand went to his forehead and he seemed to be sweating. 'What's the what's-a?' he muttered, in an orgy of growing suffering. And he fluttered his right hand on his forehead, in a continuous display, as if his hand were going to take off, catastrophically, like a one-winged pigeon. Then he spent the following half-hour in the jacks, which is a long time in another person's toilet, somehow. As Mr Tomelty's builders had not gone to town on the thickness of the walls, his distress and battle stations were clear throughout. There were groans and almost savage expostulations, and O'Casey's god was summoned to assist him. For this half-hour, as the winds battered the castle, and the rain sat upright on the windowpanes, Wilson smiled and hemmed, and laughed aloud now and then, perfectly at his ease, his stomach full. Tom was entranced again – he liked friendship expressed openly. They were like soldiers in a trench, he thought, everything raw and out in the open, bare humanity. Yes, it thrilled him. He exulted suddenly again in the presence of these young men, much as he feared them and their words. The mateyness between Wilson and O'Casey, proven now in the cauldron of the one's distress, the caldera rather, the poor man's guts surging with the lava of the Welsh rabbit, put Tom again on the cusp of weeping. Could he speak of love, could he speak of the saving graces of men? No, speechifying was not a feature of this moment, or any, or few, among mere males. He must accept that, reluctantly. Instead, he fetched an old tin of stomach powders he had used himself in such extremities, and handed it in, just the one hand and the tin thrust through the door, not violating O'Casey's important privacy. The tin was taken delicately, not violently, like a well-trained dog taking a morsel from human fingers.

In a while there was a final explosion, then a dramatic crying out, then a silence, then the chain solemnly flushed. O'Casey, pale, altered, trembling from his glad release from pain, walked slowly back into the room, Wilson beaming and nodding, O'Casey throwing the whole thing off with humility and grace. And Tom, feeling suddenly a little removed from their nice accord, maybe as a consequence of his age, wandered off into his bedroom to fetch the lilo from the little cupboard. This item of furniture had belonged to some simple cottage, he was sure, a rough, local artefact that had never seen a shop. The insides of the doors were covered in newspaper from August 1942, with advertisements for fascinators and fedoras, and war news, democratically, and now redundantly, featured. Only the passing spiders and clothes moths, and his distracted gaze, could read it now. The lilo was Winnie's bed when she visited and he was well used to fitting it out with her cut-down sheets and a feather pillow in an impressively embroidered case, the work of yet another unknown rural hand. The best things in Ireland were the work of unknown hands. And oftentimes the worst crimes.

He wasn't sure what O'Casey and Wilson could do with just one lilo, but there was always the short couch at a pinch, and because indeed he felt some panic over this, and a sense of crisis as a host, he placed the lilo and the sheets and the pillow in a little heap, and nodded his head with the sagacity of Archimedes, as if it were clear to all that everyone was accommodated, though he didn't think they were. But he had done his best, his best, and he had put the grub into them, and now he had grown weary, weary, and with a few last words as simple and worn as old pennies he went to his doss. He was up the few times in the night, what with the dicky bladder, but otherwise slept like Dracula in his clay.

When he came out again around 6 a.m. through the stumbling darkness, ready for the day, he found the lilo deflated like a great tongue and rolled up – he thought of geckos but geckos had long thin tongues, didn't they? – and the bedclothes folded with extreme neatness, and not a sign of the men. He went and had a piss in that severe silence of the solitary life, and shook his head a little at the doings of the night before. He couldn't, just that second, locate his toothbrush so he cleaned his teeth with a finger daubed in the Colgate. Shaving brush soaped up and safety razor. So then he was singing that old song, like shavers are obliged to do. Plucked hairs from his nostrils. Looking good for ghosts. He supposed they had headed out into the lightless morning to catch the early bus to town, so there would be no break in their policing, as it were, and possibly to protect from any docking of their wages. Who had had the lilo, and who the wretched couch? He might never know. Had they taken the reports with them? They had. Alleluia. Well, they couldn't be leaving them, no. Abruptly he was abashed, ashamed. He had let them down, he knew. He had played the old man, to perfection. Now he felt as if he were a murderer released only on a technicality. Now he felt as wretched as the couch. Now he did weep, serious, heart-scalding guilty tears, the tears of a coward, he thought, caught out in his cowardice. He had not given them the mercy of his opinion of the contents. He had not risen to the effort they had made to consult him. Oh, but, wise Tom Kettle. Yes, wise. Away with your trotting writing, your accustomed policeman's prose.

But he also missed them, he was stunned to discover, missed them like his own children, a huge ache of loss – which was not logical at all. They had had a nice time together, despite everything, but that was all. But he felt it like a bereavement. He had enjoyed the talk. He had. A mystery. Their warmth and kindness. He wondered should he do more of it. Human contact. He wasn't sure. It was a disturbing thought somehow, like he was betraying a confidence, a secret, but whose?

And all that day nothing sat right with him. He could not

settle. He could not 'think of nothing', which was his whole ambition. The reports floated in his mind like squabs, flapping their wings, begging for attention. Feed us, feed us, bring us worms. He would have had a lot to say about those reports, he suspected, he didn't even need to open them to understand what they were. Dreary accounts of wretched allegations. To which his heart and soul would most likely have risen, innocently, passionately, stupidly, as if one of O'Connell's bulky angels on his statue in O'Connell Street had suddenly moved her metal wings. With ruinous eagerness and strength. A sombre figure who had not stirred for a hundred years! Even poor Nelson, on his sea-grey pillar, being blown to kingdom come on 8 March 1966 (the date had stuck in his policeman's mind, he had *noted* it), had not disturbed those angels.

Having tidied his few rooms, valiantly trying to remove all traces of his guests, as if by doing so he could simply forget them, he found he couldn't tidy his frazzled mind. He was the orphan of his former happiness. But had it been happiness, or just dubious happiness? No, he thought it had been true happiness right enough, with the promise of permanence, and now something, some merciless gesture of fate, had snatched it from him. He put on his heavy coat and belted it and pulled his cap almost violently onto his head, made his door screech open, gave the beautiful rhododendron an accusing stare – how dare you look so content? – and stamped out the gates and to his left up the hill. Without the two men with him, he felt alone. He was alone. Scimitars of blunt wind flashed about everywhere, swiping at his hat, his hair, his heart. The remnant of the storm was playing the devil in the road, there was an ash tree down in the neighbouring garden, the gulls were offering their cries for mercy. Dark, high clouds moved in a sombre silent crowd towards England.

A chill rain began, just for his benefit, he thought, oh it would, and soon made free with his coat collar, without a by your leave, and wet the back of his neck, just enough to put him in mortal dread of pneumonia. But by the time he had covered half the distance to the park at the top of the hill, here was the blessed sunlight, suddenly, the rain's shy sister, not with any heat in it, but a measure of pleasing hope. He thought of those rare summer days when the whole land thereabouts would be oven-baked, every crevice and wide vista crammed with lovely, belligerent heat. Well, he was not there yet. Then he could cross down through Dillon's Park and quietly shed his elderly clothes, drag on his 'new' togs under the flapping towel, Irish fashion, and then consign himself to the deeps, exuberantly swimming, though not too far out because of the wretched currents.

Those togs. Last June, inspired by the seaside atmosphere of his new home, though not a week in residence, he had gone into Dalkey village on two errands. First thing was a haircut, which he imagined might give him a summery look, which in truth was a painful error. The barber, a mere boy of seventeen, called it ominously a Number One, like the child's phrase for taking a piss. When the boy was finished his work with the electric shaver – like you would use on a ewe – Tom was very alarmed to view the result. He looked, even to himself, who had no opinion of his appearance generally, hideous. He had no cheekbones, it was clear, and his face just seemed like a flat, failed loaf with dirty knife-holes in it. It looked to him like he had had his head shaved in a sort of unconscious gesture of atonement. I will go walking around Ireland and return when it grows back, he thought. No one must see me like this. Then he remembered there was no one to see him anyway, he was retired, and with an admirable grace he shrugged off his trauma.

Then he went on to the dark haberdasher's and asked the formidable lady there about togs. She had stared at him, taking the measure of him from the sheared head, which could only be because of lice, homelessness, missing his essential liquidity – his pension was a source of true pride – by an Irish mile, and said that she 'had a second-hand pair, if he wished to see them'. She was being humane, accommodating, merciful, astute. He had not found the words in himself to set her right, and was embarrassed even to try, so had accepted the offered garment, which was a queer sort of yellow that even Pissarro would not have used. He had snapped the material between his two hands, once, twice, and given it a kind of swirling shuck in the air, as if suddenly, mysteriously, an expert on togs, the strength of the material, the right sort of snap, and nodded his deep appreciation. He gave her the two pounds she was asking, and suffered the togs to be wrapped in concealing paper, like a demi of whiskey that was to be carried through the streets. And then he went out into the sunlight again like a man freed from a long incarceration, but, although he had been humiliated, obscurely, he was also jubilant as he retraced his steps home.

Shearing ewes. He saw again in his mind's eye the Brother from Tipperary getting each struggling ewe between his legs, holding her fast with some skill, and running the rattling shears down and down and down the ewe's body, and the cold, dirty wool coming away in solid sheets like an already knitted thing. Peeling off like an orange. Working at that all day and the boys feeding him the ewes, with cries and shouts, outside the new shed, and the drench of sweat on the Tipperary Brother's face and arms, and the billycans of hot tea brought to him hourly to fix his violent thirst. He remembered standing there at close of day and the sun like a coal setting the far heather of the sea-field alight and the boys lying on the ground beside the huge heap of wool and the Brother from Tipperary laughing from his triumph.

This present sunlight was only a distant cousin of the summer's, but it was a comfort, it was a herald, it was a joy. Now he was chuckling to himself, he was satiated, he was full, the weak fingers of this light were enough, sufficient. The time for the togs was far off, but it was coming, it was coming.

The rain that had drenched the branches of the trees had lost heart, but the wind still pulled greedily at what was already there, making the drops fly at him, fly at everything, the sunlight inserting gleams and glimmers into them, like a million silver sprat. Suddenly he wasn't so sure. He was briefly enraged, as if he were someone only in charge of himself, and not himself. The fucking Brother from Tipperary. Like he was a patient, a lunatic out for a constitutional. Then he was despondent, his boots growing heavier. His soul weighted, like a handicap of lead weights on a racehorse. Oh the good Jesus. Was he happy or wretched? Was he ruined or saved? He had no idea. What was to become of him? What was the use of him? What use was he to Winnie or Joseph, what use to suffering man? Then he stopped on the drenched pavement, and put his hands to his face, and cried again, with sobs, and shudders, in the diluted sunlight.

His unknown neighbours gazing out at him, as may be, a lump of a creature in a black coat. Somewhere in there was a famous food writer, somewhere in there the 'architect of modern Ireland'. So he had been told by the postmistress in the village. Had *he* not been a competent detective, had *he* not been appreciated for his deductive skill, his intuition, his sudden inspirations? He had. At least he *thought*, he thought sincerely, he had. No one ventures out to see a mere retired man. Retired men are to go to the devil – into the final dark, let the waters close over their heads – unless they have curious gifts. Rare gifts. He hoped it was so. Even as he wept, he hoped it was so. But he had rejected Wilson and O'Casey, he had spurned their bracing curiosity, their questions, their very ambulatory efforts to reach him. To reach the bloody hermit, perched on his wicker chair – the beloved wicker chair. The exultations of Dalkey. One day, dolphins rising. One day, the whole stretch between his refuge and the island gone silver with the tiny fish that mackerel risk everything to devour. Trillions, trillions. The Dalkey darkness that even in its pitch-blackness had a peculiar brilliance, a shining aura, like basalt stone. Oh, oh the world was too difficult for him. It was. No. Wretched lie. Lying to himself, like a maniac, like a dark criminal with crimes too wretched to admit to, even to himself. He had thrown their interest back at them, he had acted like a salted slug, he had, it was not professional, it was not even human, or admirable. But how could he have done otherwise? Their coming had unmoored him, unsettled him, terrified him, yes, terrified. Their coming out was an act of terror, but how could they know that, their intentions were so good they deserved bloody medals for them. The innocence, the sheer goodness of them, of bloody what's-his-name the chief, Fleming, bloody Fleming. I'll send you out to Tom Kettle, good sane clear-headed Tom, with a whole citadel, a museum, of experience in his head, he'll set this to rights, give us a heads-up, a way forward, a good steer, a helping hand. Most excellent, most treasured Detective Sergeant Thomas Kettle, the cream of the coppers, the heart of the rowl. What a transgression. What a betrayal. It was not good. He must cry now, cry copiously, into the flying raindrops, into the fleeting sunlight.

He had thought to go on up to Sorrento Park, to clear his head among the peculiar boulders and the trees that the salt wind kept small and stooped. There were two parks at the top of the hill, Dillon's and Sorrento, and both had their uses. As medicine. Go on as before, his little routine, the little routine of a retired man. He had thought to do so. But shaken now, shaken, *hurt*, not calmed at all, he turned back again, hurrying, and took refuge, confused and panicking, in his quarters.

He stood there in his living room, dripping. It was as if he were standing there for the first time. Alien somehow, unknown. Animal-like. His bits and pieces refusing to talk to him. Communicate any sense of home. He didn't know what to do. He wished Winnie— But Winnie was dead. Why did he talk as if she were still alive? Winnie was dead. Joseph murdered in Albuquerque. His wife June, dead, dead. What was wrong with him, that he couldn't acknowledge his dead ones? Couldn't tell Wilson and O'Casey, with an easy, grown-up voice, the little stories of their fates. Couldn't say why the contents of those reports assailed him even before he could read them. Couldn't read them, couldn't in any sense read them. Under any circumstances read them.

He dragged off his coat as if it were a mental hindrance and let it drop to the floor. Winnie's admonishing voice seemed to leak out of the beauty board. He went back into the rustic cupboard where he knew there was a length of rope. Any fool could tie a noose, it was the simplest knot in the world. Then he found himself wandering foolishly about the flat trying to find something to tie the rope to. In the kitchen there was a bracket where the ceiling met the wall, what it had been for he didn't have an idea. Onions maybe, or some sort of vanished kitchen machine. Or the pin that held the universe in its place? But he didn't think it would hold his weight. There was nothing else that he could see. He had the noose about his neck, trailing the rope like an umbilical cord, and he was walking about looking. He was embarrassed in front of himself. He stood at the picture window and the sea was a million grey dinner plates below, surging in the channel. Spinning and dipping, each one a circus trick, a clown's trick. Spin a plate on a stick. Duffy's Circus, circa nineteen-what? Was that a memory?

Dinner plates, dinner plates, exactly like that. The curious effect caught his attention, just for a few moments.

Then he saw the little boy who had arrived at Christmas with his mother, to the Turret Flat, come running into view. He had some sort of unusual stick in his hand. A black cane, with a silver knob – like Fred Astaire might use for dancing. He was flailing it about in the wind. The square of hedges around the sheltered spot that Mr Tomelty had created, or an earlier owner, was bending and shuddering, like a circle of powerful horses. Threshing the bitter grain of life. The little boy was soundless because the window was closed, but Tom adjudged he must be singing. The child was now twirling himself all about, as if the cane had not been enough of a thing to be twirling, in his short trousers, happy in the wind, the cold, oblivious.

Tom went back into the kitchen, still trailing the damn rope. He felt an absolute surge of violence in himself, of the kind, he knew, that was responsible for great crimes. But he had no wish to commit great crimes. Instead, he banged and banged on the table, assaulting the grey-green Formica as if it had done him ferocious wrong. He banged on it, he banged on it – but stopped just on the cusp of breaking it. He hovered there, with an aching effort of self-control. He mustn't forget Mr Tomelty, he thought. You must respect a person's property. It was a golden rule. It was the yardstick of the Civic Guards, as he'd tried to explain to Ramesh twenty years before. He was pouring with sweat as he admonished himself. The peace of the country, the safety of the citizen, the inviolability of property. This Formica table, which would have set Mr Tomelty back six or seven quid in

Woolworth's, was sacred. He must not cause it permanent damage. A wretched artefact, factory-made, but it *was not his*. Sweat oozed down his face, stinging his eyes, blinding him. He yearned to let his fists crash down and destroy the little table – like Samson slaying a Philistine with the jawbone of a donkey.

He was standing there, his fists raised, with something indeed of the suffering of Samson in him, thinking this, arrested, with the noose around his neck, when the doorbell rang again.

Chapter Three

What was Tom to do? Would it be the first time in history that a person seeking the solace of suicide was interrupted by a doorbell ringing? No. Except, how many people had actually knocked on his door in the last nine months? And now twice in twenty-four hours? All the fire and anger went out of him. All the strength. The world was asking him to step back into life. Oh, again, again. He was helpless against it. He felt he would be better gone, he did, and if he had found a decent thing to hang a rope from, it would have been a good old-fashioned cowboy's *adios*.

This wasn't true, but it was still a thought worth thinking. The truth was he had nearly scared himself to death. The very act of looking for the hook so fervently was now a greater terror in his mind than the actual terror that had driven him to it.

That was all in the past. He had his keel steady under him now.

Mother of the good Jesus, he hoped he would never be so self-regarding as to find himself telling all this to Winnie. Looking for sympathy. A child must believe in the strength of her father. The very vaccine of her safety.

The only challenge was crossing the floor to the door. That seemed like a long, long way. He felt like the lad and lassie on the bicycle in *Butch Cassidy and the Sundance Kid* –

oh, not their happiness, but the slow motion of their scene. With the silly song that June had loved, and hummed for a whole summer, over and over. 'Raindrops Keep Fallin' On My Head'. 1970? Funny how, after all that had happened to them, they had still been able, well able, to do ordinary things, enjoy ordinary things. Going to the cinema. Bliss, really. The Pav. Bus from Deansgrange. Her carry-all, scorning a handbag. She was a proper hippy, she said. No bloody handbags. Loon pants. Both her babies born in her twenties. The figure of a girl. After Joseph, when he was making love to her, he noticed a funny scar down there. The doctor had cut her because Joseph's head was too big for her. Now it looked like a trademark, or a tiny branding. It was just the warmth of her, sitting on the bus, her leg against his, the tight stretch of the jeans across her thigh . . . It would make a tightrope walker fall. No safety net neither. Splat on the ground. The heat of her love for him and his for her. The promise of love, always. Oh yes, and his pride in her, because now, come on, fellas, she was very unusual. She was far and away the most beautiful person he had ever seen. In the dark of the cinema didn't she only look like a film star herself. That was the gospel truth. Her mother had been a beauty too, he knew that – like Wilson's story, another beautiful mother – because she'd still had a little photo in her purse. It had given him a strange ache of recognition when he saw it – when she vouchsafed it to him, entrusting the torn photo to his gaze, sitting in a little archway in Dunleary. They had been going out a few months – a few dizzy months. His luck. It had a line of tiny bubbles on it because it had been peeled off a passport. Sacred stuff. In fact a replica of herself. Dark-skinned beauty. She showed him the photo, he held her in his arms, she cried into the cotton of his shirt. Surely they were married in that moment. So rarely did she show emotion like that. It had stilled him, shocked him, put him on high alert – just to do the right thing in that moment. Could be important. So he peeled her face away from his shoulder, it left two round marks from her tears, he held her warm face in his two hands. Even in dark winter her face seemed tanned. He kissed her nose, and she laughed. 'Wasn't she lovely?' she said to him, with the trusting voice of a six-year-old. Which was the age she . . . 'She was a beauty,' he said, like a seminarian reading the liturgy for the first time. The cigarette holder was fetched out, a Major stuck into it. Where the hell is that holder? Oh, she smoked like a fish-shed. In her kisses always was the bitter taste of tobacco, which he loved. She had a way of filling his mouth with her tongue, it just made him crazy. If they kissed in the cinema, which they liked to do, his old cock would be hurting him in his trousers. Holy God. It was because she carried in her head a whole universe of good things with the bad. All her talk, her phrases, her stray quotations, her singing – Cat Stevens, oh God, *'Oh baby, baby, it's a wild world . . .'* Her soft bra under the grandfather shirt – oh, and the underwear she carefully chose in Penneys, with the hearts on them. He lived in a perpetual state of weak knees. Her gold hair that she called 'mousey'. Never . . . He dragged himself to the door, just in time remembering the rope still trailing, un-lassoing himself with a swirling skill he didn't know he possessed. He freed himself, divested himself, and dropped the rope into the umbrella stand, which had no umbrella. It was just a long brass shell from one of the big wars. The door screeched open, and there was the chief, Fleming. In full uniform. Tom was flabbergasted. It was quite a get-up, with its braid and silver. What was he doing here? Fleming was a round man, but he was tall, twenty-two stone of solid policeman. You were getting value for money with Fleming. It was black night now. The whole of the hill above Fleming looked as if underwater, dense and pitch, drowning, with only the faint fume of unseen windows rising behind high walls. Tom was too tired to do even a quick tally of his dishevelled appearance. Fleming was so laundered, his shirt so white, Tom suspected witch-craft. What the hell time was it, though? Had he not just looked out his window and seen that boy in daylight, below in the garden?

'Arra, Tom,' said Fleming. His voice carried a pleasing Midlands burr. 'Glad to catch you. I'm not bothering you?'

'You can't bother a retired man, sir,' Tom said, with real warmth in his voice.

'I'm just there in the Dalkey Island Hotel. There's dozens there you would know. Annual dinner. Just had the starters. Prawn cocktail. Disgusting. Thought I'd pop out and visit you. Might save my life. Chicken supreme next.'

'Jesus, fancy,' said Tom, laughing along a touch falsely.

Why hadn't Wilson and O'Casey mentioned anything about an annual dinner so close to his quarters?

He had always been fond of Fleming. He knew he should ask him in, but he was worried about the state of the flat.

For many years Fleming and himself had been equal

rank. Then Fleming had been promoted over him though he was ten years the younger.

'I'm sorry I haven't been out to see you, Tom,' said the chief, as if chiming in with this thought. 'It's been a hell of a – it's been a year of mayhem. The things the Irish citizen gets up to, I tell you, would shame the devil.'

This was a joke, and Tom found it funny. He felt a new confidence surge through him, a tincture of his old self, that part of him that was always primed to 'sort things out'. It was an interesting invasion of feeling.

'Listen, sir,' he said, newly armed with this, 'let me throw on a coat, and can we take a stroll up the hill? There's something I want to ask you about.'

Fleming said nothing, made no reaction, just nodded his head.

'You grab your coat, boy, I'll wait here,' he said then, as Tom stood there, opening and closing his lips like a fish. 'Plenty of time. I hate chicken anyhow.'

Tom went back into the flat. Chicken that had died of old age, potatoes with the skin of a phone book. He wasn't long retrieving his damp coat from the floor. He returned to Fleming, waiting with a patient smile and an easy laugh, and the two men went out the gates of the castle and turned left up the hill, where just a few hours before Tom had been weeping. They were used to each other's step, like married people, and kept abreast. It had been often remarked of Fleming that he had no wife, that he was a loner, but in fact he had an army of acquaintances and friends in Dublin, Tom knew, and in Navan where his people had a carpet factory. You couldn't fault a fella like Fleming, no. You couldn't read him either, which was an advantage in a senior detective, or any class of one.

'How've you been keeping, Jack?' said Tom, risking the first name.

'Do you know, just dandy, Tom, just dandy. Last January Bríd had the little brush with cancer. Well, she came roaring through that.'

Who was Bríd? He had no idea. He didn't want to ask, and risk disturbing the ease of their talk.

It wasn't entirely pleasant out there, on the soaked concrete pavement, and the sea wind in a great huff. There was a sense of the big houses hunched against it, resentfully. Not a night to be a tramp. It was never a night to be a tramp in Ireland. The thing he had wanted to ask Fleming about, now he felt he just couldn't. Something to do with that wind maybe.

'How are you finding retirement? Must be nice to put the feet up.'

'It is fucking nice,' said Tom, and they both laughed. 'Wilson and O'Casey caught me off guard last night. Janey, I don't know what got into me. I suppose they told all.'

'They said you were very fucking friendly and made them Welsh rarebit, which was far too good for them, would be my opinion, the boyos. And a night in Dalkey. They were like fellas back from their holidays when they came in this morning.'

'Well, I'm glad,' said Tom. 'I wasn't sure I – I wasn't sure I – so long since I saw anyone, you know, from work. Strange business. They're good lads.'

'Well, they are.'

Now the two turned about and began to retrace their steps. They both could see the kerfuffle of car lights down at the hotel, though it was situated beyond the dark drop of the fishing harbour. There'd be happy excitement there, and men fixing to drink too much, and wives fixing to stop them, hoping they wouldn't get so rat-faced dancing would be out of the question. You could marry a man in uniform but could you get him to dance in it? Tom smiled to himself. Suddenly the world didn't seem quite so bare and disappointing. Old things were creeping back to him, small old things, certainties of long duration that retirement had cut away. He had had no idea he was missing any of this, not a hint. He should talk to himself more, he thought. The trouble was, he was always waiting for Winnie, waiting for Joseph. Had his life been taken away from him? He was already dead in a sense, was that it? Of course it was. But he had learned something, he had understood the glory of the wicker chair. Although the same chair was only yards away, it might as well have been a thousand light years now.

Fleming was going to try and warm himself with a fag, and with this in mind he plucked out a pack of Major, carefully hidden from the weather. A comb fell out with it, and a few betting slips, and these had to be gathered quickly off the ground – 'They're old bets,' said Jack, intimating by voice and gesture that those horses had failed him – and then he tried to take a fag out and keep the whole thing dry at the same time.

He offered one to Tom in dumbshow but Tom said no, equally silent.

'You still smoke the cigarillos?' said Fleming.

'I do.'

'You'd nearly miss the stink of them at headquarters.'

'I'm sure.'

'Kettle's cigarillos – they were famous. The crims called you The Cigarillo Man.'

'Well, only the seagulls get the benefit now.'

'I don't know, would you recommend retirement? Wilson said you seemed good on it.'

'It has its points.'

'Yeah,' said Jack. 'I'm sure.'

'It's a few years off yet, for you,' said Tom.

Then they were at Tom's gates again, and Fleming took three big drags off his cigarette. Major was a small fag enough, and it would be gone in a few more pulls anyway, but Fleming, only halfway down the stem, let out a blast of smoke, into the rainy darkness. The streetlight far down the way managed to illuminate it a little, so that for a second Fleming was in charge of a huge cone of whiteness out of his mouth, which promptly vanished. He flicked the remainder away up into the air, as if throwing it after the smoke. He smoked like a society woman in a film, Tom thought. Profligate. The Marx Brothers, your woman with the big bosom. *Duck Soup*. He smiled to witness it.

Now Jack Fleming, gathering himself – here we go, thought Tom – suddenly policeman-serious, but friendly, in deepest friendship, turned his face to Tom's, his big self somehow crammed into a smaller space, making himself smaller. Tom knew he had thrown his feather into the water and was praying to feel the sudden weight of a salmon. He knew all this, and didn't resent it. No, suddenly he welcomed it. It seemed better than the non-existent hook on the wall, the ceiling. The rope in the shell case, like a fakir's snake.

Margaret Dumont! The name slid back to him.

'You might think of – you might think of coming in to see me, Tom, would you, of your great kindness? We've an awful dog's mess of a thing to sort out, and I know you can help me, I know you can. The chief-super has okayed it, there's a few bob for things like this, you can come in in your civvies, you don't even need to polish your fecking shoes. But I fecking need you. And Wilson and O'Casey need you, they haven't a God's clue what they're doing.'

Tom was embarrassed, but by what he couldn't pinpoint. Himself? His own doubts, his recent attempt on his own life, ridiculous and unsuccessful? It was a tricky thing to get out of life, that was true. It had foxed him rightly. He felt a queer shame about it now. But he kept his face poker-straight, he did, he even smiled his old Tom Kettle smile, or as he imagined it to be, and nodded, and did his little Ramesh headshake.

'Arra, Tom, you'd be doing me a great favour, let me fecking tell you.'

They looked at each other. Tom thought of all the pieces of chicken on the plates – slaughter in the henhouse – down there in the old hotel, and the big noisy talk of the crowd, and the terrible jokes and even the good jokes, and the despair of the wives, and just the whole jolly niceness of the whole evening, and the madness of it – the inexplicable goings-on of human creatures, a mystery even to their creator, he was sure. And he thought of June, a dozen times in her best dress, going in with him to places like that, the ark of an old hotel, and the couples going in two by two, and the single men rattling optimistically in their monkey suits.

'Think on it, a chara,' said Fleming. 'You do. No bother if you can't see your way. You know where I am. Goodnight to you.' He grasped Tom's right hand. 'Jesus, Tom Kettle, it has been a great pleasure to see you again. It has.'

And with this speech, he was away.

Tom was so moved he doubted his whispered 'Likewise, likewise' even reached his chief's ears.

With sombre eye Tom watched him stride away. A giant. With sombre step he went back into his flat, with quiet hands he took off his coat, and threw it across the accustomed chair. He held the same two hands up for a moment, examining them with interest, because of late he had thought he detected a little shake in them. No trembling now. With the same hands that could have now defused a wartime bomb, no bother, he smeared more Colgate on his remaining teeth, and brushed his remaining hair for bed, as he had done all his life. The Brother had told him, if he brushed his teeth twice a day he would still have them at fifty – the only truthful thing that man had ever said. He must buy a new brush tomorrow. In his bedroom, with only the eerie light of the stormy moon, he took off his clothes and folded them, item by item, as he had learned to do in the Phoenix Park as a young recruit, with sombre mind he got in under the covers, folded his old hands across his chest, as if a conscientious undertaker had spruced him up, and with a peaceful heart sought his deservèd rest.

No one minds life as long as they are not trying to leave it. Nor death, as long as they are not dying.

Of course his story continued as he lay there sleeping, and his brain continued to tell a story disconnected from his waking self. One hundred trillion neutrinos passed through his body every second. To a neutrino, Tom Kettle was full of empty space, like the distance between solar systems, and he was so large he wasn't really there, at least not to bump into. At the top of his curtains, on the little window that looked out on the rhododendron, unbeknownst to him, were three red-and-black butterflies, waiting out the winter. The heat that might have stirred them was never there in winter, because Tom didn't believe in heating a bedroom. He believed in woollen socks, and the old stone water jar that had been his companion in the bed since June died – the selfsame marriage bed, though in another house, their old place in Deansgrange, near the famous graveyard. Up behind the headboard was a mazy mass of cobwebs, like arrested smoke, and there was a big dame of a spider there that lived off the dust mites and the woodlice. He slept in a peopled menagerie of many things. On top of the rustic cupboard were all the files and papers from his work that he thought he couldn't throw out when he retired, though he was 99 per cent sure he would never look at them again, and the little posh box for his Scott Medal for Valor was also there, though the actual medal was no longer in it. He had even prophesied the skip that Mr Tomelty would throw them into when he was gone, with never a glance, even though many a story, many a hurt, many a crime, were attached to them – his carefully compiled private notes about murders and robberies that had always helped him to reach his sudden insights, which Fleming had always so valued.

Marvelled at. You wrote something down to see it, see it all for the first time. Write it down and strive to capture it. Now these hundreds of pages lived at the top of the rough cupboard. Neutrinos passed through them also, trillions of them, neutral, indifferent, on their way down into the floor, into the earth and through the earth herself at nearly the speed of light. They passed through his tumbling mind, all its channels and sparks, the static-ridden radio of Tom Kettle, they passed through his fingers, miraculously stilled by the visit of Fleming. They passed through his vulnerable soul, itself an item so large it was not there either, at least to a neutrino. But did it speak of the unimportance of Tom Kettle that he was not really there to a neutrino? Maybe God saw him? What of the butterflies, what of the mother spider, what of the mites, striving for life and generations in the old carpet? True, true, in human affairs everything is hastiness and farewell. But there was a sort of proof in this that Tom Kettle was loved, even though he couldn't see it, as he passed through the world. He had no idea how much June had loved him, nor Winnie, nor Joe. Maybe his sleeping self knew more, intuitive, less complicated by waking thought. Maybe the love that Fleming, returning to the Dalkey Island Hotel, felt for him, maybe he understood that better in his sleep. Maybe in his sleep he actually knew why the trembling in his hands had been stilled. After nine months of solitude, the little medicine of casual human love entering his blood, entering the reservoir of his pain and guilt.

His bladder was the thief of sleep. Three times he woke in the night, and made the brief shuffling pilgrimage to the jacks. How different everything looked in the small hours. The boxes of books, the old photos in their frames, vanished scenes, vanished people, all dark and glowing in the pale soup of moonlight. He didn't like to turn on the lights because he sensed the resentment of the objects as he passed. Something in the weather had shifted outside, the thick clouds were gone, the wind was still, and a huge blue light was scarred by tatters of moonlight and the gauzy remnants of the cloud. Dark steel-blue light. The island and its shoal of rocks black and stark. The sea mutely heaving, the sleeping belly of a vast thin man. It was always strange to him, this unscheduled waking, intruding on the privacy of inanimate things – so deeply coveted by them. Chair and table, carpet and knick-knacks, wanting to be alone, like Greta Garbo. So he was content to stumble through, knock an elbow, a hip, and so gain his station at the toilet. He knew all the vagaries of the prostate because his good doctor had explained it to him. A finger had been inserted into his backside, and the swollen gland examined. Dr Brownlee, while performing this service, had talked brightly about his horses and his garden. There was no doubt in Tom's mind that he needed to find a new doctor in Dalkey because Dr Brownlee was now far off in Deansgrange, with everything else. His old life. Rising at six to drive into town. June in the old days exhausted by the babies even as she woke to another day. In her eyes the little glints of gold like gold dust in a Wicklow river. The golden hair. Not in any way mousey, unless it was a glorious golden mouse. Her gold had been left behind in his old head as if his old head were Jason's fleece. Exhausted youth is not the same as exhausted age. It can be repaired.

By holidays in Bettystown, by the lie-ins on Sundays, when he could man the fort. Organise the troops, as she called it. His wild babies. Soft, strong creatures. Leaking at both ends. Exuberant, like little dancers dancing only the vigorous bits of the dance, over and over. Boiling with life. Mad for him. Holding on to his legs when he had to go to work, trying to capture their father, keep him near all day. When you are a father your heart beats faster all the time, but not in illness. He had no idea if he was ill or well now, but he was sometimes weary in a way that had no remedy. Time had stripped him down a bit. Nevertheless he was able to piss for the moment, if with too much frequency. It boiled away invisibly in the bowl. Charybdis. The blockage in him wasn't in his urethra, that was for sure. Each time he went back to bed still mindful of the feelings of the things around him that had no feelings. He had given them feelings, the grace of feelings – it was the least he could do. They had been his companions now all these Dalkey months, they had conspired to please him, content him, recompense him for whatever he had lost. Perhaps the last spurt of urine occurred after he had trousered his pecker in his pyjamas. Perhaps that wasn't so dandy, but who was there to mind it? In the launderette he would wash out these misdemeanours, like a child in the confessional with his small sins.

About five thirty he decided to get out of the doss because he didn't believe there was much chance of further sleep now. He knew what he had to do, he certainly did. He could leave it for a few days because he didn't want to seem eager somehow, or did he just mean obedient. He was beholden to no man, he had earned that. His pension was his gun, his weapon against work. Oh but he saw the justice in Fleming's words and anyway he respected Fleming. Such trust was the bedrock of kindness and friendship. Sure he couldn't leave the prow of Fleming swinging in the wind. He brewed up some tea so strong it was like the colour of hell in his cup. Policeman's tea would put tar into your heart. By heavens it was a clement morning, almost a forgery of spring, and wasn't it spring anyway, well past the first of February. A matter of belief, the first day of spring, like Protestants and Catholics differing over the mother of God. The pagan spring, the first. June's spring. 'At least it's spring,' she would say, in the stove-black dark of a February morning. He laid his bottom onto the wicker chair and now that he was fairly certain of his course, of his next move, he was inclined not to move at all. Not even to make the chair creak, and he liked that creak. Damn it, he had three chocolate biscuits for his breakfast, he did. The sea, the island, the rocks, the lighthouse, saluted him good morning. Resplendent joy was his — did he even care it would have its term, like all joys. How he had loved June. He used to go ages when she was alive without having that thought, and then suddenly, for no reason that he could remember, he would catch sight of her in some moment, some gesture, and be stricken all over again. Just for an hour, as the morning sunlight entered his room and bathed his face, he minded nothing and no one. He cradled the memory of his wife as if she were still a living being. As if no one had been crushed, no one had been hurried from the halls of life, and the power of his love could effect that, could hold her buoyant and eternal in the embrace of an ordinary day.

The sunlight stuck its million pins into the pollocky sea, the whole expanse sparked, and sparkled, as if on the very verge of a true conflagration. Alone, alone, he smiled and smiled. He closed his eyes. He opened them. The sea was still there.

Old Dr Brownlee had warned against the cigarillos. Tom had not told the whole truth – the truth, the whole truth – to Fleming. Even those you love don't need the truth always. Far from it. He had been pretty abstemious these last months. The square tin was down between the cushion and the frame. It lived there these days, why not? It was handy. He opened the pleasing lid. It made its tiny sound. Hamlet no less. Took out a cigarillo. A short thin thing the colour of turf. He struck a match and fired the end and then it was the exciting luxury of the smoke, the heat in his lungs, in his mouth. The bitter taste of tobacco that he loved.

Chapter Four

The strange weather calmed the sea and him. He set himself to cleaning the flat as if he were going on a long journey and wanted to leave his billet clean behind him – though as far as he knew he wasn't going anywhere. But something drove him to it. He wasn't interested in half-measures, just swiping at things with a cloth, which is the method of the resident who is permanently *in situ*. No, he went into the village and got himself kitted out for action. In Prendergast's his hand hovered over the bottle of bleach but he desisted. He got a tin of furniture polish and even a chamois for good measure. He felt the housewives in the shop might be admiring him. Was that possible? There were three of them, just ordinary ladies in their ordinary coats. Glancing at him from under rigid perms. Of course they would have the secret knowledge of surgeons, say, or astronauts, the equivalent, when it came to housekeeping. It gave him a curious jaunty feeling, he was almost dancing along the shelves. Those blue cloths, and Fairy liquid which was so kind to hands, apparently. And he couldn't resist, now he was warmed up, a scrubbing brush with a boar burned into the handle, and a nice cake of carbolic soap. Jesus, he would give the place a great rinse-out. Mr Prendergast, a little gouty fellow with the fat red hands of a man who was obliged to wash them often, seemed uncomfortable with Tom's purchases, as if Tom had strayed across gender borders, and as he packaged them up, in waxed brown paper and unwaxed brown paper, and thin white tissue for the loaf of bread Tom threw in with the rest, and a pink toothbrush, Mr Prendergast kept silent, as if struggling not to vent his vexation. Or so Tom imagined, trying to read the little person. 'You must eat more fruit, Daddy,' came Winnie's voice, but he hadn't bought fruit. Mr Prendergast was wearing a jazzy striped shirt under his apron. A stray garment of Carnaby Street. The apron was marked in an interesting way by the various wet items in his shop, not unlike, in some ways, a murder scene. Tom had worked long enough to enter the era of forensics. You were more likely to get information by banging a man's head against a wall in the old days. Or a barrage of questions, the more frightening the better. Fear was a loosener of tongues. But forensics was impartial, impersonal, elegant really. You could find out a thing and then ask the culprit about it, and know the true answer. Have it up your sleeve, like a glorious riposte in an argument. Old items long kept in evidence bags, even from twenty years before, could be fished back out and bodily fluids examined. Mr Prendergast's apron spoke of sliced ham – a hefty thigh of it hung pinkly on the slicing machine, stabbed with holding pins – tomatoes, the slurry of a broken egg, mysterious green splashes, soil from lettuces, and the traces of things requiring to be rolled up across his stomach, unwashed carrots with their green wigs, and on Fridays – more reds, greys, even yellow dye – fish. The poor haddock with a bad case of jaundice. Tom watched little Mr Prendergast and began idly to wonder about him. Was that his wife in the shadows, the stout grey woman emptying out a big sack of pea pods onto scales, the green things wiggly and rushing like a shoal of little fish – were they happy together after all the years? Who owned the white Ford Escort outside the premises, as clean as a baby's soother? Did he work long hours, and in the Dalkey evenings, having pulled down his shutters and turned out the light, did he pause in the dim shop and light a fag and think about his life? Were there any crimes long hid from understanding? Had he maimed, hit, hurt, struck another human being? Was he burdened by debts, by unpaid taxes? How could Tom know? The 'new' boys and girls in the forensics division, geniuses really, they might be able to tell from that apron. Mr Prendergast fed the numbers into his magnificent register, all steel and brass, hitting each key with his finger like a heron striking at little fish, and there was the sum owed, which he didn't seem able to say aloud either. So Tom went with the dumbshow, nodding and peculiarly contented, and gave the shopkeeper his money, and put his wrapped goods under his oxter like you might a wounded animal. The three women seemed to bristle against his presence now, as if he were holding them up from the strict marked card of their day. They were tipped forward, weight on the balls of their feet, like the marathon runners on the starting line at the Olympics. They're off! But very slowly.

'Thank you, and good day to you,' said Mr Prendergast, with surprising lightness and warmth.

'Oh ho,' said Tom.

Well, so, there was a lot to be said for what was in a person's voice, if you could get them to speak. Just looking at them was only a bit of the story. If the sea could speak? The deeps between land and island? The birds of the air? Now he carried his little burden of cleaning goods et cetera in the colour-scratched plastic bag he had brought with him scrunched up in a pocket. The main street of the village curved away from him, as if following an ancient way of cows. The citizens in their variety passed him on the old pavement. It was still difficult for him to include himself among them. He still felt the old instinct – professional distance. The curious aloofness he had perfected, especially in the vicinity of bloody crimes. When children were killed, or even animals. When young girls were struck down, felled by fists, by shoes. In the old days, when wives were bloodied and beaten, you were not to go further than the front door. Ah yes. You could check if a person was still breathing, but no more. A child of the house could be lathered into a state of utter distress – you had to leave that alone too. You learned these rules off the station sergeant, off the tough detectives. The lowliest of men were kings of women. Girls fleeing from laundries, children fleeing from orphanages, all had to be returned. There was no statute he knew of requiring him to do so. It was a matter beyond the law. It was what everyone wanted. That was a quare form of policing, but he had never done anything but buckle under. Never done anything, but just the once.

He stopped by the stationer's and a girleen behind him with a pushchair nearly rammed into him. She was wearing those leggings that all the girls sported. Yellow. The little bit of fat on her after giving birth in no way interfered with her beauty. Sorry, sorry. Both times June was pregnant he had

had to try and calm his erections. He had pegged away at them in private, to take the jump out of them. He gave a little laugh, laughing at himself. It seemed like a happy problem now. Privilege. To be lusting after your wife, when her task was to keep her breakfast down, or more often not, retching and moaning in the jacks – she'd had morning sickness all day – whispering to the good Jesus, and to get Winnie and Joe out at the allotted time and not before, and more than whispering then, caterwauling, shouting out shouts the width of hills. He had come out without his damn cap and now the February sunshine was beginning to cook his scalp. He checked again in his coat to make sure he hadn't sequestered it in an unaccustomed pocket. He sometimes did that. Confounding himself. Put things in the wrong place, set down things without a clear thought about them. Someday he would put himself down somewhere and forget where he had left himself. In all likelihood. He wished he had a handkerchief but instead he laid the back of his right hand across his brow and mopped it that way. The big change after sixty he had noticed was not just the rising to piss at night, but a hundred other little intimations of infirmities ahead. His very footstep seemed to him less recognisable. Where once he had stridden forth, now he more or less was on a shorter rein, he had taken in his stride, tailored it, like the gansey of a famished man. The old Victorian buildings went straight up as always, but they also these days were inclined to sway about a bit, just at the tops where the flourishes were, the inspirations of architects, little Greek temples, dates marked on decorative tiling. A date in Ireland was always a bothering thing. 1911. Was that the Wexford

Lock-Out or the visit of the English king? It was both, but it was never both in Ireland. To the left of the stationer's – the *Dandy*, the *Beano*, *Woman's Way*, *Ireland's Own* made a damped fire of colour behind the serried interruptions of the plate glass – was one of those intimidating restaurants someone of his soul's mien would never patronise. Out of the doorway with its proud array of plaques and metal ribbons stepped Mr Tomelty, polishing his glasses on the lining of his Crombie coat, and then perching them on his large nose, and then gazing out under a shadowing hand at the quiet street. All the other actors seemed to have disappeared into invisible wings, so Mr Tomelty had no choice but to notice the rather bedraggled tenant of the annexe. It would not have been Tom Kettle's choice to bump into Mr Tomelty, largely because he didn't feel he knew him, or would ever know him. But Tom noticed the spruce coat, even now with traces of the brush that Mr Tomelty must have used on it, not unlike a horse with a close clip. He wasn't in his gardening rags at any rate, and was dressed more like the rich man he was. He looked so much trimmer, younger, in his dapper clothes. Could Tom claim acquaintance with Mr Tomelty, was that within the bounds of decency? It seemed not only could he, but Mr Tomelty showed a certain eagerness to greet him.

'Oh, Kettle,' he said. 'Mr Kettle, just the maneen I wanted.'

Tom gave him a quizzical look, and smiled, aiming for benign and easy-going connection. He knew not what else to do.

'You have no idea,' Mr Tomelty said, 'the comfort it is to

me and my good wife' – Tom had never sighted the wife – 'to have a member of the Garda Síochána in residence.'

Tom nodded his head, gave it a few seconds, so as to take any false hint of criticism out of what he was about to say.

'Retired,' he said.

'Just,' said Mr Tomelty. 'Just.'

'Nine months now, nine months now . . .' said Tom, graciously, easily. He had walked on a few steps and now was obliged to turn on his shoes to accommodate Mr Tomelty's walking further out onto the pavement. In the distance Tom could see the old hotel and the remnants of two castles – real castles, not like Mr Tomelty's gaff. He was instructing his whole being to be at its most relaxed. Somewhere inside all this he was making a huge and taxing effort.

'Listen and I'll tell you,' said Mr Tomelty. 'Our new tenants in the Turret Flat' – Mr Tomelty didn't pronounce his *r*'s in their entirety, but just a little burring sound instead, so it sounded like Tut Flat – 'well, she is an actress, you know.'

'Oh?' said Tom.

'Oh yes – but just last night arrived in an older gentleman, I had no notice of it, she is very young, I suppose he is her benefactor, I have no idea, you know, Mr Kettle, I am sure we are both men of the world, but . . . Can I persuade you to turn a blind eye? I know a man of your probity – might . . . – well, I don't know – might be uncomfortable – and rightly. But.'

Tom Kettle suddenly felt cooler and the little feeling of unwellness left him. He had thought he knew what Mr Tomelty was going to say, and had feared that it was going to be much worse than asking for sugar. He had feared Mr

Tomelty was going to ask him to find out who the older man was. As an ex-Garda. Skilled in the arts of detection. Well, he had thought immediately, and this was what had made him feel a little unwell, Mr Tomelty was going to have to do his own spying in his own house. But then, Mr Tomelty hadn't said anything of the sort.

'I feel,' said Mr Tomelty, with more than a trace of self-regard, certainly an intended display of his own generosity, 'in the modern age, in this age of changes, that we must be more tolerant, and Mrs Tomelty – well, she is my guide in a matter like this. If this old chap is – is – as we may suspect – well. Even to say it is inviting scandal, but we must – I hope – you won't take exception to the young woman and her arrangements. We must live and let live, I believe. This is the new Ireland. In our youth, Mr Kettle, there would have been no mercy for such a person. None. Denounced from the pulpit in the . . . By the Catholic . . .' Tom knew instantly the good Mr Tomelty was a Protestant, the way he didn't finish the sentence, but floundered in that special mire of Irish social intercourse.

Now Tom suddenly realised he was taking a liking to Mr Tomelty and his strenuous open-mindedness. He laughed. He was pretty sure no one in Dalkey gave a damn about such things. Maybe down the country in remote parishes. Where priests were still kings. An old Ford Cortina puttered up the street, relic of a distant era. There was a little smattering of passing starlings, as if the laugh had made them veer from their course, who all shot up onto the roof of the stationer's. He nodded his head.

'It's of no concern to me whatsoever, Mr Tomelty,' he said,

finding something of Mr Tomelty's diction in his mouth.

On his way home he thought about the young actress and her 'benefactor', up there above him in the Turret Flat. He tried to picture them in that particular aftermath of human reunion that he had often felt himself when he'd been away from June for a few days, on the track of fugitive criminals down the country, as may be. You'd sometimes be called in to help with local emergencies. Kidnappings, rural post offices violently raided. Big-world crimes in little places. The glad embrace, just on the verge of embarrassment, as if a few days apart had nearly made strangers of each other, and the options open were: fall in love again, or flee. The weird giddiness of it. He was sure mere age couldn't blunt that. He trod along between the beautiful houses, their high walls, their perfected oldness and rightness, thinking of what it would have meant to him to grow old with June. Was it not one of the ordinary rewards of love? Crawl with each other to hospital appointments maybe, but also revel in the allotment of days still left. Talk about the children with the reverence and pride of former owners. He could only imagine it. It was given to you either to live, or not to live, there was nothing else. A soul like him left on earth without the person he had loved – what sort of creature was that? She would have remembered what he looked like when he was young, or youngish, in the sixties. She always said, as if it were an article of absolute faith, that he was 'a very good-looking man', though he knew for a fact he wasn't. But he would have gone on with a woman who thought that, well past any debate on the matter, with his large, bandy body, and his belly, and his beat-up boxer's face.

It nearly made him angry now – and he knew it was illogical, he probably looked a great deal put out and vexed, though no one was on the road to see it – that she was always in his mind as the person she had been when she departed. Not young, not old, but human and beautiful. Why would that make him angry? He was angry with who, with what? It was his duty to remember her. It was his duty to remember her. But he was old, he was old, and he had never wanted another, never. He was old and she was gone, never herself to be old. His fists were so clenched now, his nails – which he must cut soon, damn it – nearly sliced into his palms. It was still June he thought of, it was she who floated in his head. The small of her back where there was a triangle of skin aglow between her buttocks and her spine . . . Like the bit that joined her together. How her breasts pointed down at him when he lay on his back, pointed down at him, pointing him out as her elected beau. How her smile made her green eyes brighten, sparkle, so much kindness, and a crazy little roughness, an outlaw giddiness, and the little violence in her when she climaxed. She'd nearly slap your face! And what had taken her away? What had taken her away? Only the most perfidious dastardliness, only the most contemptible vileness. Oh, he wanted her, he wanted her.

Just then an old car pulled into the kerb, the engine making its noise like one of the big cats. He had seen it parked at the far end of the castle – of course, it was Mr Tomelty's Daimler. Six litres, a thirsty beast. Never do for a cop car, it was a stately galleon of a machine.

Mr Tomelty opened the driver's door and half emerged, like you do, awkwardly, just enough to talk to him coherently. Tom puzzled himself by giving a shy smile. He wondered what age Mr Tomelty was. Seventy, eighty? It was impossible to tell. Good lunches and dinners had kept the lines out of his face.

'Lift?' said Mr Tomelty, with a touch of theatrics.

It was only a few hundred yards to the gates of Queenstown Castle. He'd walk it in four minutes. And he had been looking forward to just gazing down the slipway to the harbour, where the tiny huts of the fishermen, that held their nets and gear, descended in raggle-taggle order. It was nothing, the nothing he was growing to love. He wanted to see the clear water in the harbour itself, and salute the gulls, the survivors of the hooks of wicked boys, and all the rest. It would calm him, just as this weather had calmed him in morning-time. He was not beyond calming, Tom Kettle, he wasn't. But there was something in Mr Tomelty's gesture that also pleased him. Soldiers in wartime, comradeliness, easy camaraderie. It was the thing Tom liked best in men, when they had these qualities. If they didn't, he could take them or leave them. He climbed into the passenger seat, and it was the frankness of his nature that admired the leather coverings and the rich veneers around the many dials. He was laughing again as he pushed his backside into the soft seat.

'Do you know,' he said, 'do you know—' But he didn't get a chance to complete his question, and instantly he forgot what he was going to say, because Mr Tomelty, his foot to the accelerator with a youthful flourish, made the engine growl, growl magnificently. Mr Tomelty was laughing too.

Although the evenings were lengthening, it was still dark at five thirty, and it was five thirty now. Between the pick-up spot and the parking spot, the sun abandoned everything for one more day, the sea blackened, and the islands blackened even darker, more black than black, and the sky looked shocked and empty, as if not fully trusting that the moon would rise soon and her cohorts of stars crowd in like figures at a hajj. Now Mr Tomelty inveighed upon Tom to follow him into his own quarters, through the main door of the castle no less, and into a small, battered hall. There was no baronial flavour to the place at all. And coming down the steep stairs, treading firmly, was an unknown man, a smallish figure with white hair combed back, and a tweed jacket, and in truth a decent pair of trews. Tom knew a gent when he saw one. This was not the clobber of a jailbird, anyhow. The descending man was looking neither right nor left, nor even up or down, he was in a private reverie of his own, and even as he passed Tom Kettle there was no greeting or other human sign. As if Tom were not quite there, a Victorian ghost in a Victorian mansion. It crossed his mind that the man thought he was a servant of some kind, or a tradesman, not worthy of true notice. But how could he tell that? Maybe the man was in some unknown distress, preoccupied, hurrying out to deal with some harsh news. Anyway, the front door opened and closed. Tom hurried on after Mr Tomelty, the plastic shopping bag banging his leg, suddenly afraid he would lose him, or be lost himself somehow. Actual panic.

But Mr Tomelty was waiting for him, with his smile. Between the dark of the hall and the lights in the room behind him, his sparse hair was lit in relief, a halo, like the painting of a medieval saint. There were no saints in any era, Tom knew, just good men and bad, and sometimes both in the one bottle. Mr Tomelty made a head movement after the vanished gent.

'The boyo in question,' he said. 'Ah ha.'

But Tom felt he was breasting a fresh wave of challenge now, and said nothing for the moment, and followed after Mr Tomelty with obedient tread.

Here was a fine big room after all, not poky like the hall, that took Tom by surprise, with three tall windows framed by trimmed and gathered curtains, still open so the expanse of window glass glimmered darkly. The clerk's-ink of night had spoiled the view, but well he knew that view already, Tom, from his own perch in the wicker chair. And he thought briefly it was *notable* that they were all living with the same glad sight, and yet closed off to each other, strangers and worse. There were family photographs all about, wherever there was space, almost a superabundance, as if they had profligately bred, these Tomeltys, almost too profusely. And books on shelves, upright, fallen, like the integers of a primitive computer, and library lamps throwing light onto their shoes.

A little woman came forth as if to block his further progress and took his right hand. The gesture shocked him. Her dress was the same colour as the shadows. Again he could only think of ghosts. Her two hands that gripped his felt as if they had just been taken from being warmed at a fire, but he could see no fire. The room was made bearable by a long Dimplex heater that gurgled softly in counterpoint to her smiling silence.

'How do ye do?' he said, making a great effort not to follow it with 'ma'am', like a fool.

'You'll have a drink, Detective Sergeant?' she said, again flummoxing him and breeding silence instead of explanation. Retired, retired!

'I will, ma'am,' he said, 'sure I will.'

'You're not on duty,' she said, humorously, shaking her narrow shoulders at him. Her necklace of small garnets – rubies maybe, more like – held tense on her lined neck, like insects on the very point of dispersal.

'I am not, nor ever again,' he said, finding his feet in the dose of humour at least. She asked what he desired and he asked did they have a cordial, a lemonade, a fruit juice, anything, and didn't she, she did. And she went and poured him this, and Mr Tomelty gripped his own glass of unknown liquid and smiled, and he laughed for an unknown reason, and Tom thought it was a very rum world when people were revealing themselves to be not at all what he had thought them, as if in refutation of his old inspired self as a Garda.

As though hearing this thought, Mr Tomelty said:

'And how are you finding retirement?'

He was handed his long glass of lemonade – pink, he could just see – and swallowed a morsel of it down, because he was afraid he might choke on it, though there was nothing wrong with his throat. He wasn't confident the gods would allow him this encounter without vexation. His left hand still clutched his shopping.

'Do you know I—' he said, before he had even formulated the rest of the sentence in his head. 'I think I can say—' Again no fuller thought came to him. 'Are you yourselves—?' Why could he not complete a sentence? He blushed in the merciful half-light.

'Hoteliers must take bookings till they drop,' said Mr Tomelty, with all the force of a practised phrase, as if his life were a play and on this page of the script, this is what it said, and he was going to say it well, and with quiet force.

'I can well imagine.' Tom knew nothing about running hotels.

'Let's sit on the chairs and take our ease,' said Mrs Tomelty. 'I am so happy to meet you, I really am. We were in need of a strong presence without fully knowing it. Especially now we have children in the house. That lovely little girl, and her brother.' She looked at her husband, as if not wanting to exclude him from this conversation. Tom had not seen any little girl. Did she mean the people in the Turret Flat? Mr Tomelty beamed, like a torch switched on. 'These dark nights have seemed brighter for your possession of the annexe. The older you get, the thinner the arm.'

The older you get, the thinner the arm. He was thinking to himself, without purpose, she is from Roscommon, Leitrim maybe. Sligo at a pinch. They sat themselves down in chairs as she had suggested. He was quite content to sit with these nice people. He was quite content to be a strong presence with thicker arms. The moon rose far beyond the island as they spoke on, and each time he looked through the dark windows it seemed to occupy a different pane. There was a sense of quiet music although no music played. Mrs Tomelty had invited him for a drink, she had in a sense invited herself, they were all of a mind to speak of nothing, and speak of nothing as well as can be, and they did that.

Soon they knew he was a widower, and that his children were gone. Soon he knew that Mrs Tomelty was the Irish authority on tea roses, apparently a vast subject. He perhaps had innocently thought there was only one tea rose, or had never thought about it. He had made a little study himself of wildflowers, as they pertained to corpses, and the environs where corpses were found, and what could be picked out of a jumper or a hairdo, but he said nothing about that. She showed him a book published by the Royal Dublin Society that she had in fact written, with the title in elegant stamped gold, *Tea Roses*. Eliza Tomelty. It looked like a family Bible, fat and leather-bound. Mr Tomelty left inches around all the talk of his wife, as if he had promised himself he would never talk across her, or interrupt her, whether out of fear of her or love Tom was not in a position to say. Perhaps it came to the same thing, theatrically speaking. He admired them. The dark print dress she wore was made of nylon. Were there miniature lightnings fleeing across her thighs, as she crossed and recrossed her legs in her static-rich stockings? It was only now, so late in the day – this replenishing, soft spring day – that he noticed Mr Tomelty was wearing a bow tie. It was the green of gooseberries. It was difficult to square this with the man in tatters who had asked him months back for a loan of sugar. He was struck again by the strangeness of people, their mystery, but also their recognisability. He felt he knew these people immediately, which to him suggested a certain homogeneity among humankind. A general familiarity. As if there were only ten different varieties of soul after all. He had often thought that, in his dealings as a copper. And yet if he had been put on the rack to tell the truth, he had also to allow that they were intensely individual. So that they were known to him instantly, but also not, and possibly never to be known.

In the corner of the room stood a unicorn, with a silver horn, or possibly white gold, raising its delicate right hoof, and innocently staring out through quiet eyes. Mr Tomelty and his missis made no reference to it. It was just there, verifiably.

Chapter Five

If he wasn't exactly sleepless – he kept nodding off and waking abruptly – he couldn't sleep properly. Tomorrow he would go in and see Fleming. Or the day after, when he had got the flat sparkling. He had cooked himself frankfurters and mash, a great favourite, and now they lay in his belly like an early pregnancy. His pyjamas were old but all pyjamas seemed to be born old. His even older stomach was mottled here and there with skin tags and dark, round, coinlike things, which the good Deansgrange doctor, the indefatigable Dr Brownlee, had declared to be benign. They were still unsightly. But who was there to sight them? No one. The burden of getting older was borne alone, but also as if by someone else, because he often couldn't recognise bits of himself he caught in the mirror. Whose newly scrawny legs were those? Why was his head sitting further forward on his neck? Was it really kind of the gods to do this to the skin of his face, as if a child had been let loose with a brown marker? Beside his old bed, on the bedside table much prized by June long ago – 'though no one sees it but ourselves,' she had said, in the old house, the day they moved in, and rolled out the carpets, oh momentous day – was the book he *wasn't* reading, just wasn't, though it had attracted his eye in one of the boxes. It was a newish history of Ireland but he didn't have the strength for it, the signal within.

Who was he anyway, he didn't know. Was Kettle even his name? Was it even *a* name? A pot in the kitchen. Joseph was well up on Native American kettles, though they didn't use them in New Mexico. This was the sort of thing Tom liked to know – so-called useless information. He couldn't be told about enough useless things. Before Joseph got the final nod for his green card in '91, he had been looking for books about tribes, because the only job on offer was as a locum on a pueblo near Albuquerque. He was so happy to be going off and getting out of Ireland, so happy, after everything that had happened, and though Tom was stabbed by the happiness in a way, ah yes, but, he understood it. Adventure. Renewal. Give the whins to the plough horse and turn the earth over. 'Mind the rattlesnakes,' he said, as his son went off that day at Dublin Airport. 'I will, Da,' said Joseph. They were both smiling and laughing. Tears brimming, tears brimming.

They didn't have long in the new house in Deansgrange, in truth, before the little changes. At night she would go to sleep like a body interred – he could barely hear her breathing. She lived so lightly the traces were hard to see. He would hunt for signs of her. Traces of June. Later, a good few years on, he'd come home of an evening and go about the house, looking for her and the children. When he called out to her she mightn't answer, because sometimes she wasn't there. In the last times, when he called out, and she was there, she never answered either. Even alive she was every so often like someone you remembered that you had loved. There was the stick of mascara in the loo without its top screwed back on. As he would make that good, he might wander then into their bedroom, and there might be a pair of her jeans left in a heap, like she had suddenly evaporated. Winnie got out of big school at five, Joseph little school at four. She began to go on epic bus rides with them, he knew not where. He had no way to reach her sometimes, even when she was home. She'd be like a telephone not plugged in then. Billy Drury at work, a Roscommon detective he had a great grá for, and who he could just about talk to, said she had the blues, the blues, the housewife blues. But Tom didn't think she had the housewife blues. That was another thing. He liked to do the housework anyhow, in the evenings, running the carpet cleaner around the place, rackety rackety, having a bit of a scrub at the loo. She gave the kids a bath, which they adored, and dried them cyclonically in the big white towel, and smothered them in a dust storm of talcum powder, and read to them in their beds, their happy, sleepy faces still smudged with white. Beatrix Potter, Peter Rabbit, Mrs Tiggy-Winkle, he used to eavesdrop on the stories, liking them well enough himself. Sally Henny-Penny, have you seen my pocket handkerchief?

Or was it himself read the stories mostly?

In the early days she was as right as rain, wasn't she? As right as Irish rain. And to him everything had been verging on the miraculous. He was so old, all of thirty, and he had long given up hopes of a deep love like that. And it was a deep love. She was just a girl that worked at the Wimpy café in Dunleary. He and Billy Drury were down there for three long weeks trying to dig out evidence about a murder. Another girleen had been found murdered in a graveyard, and himself and Billy were much exercised to uncover the villain. It was a disgusting case all told, a beautiful young woman left like rubbish in a big grain sack, in a weedy corner of the quiet yard. Wolfsbane, summer-stocks and giant dock leaves, trying to make a decent guard of honour for her. The hands were only found years and years later in the Dublin Mountains, dug up by a Labrador on his walk. But they never found out who the girl was. She had been killed in an atmosphere of total anonymity. They thought she had maybe just arrived on the mailboat from Holyhead – in despairing moments, they wondered had she dropped from the heavens? An angel with severed hands. In the sixties it was so hard to put names to the dead sometimes. And around 11 a.m., having traipsed about from house to house, up and down Patrick Street, the curious snake of York Road, which started among the working-class houses and their damp little yards and ended among resplendent mansions, hanging gardens, he and Billy would drag their sorry arses into the Wimpy café, and get that weak coffee in the opaque glass cups, white as seashells, and stick their sore legs under the Formica tables, and Billy liked to play the jukebox, and that's how they got talking, himself and June, mocking his dubious taste in country and western.

'Nothing wrong with Johnny Cash, though,' said June, in her blue outfit, and the white bib thing like a nurse's nearly. He would laugh, and Billy, being an easy-going head enough, yes, he was a lovely lad really, would laugh, and call them bolloxes, under his breath, because he didn't want to give scandal to the schoolkids that infested the plastic benches. Joe Dolan and the Drifters. And Billy would go on writing his notes, his endless notes – he was the best, most meticulous writer of case reports in Harcourt Street. And then there was the famous day – famous for evermore in his heart, anyhow – when he and June went walking down into Monkstown, on a sort of date, and went out far onto the pier there, where the summer grasses were left to grow like a long narrow meadow, and the sun was so hot on the wooden seats that the blue paint blistered. And they sat together smelling the salted air that was stocked so thick with fishy smells because just a few yards across the oily water was the stubby pier for the trawlers, the heroic fishermen of Dunleary, with their wellington boots as creased as the skin of elephants, and the boxes of otherworldly ice. They sat together, picking at the paint blisters with their fingers, June's bare legs covered in an almost imperceptible suggestion of downy hair, also something of a strange meadow, and her skin as brown as almonds, and her cotton dress on her trim form, and the crazily perfect face, as it seemed to him, someone so lovely he could barely breathe to think she was with him, him, a mere copper of dubious extraction in his thirtieth year.

The touch of her hand not obviously like fire but burning him all the same, burning his hand.

She told him almost nothing about herself for ages, and he told her almost nothing, because what did they have to tell? But they soon clicked that the reason for this was the same reason, in each of their cases. *Cases* was the word. Their whole lives seemed to him like crime scenes, of a sort. And yet here he was, a detective no less, and here she was, a lovely waitress, and here was the sun of Dunleary, the same sun whose heat was much stronger inland, even close inland, like the back of Monkstown. And one lazy Saturday on her day off they sat in a bar in Blackrock and lent half an ear to some ould match on the radio, and drank cider, feeling like a king and a queen of the world, and walked all the way past the Carnegie Library, and the posh Volkswagen garage, and along the high road built along what must have once been a wild coast of cliffs and rocks, where ships no doubt came to grief, tamed only by the racketing railroad, and the enormous mansions that fronted the way, the salt wind attacking their facades. And they walked hand in hand all the way along the tremendous seafront of Monkstown, the little bodies of people below shivering on their towels, or braving the wretchedness of the Irish Sea, and they went down a little way past the big iron gates of the hotel, and past the tennis club lurking in its cowl of woodland, and crossed the iron bridge, their shoes going clack-clack-clack, and got out onto the old sea-field at Seapoint, luxuriant with the August grass, tall and shedding its seeds, and they found a discreet hollow like thousands of lovers before them, and hoped no boys would be nearby and lob rocks at them, and kissed like crazy kids themselves, falling deeper and deeper into the bottomless pool of love, and made love like moaning demons, and if they didn't make Winnie that day, he was a Dutchman.

Would the gods forgive him for weeping in his bed now, in far Dalkey, thinking these things? These were the gifts given to him in his life, there was no reason to mourn or complain. They could only be experienced the once, there was no need for repetition or a chorus to that song, he had once been that man and she that woman, on old Seapoint, so drowned in the sea of grasses that they might as well have considered themselves inanimate beings, or the dragonflies that fired past, or the very smell of the grass as they flattened it, the upsurge of joy as they came, and cried out, crying out to who? To the betrayals of the past and the future he sensed then only as a recompense.

But who was she? Almost as unknown as the murdered girl. Was she in effect a murdered girl, a long-drawn-out murder like death by a thousand cuts? Lingchi. Yet there wasn't a mark on June, for all the cuts she had endured. They were cuts of another kind, of course. Of course they were. Cuts he knew himself, understood himself. Was it a good thing, then, that they were both so cut into – since, after all, that's how they knew each other? Recognised. Didn't need names and families, grandparents, mothers, fathers, in fact the lack of them gave them their love, if only for a while. Was that while worth all the years after? She had only been three when her mother died. Her mother as beautiful as herself, according to the little photo. Where was that photo now? He hoped he hadn't lost it. What was her mother's name? June had no way of knowing. Those bloody nuns would never tell her a thing. She had nearly found out. As a little girl of eleven she had sneaked into the orphanage office to try and find her file. The other girls had said there were files on them all in the office. It was a big gloomy place, June told him. She found her file alright, her name on a folder, in a long desk, she said, she lifted it, and the little photo fell out. Otherwise the folder was empty. Just then one of the nuns came in, and then there was caterwauling, and raging, and punishment. But she had put the little photo into her knickers and it was hers. She had seen no names, no facts, no dates, no nothing, but her mother had fallen down into her hand, and the nuns knew nothing of it. She believed it was her mother, though there was nothing on the back, and Tom could vouch for the fact that they looked so alike.

And then worse and worse, that bloody Mrs Carr, the only person at their wedding in any way family, in that she had been foster mother to June for a couple of years. And took this as a licence to haunt her. Which June very mysteriously allowed, wouldn't tolerate his wish to banish her, banish the witch. Because June was kindly, astute in a subtle way about human persons, knew something about Mrs Carr beyond his ken. They had Billy Drury and the golf wizard McCutcheon and his missis and a few other lads, and Tom's Nigerian pal from his army days came over on the mailboat, dear old Peter, where the hell was he now? Mrs Carr spewing discord like a cobra. With her black dresses, and her legs like big stabiliser posts on a fence. And her hair tortured into a leprous perm. Who worked long and hard to drive a wedge between him and June, but never managed that, never. And only got her walking papers when she suggested to June that Tom looked like neither of the children, and was she sure he was the father. Goodbye, goodbye, and lock the door after her. And good riddance.

It was the small hours now, those well-named hours.

She didn't know who she was, but she knew where she had been. When she talked about where she had been, she sat in a certain way, she shifted her body forward in the chair, and squared her shoulders, and spoke with a different voice. She could talk for two hours and still sound like she was summing up.

For so long she was quiet and never spoke about those things. They'd been going out for a whole month, him fairly killing himself to get out on the bus or the train to her, from his lousy digs in Glasnevin, or his work in Harcourt Street. He tried to see her every day. If only the old train station there had still been open, oh bejesus, but he had to gallop all the way across Dublin, through the Green, down Grafton Street, skirt the college, stampede up Abbey Street and onto Talbot, and go like the clappers to Connolly station for the 5.30 to Bray. He was younger then and fit but it was summer all the same and he was obliged to change into a spare shirt in the tiny jacks as noisy as a drumkit, and wash the sweat off his chest and arms into the bargain. After a month of this he might have qualified for the Irish team at the Olympics. A whole month, a fortune in train fares. Couples might be expected to talk through their life stories the first night – not June. She liked to tell him all that had happened that day at the café, maybe in just a little too much detail, but he could bear it. He liked her in the aftermath of her work, weary but not bone-weary, her feet aching. She'd have thrown on her jeans and grabbed a jacket. Her lovely denim jacket, the very height of hippy fashion. The jeans she had worn into the bath as instructed by the label, and let shrink on her legs, skin-tight. She would never meet him in her digs, of course, because it was some kind of religious gaff for the protection of Catholic girls – Mrs goddamn Carr lived in Stillorgan, far away from the Wimpy. Not that he even knew about Mrs Carr then. He knew nothing. She loved to natter on but she never talked. He supposed that was it, that was how she was. In a way he was relieved she didn't go serious on him, because he was the guardian of his own silences, had been all his life.

Tom could see them in his mind's eye still, the cluttered blaze of sunset making Howth Head seem very close, though it was seven miles away across the bay. They were passing the yard of Irish Lights, where the poignant deep-sea buoys and floating lights were kept. For storms and the darkness of winter, he supposed. He had stepped down from the train in a flurry of simple happiness. Meeting his girl, under the ancient face of the town hall clock, and Queen Victoria's ruined fountain. They didn't care who saw them kissing and they'd kissed on the platform. Now they had trekked seaward, among the little industrial privacies of the front, between the mailboat jetty and the pier before Seapoint. There would be no use heading down to Seapoint now, though he longed to, because there was a fierce persistent rattle of summer rain coming down on them, and so they sheltered under a stone arch of unknown purpose, maybe an entrance into somewhere that was no longer there.

She said she was cold and they perched their bums on a granite ledge and held each other close as they could. He was holding in his arms the best thing he knew in the world. This human girl. For all her saying she was cold, her very heat was in her clothes. Her very softness signalled to something in his brain, releasing the optimum amount of pleasure he could feel. The dial turned fully up. That was the truth of it. Why not? He knew well what unhappiness was, and here was happiness. How precious she seemed to him, how complete, how perfected. Where were her flaws? He couldn't locate them. He rested his face on her hair and breathed so deep he wasn't sure if he was dead or alive, and couldn't have cared less. He knew minutes before she spoke that she was going to say something to him beyond an account of her working day. Any human creature can sense these things. The rain, the arch, the hour were conspiring to bring her to this moment. He had no idea what she was going to say, no idea that what she was going to say was in the upshot going to be his salvation and his ruin. But he knew she was going to say it. It wasn't so much about her mother as what she said after she told him about her mother, although this was the time she did tell him that also.

'I don't know who I am. There's just no one for you to marry.' At this point he didn't believe he had mentioned marriage. But she spoke so sadly, so precisely, and so bravely, that he certainly didn't say so. And he immediately thought, by God, if she wants to marry, I will do that. Had it even entered his stupid head? It must have. Tom couldn't remember. She sat on in her denim glory, the jeans like a second skin, or a skin she could shed, with that gathered, collected set to her shoulders. She had a little purse with a heart on it – like the knickers. More of a wallet maybe. It was then she extracted the sacred photo and told him the story of how she had won it, how she had stolen it from oblivion. Those damnable nuns.

But then, by her courage, she released him to tell her his story, his own sorry bloody tale of woe. All the dead mothers!

He was gabbling, excited. He was aware at the back of

his head of his lousy pay, detective though he was. That wasn't the point. They'd manage, they would. And who the hell would they have at any such ceremony? That wasn't the point either. Nothing in the normal way seemed to be. Because he knew she wasn't finished. There was something further to say, he could see it as if it were a raven sitting on her shoulder. They had come to a huge decision about their lives, almost by happenstance, by things benignly conspiring, but she wasn't finished. The shoulders were still set. She wasn't finished because she never would be.

Quoth the raven, never would be. Here was now, a light year removed from that reverberating day, and all the things that followed, all the hard things, the happy things, the happier things. The usual fog cleared a moment from his mind. The small hours were refining him down, like a rough whiskey. What would God want to take from his story, he wondered. St bloody Peter at his gate. What was important in all this, his life, his life, like any other life? He thought suddenly of all the detectives on the earth, and all the detectives that had been on the earth – would it be hundreds of thousands? Would they be herded into the detective enclosure? And made to race against each other like horses? All the detectives – the violent crimes, the rapes, the murders, the con jobs, the robberies, the frauds, the very waterspout, the waterfall, the great flood of crimes in human stories. The hubbub, the hubbub. That had so concerned them all. Like the waterfall in Powerscourt, pouring down, pouring down. And all these men, in all the languages of the world, all the races, all the forces, trying to peer in, to weigh up, to come to conclusions, to strike it lucky, cop a break, to squeak a case through by the skin of its teeth. What was their worth, their own weight? And what was at the heart of it? His life, his little life? The fog edged away from the shore of himself, the sea opened like the stage in a theatre, the helpful sun burned in its element, there was a truth told to him, a truth, in his curious age, in his palpable decay, that there at the heart of it, there at the heart of it, for ever and always, was June. Winnie and Joseph and June. But June.

Chapter Six

And he would have gone in to see Fleming, of course he would, that day or the day after, but that, unannounced – the right of any child – Winnie arrived the next morning. And what a morning. When he went to answer the door – he was going to have to fix that screech if this went on, it was well-nigh embarrassing – the early-spring sun was already more or less frolicking in the front garden. The rhododendron flowers were just beginning to brown at the edges, but they were still burning with their purple. For a second he thought there were bees gathering the nectar, he could hear a vast humming, but more likely he thought it was just in his head. And here was Winnie, in her leggings – a good choice on her, since she had June's legs – a sombre grey, very elegant, and her dark-grey woollen dress, and her wonderful mustard coat that had made him laugh when he first saw it, because the back of it had been painted by a designer, in actual paint: the face of Marilyn Monroe. He couldn't see Marilyn just yet, only the lovely familiar face of his daughter. Oh, but he wished he'd had time to clean the flat now. Oh, she would be 'gazing about'.

'Ah, Winnie, Winnie,' he said. 'Sight for sore eyes!'

'Hiya, Daddy,' she said.

So he brought her in, with all the little bustle of an arriving dignitary, took her red gloves, now her coat – a quick dekko at the back, a quick look at her, and laugh of appreciation, 'Marilyn!' – and set her down in the wicker chair. The rear of the castle was in shadow as yet, but a rich, interrogatory, radiant shadow, with the strange promise of a sunny day. Could it be so in mere Ireland, for a second day in a row? Miraculous. In Malaya he had endured days so hot they were intolerable, as you boiled in your uniform, and regretted life itself. But an Irish spring day could be clement, choice, and kind. When Irish weather stepped up to the plate you couldn't wish to be anywhere else in the world.

But then Winnie was her own kind of sunlight. The living room was all the better for her presence. The red gloves lying now on the dark-yellow coat, and Winnie stretching out her legs. A sort of wondrous painting. Oh, his magnificent daughter. In dumbshow he indicated the possibility of a cup of tea and she answered in the same fashion. Father and daughter, no need of words. After all the mud of life they had traipsed through, as if in clogged boots, that she could still visit with sprightly mien, was his idea of recompense and benison. He wasn't ever going to question it, was he? The very solidity of her, the arms, the legs, the head, the torso. Something he had made with June. If not on that happy day in the dip in the field at Seapoint – perhaps that was just a wild thought, when he counted the months till their wedding – then later, later, with just as much passion and inspiration. To make a girl. What a miracle. And this girl.

'Oh, this place, what a great spot,' she said. 'You were so clever to find it, Daddy.'

'But I didn't make the slightest effort,' he said. 'You looked in the evening paper, and it was there.'

'I looked in the evening paper, and it was there. Yes, yes.'

So now he was in the narrow kitchen, getting the kettle to boil. Stubborn beasts, kettles. She herself had bought it in Pete's Electrical, on Parnell Street, as a housewarming gift, nine long months before. 'A kettle for a Kettle,' she had said, inevitably. Surely that was so.

'*Press-a-Herald, Press-a-Herald!*' she sang, quietly, which had been the street cry of the newsvendors in O'Connell Street long before she was born. Straggly dark lads with the papers laid over one arm, and then plucked forth and folded and presented with one fluid movement, to a hovering passer-by, money taken as if a moment in a ballet, as he had often described to her. Before he made detective, his beat had been all that part of the Northside, from the river to Mountjoy Square. He had loved the queer sense of citizenship – to protect, but of course also sometimes to correct, to harass, to arrest, his fellow Dubliners. The harmless 'ould wans' with their wheelers, the fiddlers and the flute players begging for coppers in the street. The tuneful crime of vagrancy. The tired tide of office workers in the evening, coming into the street like shallow floodwaters, seeping out to bus stops, taxi ranks, headed for a dozen, for fifty, destinations. The hucksters and the pickpockets and the drunkards, the fancy women and the boys in their flashy shoes, the street traders, the strolling priests, the nuns in their headgear of many shapes, the middle-class ladies who had shopped in Arnotts, the lower sort of ladies who had shopped in Clerys, the pretty shop girls in high-voiced gaggles, arm in arm, as if floating along, untouchable in their beauty, exuberant and triumphant, the rough-looking countrymen maybe bedding down in Wynn's Hotel, and the local boys from all the little streets behind the grand buildings, with an eye on the main chance. 'Who you lookin' at?' was their menacing catch-cry, should you even so much as glance at them. Unlettered Cúchulainns. The boys in posh school uniforms, CUS or Belvedere, going to the pictures at the Carlton or the Savoy, hoping to get in to *Viva Las Vegas* with Elvis Presley, over-eighteens only, and the scutty little children with green-running noses, a delta of filth on their ganseys, in big black prams and greasy pushchairs. His people. And Winnie loved to hear all about that, his city when he was a youngster, a young copper, younger than her now. And maybe she still did love to hear it, except she knew it all, chapter and verse, there was no need for words, she could hear it any time in her inner ear.

So he gave his luxuriating daughter – she professed to love that wicker chair too – her tea, two sugars, 'and just a tiny bit of milk, now, Daddy, mind', and phoned Harcourt Street. Although he hadn't phoned to say he was coming in, he thought he had better phone to say he wasn't, and that he would make it in tomorrow, God willing. The sweet-voiced lady on the other end, who knew him so well, instantly recognised him, how very satisfying – 'Yes, Mr Kettle, sure well we'll see you then, won't we?'

'We should go out to the island in the summer, Daddy, we must, don't you think so?'

'We should.'

'We really really must do that, Daddy. Now, make a note of that, Detective.'

'Oh, I will.'

'Come May, now, and I'll be reminding you.'

'June in May . . . Noted. We can hire a rowing boat on Killiney Strand, sure, and we'll row out to the island. Of course we will.'

'We can take a picnic,' she said, 'so we can. I'll make Scotch eggs, I'll make sausages. I might even make – chocolate pancakes, Daddy, now, your favourite.'

'We have Mammy's picnic basket.'

'Do we?' she said.

He was suddenly not so sure. 'Well, maybe,' he said, looking around vaguely. He hadn't seen it for a few years, right enough. Not to register it in his memory. Might be here somewhere. Did it even make the move? Did he throw it in the skip with a thousand other items too worrisome and painful to keep? June's snazzy clothes, her three coats, her underwear, foamy masses of it, her socks, her dozen pairs of shoes. He couldn't bring them and he couldn't leave them either. In the end he darkened his mind and bagged them all up and . . . The shoes he had bought her that time they were broke – bought them with his last few pounds. In Brown Thomas's. Loony extravagance. As a challenge to their penilessness. He filled the skip, going a bit mad maybe, he might have sold some of the things, he supposed, some of the 'bits', but how could he, and he was nearly sure he had thrown in all their photos by mistake, good Christ, because he hadn't been able to locate them ever since either, and next morning when he went out to see what in fact he had discarded, the eejit, it was completely empty. The travellers had come by, his neighbour told him, and picked every last thing out, and put it all in their van. He might have saved himself the forty quid for the skip.

'And are you going into town later?' he said.

But she made no answer.

'And, Winnie, where are you living?' he said, suddenly unable to remember. It was very strange. A father should know where his daughter was living, surely. He knew where she was living but where was it? It had just slipped his mind. He was growing demented, he must be. 'Where are you living?' he said, in some distress now, a bit of a headache brewing.

'Deansgrange, Daddy, Deansgrange.'

'But we've left Deansgrange,' he said, again with the note of panic and misery in his voice.

'Well, but I'm still there, Daddy.'

'Not the cemetery!' he said, with a small cry.

'Yes, Daddy, the cemetery.'

When she was gone, as she soon was, or so it felt like – it was late afternoon and the day had just whizzed by, uncanny really, oh, but he knew why, *because he was so happy* – he washed out her cup in the sink, swirling the water round and round to defeat the possible tea stains. He knew the deviousness of tea. Swirling it round. How he loved her. The simple, complete set of her. His head doing the Ramesh shake. A daughter *set*. Like a tea set. Arklow pottery, which he and June were given as a wedding present by Mrs Carr – and every last cup and plate broken by themselves and the children over the ensuing years on that bloody stone floor in the kitchen. Well, he might have the milk jug somewhere. The soup tureen? Maybe. Winnie, Winnie. Just how she had arranged herself in the sitting room, on the sacred chair, like a painting, yes. He couldn't imagine a world without her. He loved his Joe, he loved his Joe. But he couldn't quite grasp a world sans Winnie. Her confidence. He was chuckling to himself now, drying the cup with a cloth, going on long after it was dry because he liked the motion of it, ha ha ha. He rattled his head. Her ability to get on. Earning more money than he ever had. A novice, a beginner, helping Mr Norris, the barrister, at the Four Courts. A runner, a dogsbody, a tea-maker, a note-taker. But someday she'd take silk. Oh yes. She'd don the white wig. Watch out. She was going to clean out the constitution of all its woman-hating nonsense. The special place of women in the home. That got her goat. McQuaid and de Valera, priest and president. With lawyerly Vim she would scour it all out. Mount a challenge to it. In honour of her mother and all the mothers. Fuck housework. Down with dishcloths. Let's have raging, ragged, ruinous, riotous, ravening, rabid women. Real women. None of these man-made fucking women. That's what she used to say, no doubt would still say it, in Deansgrange. No doubt she would still say it, wherever she was. Deansgrange, come off it. She was not still in Deansgrange. The very idea. Swirl out the stains, swirl out the stains. Ha ha ha.

    McQuaid. Now the dark name had cropped up. He must be thinking about McQuaid now, before talking to Fleming. Everyone knew that the whole fucking mess started with fucking McQuaid. Archbishop of ruinous bullshit.

Maybe not everyone. Himself and Billy Drury, anyhow. He missed poor Billy just as much as anyone – two murderous boys doing for him in five seconds at a stupid robbery in Clonsilla. He wasn't even on duty. Saw these two boyos running out of a little bank there, as he was passing in his Ford Anglia on the way to work. Neat little light-green gluaisteán. Early risers, those robbers. Professional. And armed, with a proper gun, not a plastic popper as they called them, no, a real gun with real bullets. Billy leaping from his car, like the brave fool he was. And how was he going to catch them both, with only two hands and a big voice? He had a lovely big voice, very handy, and anyone that heard him sing the high note in 'Danny Boy' knew they had heard something special. Billy wasn't married, never had a sweetheart in his whole life. He was only getting started at the big stuff. Still lived in digs with another lad, like recruits. Sort of a simple lad in a way, his father a small farmer in Connemara, where the only crop they grew was rocks, but also a kingly lad. Loved the police – one of those rare boys that go in to do good, and stay to do good, and do good. Pity then that he's the one was killed. Father came up from Aughris Beg. Tom had seen lots of grief, buckets of it, in his time, but that little man with the dark weathered face. His son. Oh yes. The dark page of policing, the one you can't read when you join up. They just shot him in the chest, bang, like that. End of Billy Drury. But that was years later. When the thing with the priests had boiled up over them, burning their hands, scalding their faces, Billy had had McQuaid's number. They never even met the old bastard. It was just his word was everywhere, ran everywhere, through everywhere, like rat runs in an old barn. How young they were, him and Billy – late twenties, but also just raw gossoons, in a way. When you got old enough, these old matters changed in your head, took on new meaning. You saw more clearly what the gift of life could be – something precious given, then snatched back by the mean gods. How rare was a man like Billy. When you were young you thought there would be a succession of Billys. But there was only the one. Best man, in more ways than one. With this ring I thee wed. Thought June was a wonder, a beauty, a queen. 'I know my pal Tom a good few years, and know how precious this woman is to him.' That was one of the lines in his speech after, at The Tomelty Arms in Dunleary. Holy Jesus, how had he forgotten that! He must tell the Tomeltys next time he saw them. He had had his marriage supper in their bloody hotel! Jesus, what was wrong with his brain that he had forgotten that, till this moment? That was bizarre. He had never put the two things together, ridiculous. And the burnt chicken dinner, maybe that wasn't to their credit. Mrs Carr, outraged, and raging at the waiter. 'You could as well cook it well as burn it,' she said, her whole body shaking. Which was true enough. June laughing, then everyone laughing. They got chips in the Ritz Café, and ate them on the bus to Rosslare. Ah sure but he wouldn't mention that to the Tomeltys, bless them. All water under the bridge. Ferry to France, the two of them legal in the double cabin, and the storm coming up near the boot of England, lashing the porthole. The two of them twined like pythons, his head burning with her, essence of June. June Kettle. Oh, the wildness. Young.

'Twas in the hotel in Cherbourg she told him. They had

been walking hours and hours along the coast, just strolling in the Normandy sunlight, marvelling at everything. The strange pier not connected at all to land, she couldn't get her head around that. Just like at Rosslare, the endless beaches and the boats. He thought he was going to die, he was so happy. Weren't things meant to go sour in life? That's what the other lads had said, or that's what they'd meant when they gave sort of mournful congratulations in Harcourt Street. Oh, the end of freedom. Oh, no, oh no, the beginning. This magnificent woman, who had chosen him. That was the true feck of it. The true feck of it was she loved him, and he loved her. What was human love? Who the feck knew. But that was their possession and their wealth. Even when it came to sorrowful revelations. He thought they had tucked it all under their caps and could carry on. The rapes, the bloody priests, the nuns, the hardship, the sorrow, the cruelty, the mess.

'I'm after marrying you,' she said, 'and I've not even told you the truth.'

They were sitting in the elaborate covered balcony of the hotel, in a line of slightly grubby chairs, the other chairs occupied by grizzled denizens, old folk whose loves seemed to have stretched this far at least. It was encouraging. There was silence there in the main, with the nice geometric tiles, and the evening wind baffled by the tall glass, and the uppity waiter from Paris who seemed to think Normandy and they themselves deserved no courtesy, but they didn't care, he brought them the sambucas anyway, good enough. Tom hadn't calmed down enough not to be wearing his decent clobber, his tweed jacket from Kevin & Howlin's, and the bawneen tie, a gift from Billy. Not very rock and roll, really. But she had her jeans and T-shirt on, no revolution too large for her, the proper sixties girl, he thought. Vietnam was *her* war, though she had never been to the States. *Five, six, seven, open up the pearly gates.* Country Joe and the Fish. *Whoopee, we're all gonna die.* You could have fitted her in anywhere at an anti-war rally. You really could. Now her shoulders were set. She was drinking the sambucas like Coca-Cola. Flames and all. The fiery little glasses, the tiny smoke wafting along to touch on the quiet couples, and then slowly, the sun plunging down, a burning orb of molten gold, making everyone gasp and clap their hands. Oh là là. Sacré cœur. That's what did it. She asked him what *sacré cœur* meant, and he said he thought it meant sacred heart. Yes, she said, I thought that's what it meant. It was Sacred Heart Sisters had been her nuns, she said. Her nuns. Like she had had a herd of them. Out grazing in the nunnish fields. It was them, she said, Sacred Heart nuns. Mam died and who was to take care of her. Well, she knew nothing about all that. Maybe she hadn't died, maybe the nuns just said that. The spawn of evil. Did she have a father? Lots of girls had fathers but they never came. Fathers they knew of, she meant. She didn't know of one. But when she was older she saw the children coming in, one by one arriving, over time, sent down by the courts, so she supposed that was what had happened to her. She had told Tom she was six when it happened, but it wasn't so, she said, no, she was only a baby. That's what the nicer nun said, the one she thought would help her. But she wasn't that nice. Oh, Tom, she said, Tom, I was so lonely. Can you imagine? A room with a hundred girleens. And babies, babies to beat the band. Babies the girleens reared, really. Nuns cared more that the huge floors were polished, the girleens down on their knobbly knees, a long row of them, fifty, with the big polishing cloths. The hands lost in them like stones in snow. And the ould nuns walking them down the floor, herding them, with the sticks and the belts. But that wasn't the worst of it, it wasn't the loneliness, and how could there be loneliness in a great crowd like that, but there was. No one to touch your face, to have you on their knee – and Tom, we're going to spoil our kids, we're going to fucking spoil them, there'll be no limit to our love for them – no hugs, no kisses. Unless it was that fucking priest.

'What priest?' said Tom, kind and quiet as could be. She knew she could talk to him about all this. She knew about him, he had gabbled it all out long before her. Sure he was brimming over with it, like a little glass of sambuca. Like the egg cup under the waterfall in *Mrs Tiggy-Winkle*, which he had read three thousand times to Winnie and Joe when they were of the age for bedtime stories. Yes, they had been as good as their word, they had heaped love on those babies, they certainly had. But he nearly wasn't prepared for it. In the aftermath of the sunset, when a strange darkness began to seize on Cherbourg, a black army from the west, it looked like, painting over the wide vista with relentless brushes heaped in black paint, cancel, cancel, there goes the harbour walls, the strand, the scrubland between sand and dwellings, someone turning on a light there, far below in their salty house, like a votive candle, ping, a stray dot of light in the new darkness.

'What priest?' he said again.

'Oh, he was called Father Thaddeus – Father Thaddy, the nuns called him – he came in to say mass every morning,' she said. 'They had us up at five, our faces scrubbed, I mean even the doors of the nursery were left open, so the holy words could reach in to the babies, and that was supposed to be a great day, when you were old enough, well behaved, you know, to sit in with the big girls and hear the mass. Father Thaddy. A young man, the girls all thought he was so handsome. He was handsomer anyway than Mr Gill the gardener, who had the skin of a big bramble' – 'Good merciful Christ,' said Tom, involuntarily, without fully knowing what he meant – 'and there was another lad, a Mr Gingham, a poor *Protestant*, fancy, the nuns were so *thoughtful*, that did all the odd jobs. And Father Thaddy was as friendly, friendlier than any nun, even the nicer ones, oh yes, and *he* put you on his knee, and made a great fuss of you, and said I had lovely curls, and wasn't I a lovely girl, ho ho ho, and this was in the parlour, you know, the nuns' little outside parlour, it was a great treat to be in there, where the outside world began, you know, which I knew nothing about, because I had gone in as a baby, hadn't I, I was never anywhere till I was six, and I was six now, and there I was, Tom, in the fucking parlour, where no one came in, now I think of it, when I was there, with fucking Father Thaddy, "spoiling his girls", the nuns called it, for Jesus' sake, oh my *God*' – one lady among the couples, with a floppy hat, looked their way, leaning forward for a millisecond – 'so nice, so kind, so soft, so different, and me staring up at him, what was all this, it was nice, so nice, and Tom, and Tom . . .' He suddenly was wondering where the orb of the sun was, of course he knew where it was, yes, the earth was spinning, the earth was in orbit, darkness was closing over them because it was the time for darkness, the gigantic, enormous, measureless vastness of the earth, the obedient child of the utterly measureless, unimaginably stupendous sun, and . . . But the sun in old stories was a different story. It was a story of the sun being quenched by the ocean, being put out like a candlewick in water, and who was to light it all again when it pulled itself up in the east, the waters cascading from its shoulders, who was to put the match to it, the merciful life-giving match – and look, her own shoulders set like a boxer, the weight on her left foot even though she was sitting down, ready to punch, to defend herself. 'Tom, will you forsake me if I tell you?' 'Will I what?' he said, just for an instant not understanding the old-fashioned word. Forsake. Never! 'I will never,' he said, oh, and thank God that stayed true, thank God, my June, my love. So when the little story came out, it came out with her smallest voice, but there was a seam in it of strength, the strength she had won for herself in her life. The strength maybe even of their present love. 'You don't need to say more, if you wish,' he said. 'You really don't, a ghrá.' He didn't think he could bear it. His wife as a little girl in a nuns' parlour, long ago, on the knee of a priest. His own memories of the Brother, and the smell of urine, and the merciless lashing, the stick on his back, on his legs, every night for a thousand years, world without end, and him getting off lightly, compared to other boys, the Limerick lad that he supposed was murdered, ran off and taken back by the guards, the guards, and then left out in the yard for the winter, the winter, for weeks and weeks, and who knows what became of him, disappeared really, one morning wasn't there, never spoken of again, poor Marty, they said to each other, what happened to him, they didn't know. Tom only wet the damn bed, he wet the damn bed, and was beaten for that, but also Brady, a kid two years older, the Brother's pet, trying to skin him with a knife, stabbed his thigh a dozen times, little pinpricks, while his cronies held him down, laughing, look at the little fucker, well, Tom had all that in his head as June spoke, and she knew all that.

She nodded her head, so silent now his ears seemed to pop, like the air pressure in the veranda area had changed.

'I'd better say it now,' she said, 'since these fecking nice Frenchies can't understand a word of it. The poor wee things. The poor *crat*urs . . .'

Now suddenly she laughed. It was an actual giggle. There was a little stir among the nearest couples. Giggles were a good thing.

'But aren't they *lovely*,' she said. 'I *love* this hotel.' And she well-nigh cackled again. 'My God, Tom,' she said, 'it's a wonder we're alive at all, us two.'

'It is a wonder,' he said, and his hand stole over to hers on the wicker arm of her chair. And when she took her hand away gently it wasn't meant as an insult. She couldn't say anything when she was connected to him. He understood that.

'You can get rid of me now, if you want to,' she said, again with a giggle. He was very much at sea, but at least in a boat of some description. He wasn't drowning. And nor was she, not then.

'That man raped me, Tom, I was only six, remember.'

Her voice was so low he could almost not catch the words. She didn't trust that some of the couples might not have English, though even the waiter had no English. 'Maybe you should get rid of me. The nuns said it was my fault. On and on, till I was twelve. Can you imagine? Twelve is a big girl, Tom. Every few days. Coming for his kisses, he called it. "I've come for my kisses, June," said he. His kisses, his fucking kisses. His yoke inside me like a burning poker, do you know how much that hurts when you are a little girl? I was about two feet tall, he was tall as a giraffe. With his hairy belly and his beery breath. His big yoke like a rod of steel, piercing into me. At the age of six. Tom, Tom, I am sorry. I want you to see it. I want you to know it, beyond a shadow of a doubt. So you don't misunderstand me. So you don't mistake me for who I am. Just in case you think I am someone else, Tom. And if the nuns knew, they never said. And if the nuns didn't know, they must have been blind, deaf, and dumb. Because he did it to a dozen girls, over the years, how many I couldn't say. Oh, and always so nice to him, Father Thaddy this, and Father Thaddy that, they *worshipped* him, and baking three cakes for him every now and then, his thank-you cakes, they called them, and he'd give me a slice of the cream one that I liked, and I'd eat it like a little animal, a little fox cub, and one time he tore me, you know, in the backside, and the doctor had to come, and he said, hmm, hmm, yes, yes, she has *colitis*, saying it clearly for the nun, the poor little thing, that's very sore, he said, I'll give you an ointment, and if it doesn't clear up we can give her a stitch in the hospital, because that little anus is ripped, Sister – yes, Sister Brenda was there, while he was fucking scoping my bits, Tom, and all the tut-tutting of her, and the hands of her going like a butterfly, dear me, dear me, how on earth does that happen, Doctor, oh, sure, says he, they're only little, you know, delicate, things get torn easily enough, she might have sat on a twig, and no one knows what causes colitis, no, not even the big doctors in Boston, where they did a study of it. Is that so, Doctor, is that so, says Sister Brenda, with her butterfly hands and her big moony face, and the smell of carbolic soap off her habit. Now, Tom, now Tom – you love me now, if you can.'

But Tom didn't have to start loving her then, he already had started that, and he hadn't stopped. Not any word, or vision of horror, or intimation of violence and pain, could stop it. He could see it all perfectly, with awful, experienced eyes. He knew how small six was, and how small even twelve was. He thought of her there as a big girl, and that sweating, murderous priest. Murderous. Many a soul put out like a candlewick in the sea of that lust. The ocean of lust pouring down on a little light, and never to travel again the bright breast of the earth, and come up again like a daisy, a bright yellow daisy of light, on the other side, as the gathering sunlight of a new morning. Quenched and obliterated. He had seen it with his own eyes, the boys the Brothers were raping, with the light in their eyes put out. Boys put to the sword of their lust. For ever. He had seen it. He had witnessed it when he didn't even know the words for it, when he couldn't have described to anyone what he had seen. The little wicks of their eyes put out. Eternally. How had she managed to bring her soul along with her, his June? To come as far as here, among the proven couples, in a darkened veranda, with the lights just now being switched on by the surly waiter, and her face being touched by the new light, like a girl in the sunrise, her hair not blown back by wind, of course, but blown back by something, her famous 'mousey' hair, her golden hair. Her lovely nose and her quiet eyes. Her moon-bright skin. Not a tear on her cheeks, as if she were far beyond tears. The tears of a little girl. The dry, cool face of his wife.

He sort of came back to himself then, standing there in the kitchen, with a cloth in one hand, and Winnie's cup in the other, dry as bones.

Chapter Seven

Next day he offered his famous Travel Pass to the agent at Dalkey station but the man shook his head. There was a red stubble on his cheeks, and the long ginger hair was in a ponytail. The first intimations of baldness had thinned his hairline.

'You're too early,' the lad said. 'You can travel for free after eleven. Sorry, bud.'

'I suppose I can buy a ticket.'

'Indeed and you can, you can always buy a ticket.'

Tom had dressed 'with care' that morning so he was as dapper as he ever would be. The coat was a sort of mercy shown towards the oldness of his suit. He was no clothes horse but he didn't look too bad.

'I'm going into work anyway,' Tom said, with a jocular nonchalance he in no way felt, handing over the few bob.

'Oh yeah?' said the man. It was the first train and the working crowd hadn't shown up yet. Soon he would be bewildered by the many hands and faces coming at him. At close of day he would go home to bathe his feet in Epsom salts. Like a copper off his beat. He had a transistor radio handy in his breast pocket, a little Japanese yoke.

'Were you listening to the match?' Tom said.

'Liverpool on Saturday?' said the man – an elderly boy, really – with a sudden ignition of interest.

'Yeah, yeah, Liverpool.' Winnie was a great fan, and had been since she was six. A little girl on her pink plastic chair in Deansgrange following a team in the far north of England. Tom tried to keep up with things for her sake. In secret he followed United. Never breathed a word of that to Winnie.

'Oh, Jaysus, mercy, but Leeds got a thumping,' said the agent, with delighted ferocity. He bared his teeth. His ponytail shook like a small russet creature.

Tom was only in the carriage five minutes when the rain started. He had a plastic New York cop's hat-cover that he liked to wear without the hat sometimes. Joseph had sent it to him, when he stopped over at Kennedy on his way to New Mexico. It looked like a jellyfish when you set it down to dry. He patted his coat pocket to check he had it. The last thing he wanted was to arrive at Harcourt Street like a drenched rat. A Garda's uniform for reasons unknown used to be made of some kind of felt, so if you were house-to-housing with your damp questionnaires, you were soon carrying extra pounds of weight in rainwater. Squelching along then. And the black shoes bought in Marlborough Street that declared themselves on the box to be impregnable. You got a little tin of dubbin free with every pair. You might as well wear blotting paper. Ah but sure it was all part of it. Nothing was what it was made out to be. The truth included. The Gardaí. The country.

The old railway line was inclined to follow the coast whenever it could. Some of the best bits were behind him, the mysterious Wexford inlets, Killiney Bay. Where the handsome boatmen hired out their boats. Between Greystones and Bray, Isambard Kingdom Brunel had blasted through the rock face along the coast only to find he had gone too close to the sea. So he'd had to change tack and bring the line in by fifty yards. Long ago in the seventies a body had been found quietly deposited in one of the never-used tunnels. A lofty cathedral-like place, where likely hares and cormorants and seagulls held sway, the marks of the holes drilled for dynamite still in the solid rock, as fresh as yesterday, and the sea wind making a howling wind instrument of the place. And the body of a young man, in his 'going-out' clothes. And they could never find out who did that murder, if it was a murder, though the lad was a local boy that used to fry the chips in the chipper back at Greystones Harbour. Some said he had killed himself because a girl had jilted him. But there was nary a mark on him. No trace of pills or poison, no rope or razor. That boy lay there in mystery, and the mystery survived him. Tom could still see himself and Billy Drury and the other men, technical boys, in their coats, gazing down at him in sombre contemplation. A handsome young chap, erased. They had him taken off onto a trawler when the tide was right, and he lay there like a dead dolphin on the cold boards. It was a terrible thing when you couldn't solve a murder. Like a house falling down on a builder. Of course they hadn't had the benefit of DNA in those days.

He shifted in his seat. Let them think it's haemorrhoids, these lads with the wires in their ears, the young women looking out on the bay. It made him uncomfortable somehow, to be among them. He was too old for travel, free or otherwise. The rain had stopped and a drizzle of gold threads suddenly blew across the patches of open sky, what there was of it. The wideness of the bay was a great comfort to him. It made him think he would never reach his destination. In his mind's eye flashed Monkstown Pier, and Seapoint, far ahead. Blackrock. Booterstown. Irishtown pushed over to the east, the line making a dash for the old city. Every single place would be a peg with a memory hanging from it.

The train line from Dalkey was a creeping thing. It avoided the sea now and snaked between the rich men's houses, through Glenageary, Glasthule, Dunleary, nearly underground, navvies long ago had dug a deep trench for it – as though it was ashamed of itself. But after Dunleary it burst forth on the coast again. Tom's actual eyes saw Monkstown Pier now, an arm with three elbows. It pierced him through with memories of June, of their innocent walking. And through his memories of the sea-field at Seapoint the train rattled and shook. Oh, he bowed his head from the assault of it, the banks of ruined gardens thrown up on the ancient cliff, the sand spreading and contracting as the tideline found its gauge against the land. Suddenly the old bay filled his head, stuffed it with light. He wanted to shout out to the passengers, look, look, the bay, the bay, the pouring rain has stopped, all that light, all that light, rinsed and silver, rattling the little pegs of memory, you can hold nothing in its place now, two thousand known years, back to Romans and Vikings and God knows who, in triremes and boats with great dragons on the prow, and all the little histories of the trawlermen, the fishermen of this lovely place, and Howth like a woman's pregnant belly, and the Kish like a jewel in the belly button of a goddess . . . He was sitting up in his dusty green seat. Like June squaring her shoulders for the telling of atrocities, he had lifted his hands in some strange way without really knowing, as if, like a little baby, he was trying to touch light itself. He felt he could sign the old canvas of the bay, with its thousand acres of hundred-coloured waters, writing *Tom Kettle* on it, *Tom Kettle*, *Tom Kettle*, as if by right, as almost a Dubliner. If he were looking for citizenship, it might be of this miraculous bay. Child of nowhere, he could claim rights over this, this vast vacancy queerly filled, both empty and full. He was just an old policeman with a buckled heart, but if he had known how, he would have sucked the whole vista into himself, every grain of salt and sand and sea, swallowed it whole, like one of those old whales in the loved museum, like a monster in an ancient story. All this blue and different blue and greens and acres of blown white, and the mysterious golds and silvers of the after-rain. He knew, he knew he was in trouble, he could sense the trouble with his copper's instinct and didn't yet know its shape, but the bay also released him somehow, let him go for a blessed minute into some wild freedom, so that his heart and soul were both shaken and renewed, in the same moment, in the same breath. If he stayed on this train, if the bay would only stretch to the distance between the earth and Andromeda, if it would only so oblige him, thank you, thank you, he would never die.

He got off at Westland Row station.

City of death. Lincoln Place Gate, South Leinster Street. Now he had made his way along Westland Row itself, and memories were lying in ambush everywhere. May 1974.

Merciful God. Up in Harcourt Street they had heard the three explosions. Fleming was in his mid-thirties then, still his equal in rank. The two of them went down like hares through St Stephen's Green, searching for the source of the noise. Galloping between the rose beds, the pushchairs, the bonny babies, the tuppeny deckchairs, make way, make way for the boys in blue. Or grey suits, anyhow. Sirens now and fire tenders and the silent forms of people looking back towards the sound, not in the least knowing what it was. Down Kildare Street, their bodies sweating, their boots a dreadful weight. And in the distance something to make your heart quail with dread, even a policeman's hardened heart, things lying on the road below that looked like cuts of meat, had someone blown up a butcher's? Slowing down then to take in the scene, then stopping, panting, *trying* to take it in, trying. Shoppers right enough, or people heading home, they must have been, in the instant before the explosion. Standing at their accustomed bus stops, getting a last message from a shop before it closed, checking in their minds they had all they needed for the tea, would Joe or Janet or Bill or Brenda be home yet before them, all the secrets and the honesties equal before the blast, and then the blast, bursting everything known and usual to smithereens, every window in the street blown in in a violent cascade, and the bomb debris and the looser items of the street, and the window glass, all turned into weaponry now, against the soft bodies of the citizens, and rending them, and tearing them, and undoing them, till Tom saw more clearly what he had thought were the cuts of meat, black smoke everywhere and the cuts of meat, some of them neatly squared, smoking, blackened, but it was sections of those just recently living souls, oh some still living, a head and a torso with the mouth moving, the eyes open in bloodied faces, and some still whole, in their blast-torn coats, here and there kneeling to the imploring faces, saying words that Tom could not hear, prayers maybe, or whispering, he could sort of lip-read what they were saying, though he didn't have that skill, not until that moment, well, it's not too bad, hold on if you can, the ambulances are on their way, don't worry, dear, don't fret, my friend, help is coming, lie quiet, lie quiet, you'll be okay, don't worry, don't fret, ah sure Jaysus, ah sure Jaysus. And all the vowels and consonants trying to fashion good speeches, offer simple words, but it was the kneeling figures that nearly hurt Tom most, and Fleming appalled beside him, the two of them rendered into mere witnessing humans, the long Georgian street of blood and body parts, and smoke still rising, and the cries suddenly of the terribly wounded, coming into his ears as if he had been temporarily deafened, and now the cries were in his ears, and now the words of the dying, oh sacred mother of Jesus, protect me, oh God, oh God, tell my wife how I died, and that I love her, I love her, will you tell her that, please, and I will, and I will do that, and I will.

There are worse things and worst things, he remembered thinking. The two of them kicking into gear, helping the young Gardaí who poured in to block off the side streets, Leinster Lane and the like, and close the roads at Clare Street and Nassau Street, and be on watch to let in the ambulances and the other personnel of catastrophe. They had no idea what was happening or why it happened or who did it, only that radios crackled out that there were fearsome casualties in Parnell and Talbot Street – Talbot your man who wore the chains anent his body, a penitential man. What terrible penance was this, thrust on these ordinary souls, going home of a May evening, their day in town done? A girl with twins in her stomach in Parnell Street, June told him when he finally got home himself, as weary as a hunting dog that had run over rough ground from sunrise to sunset. On the news at nine there was a shot of South Leinster Street, taken from behind the barrier he himself had helped erect. He thought he could see himself, away there in the distance under the railings of the college, just for a moment, busying himself with spontaneous tasks. There was no training for that. Far away in Deansgrange the two of them sat, counting the blessings of their children, of their lives. He began to tremble in his chair, seismic trembling, and sweating, and he was groaning so loudly the children climbed out of their beds and came down to sit with them, curling up against them both, Joe in his Thomas the Tank Engine pyjamas, Winnie in her new nightie all the way from London. There were worse things and worst things. His trembling got so bad June called Dr Brownlee, who hurried down from his house in Monkstown. Gave him two tablets to calm himself, his bald head nodding, his eyes anxious and sympathetic, many miles beyond the call of duty. Political bombs with personal outcomes. Dr Brownlee nodded his head again.

'You've had a terrible experience – your body is in shock, just like after a battle in a war.'

'I was in Malaya,' said Tom, 'and I never trembled there.'

'This is different,' said the doctor, 'this is close to home.'

'My home,' said Tom, as if to say so was a home in itself, a destination. All he needed to say. 'My home.'

And he felt the very rooms of the little house around him like an embrace and a solace. But all the same the next morning he was trembling again, and he trembled for a week. And he had only been a helper, a policeman running to assist. What earthquakes must those others be enduring. The kneeling people. The supplicants on the tar road. The spouses, the aunties, the uncles, the fathers, the mothers, the children – a plague of trembling. We tremble before thee, Lord, that you have sent this calamity on our houses. My beloved city, Tom thought, that is not my city. All the more beloved. I must guard it, I must guard it. For years after no cars were allowed to park on the streets, in case there would be a repeat of this enormous offence. It was bombs left in cars had done it. Cars left in the streets by human hands, the drivers walking away, leaving the ticking things behind them. Oh blessed shoppers, oh blessed wayfarers, oh blessed babies in the womb.

Was he even trembling a little now, these twenty years later? He was feeling the stirrings of old responsibilities. He hurried on to Harcourt Street. There were gangs of gardeners in the Green, the flower beds all raked bare, being readied up for summer, putting in little plants to a strict design. Knocking them out of the pots, dextrous. Kneeling. Like penitents, like survivors of an outrage. The dark-red daisies. Some men make flower beds and some men kill. Then he was thinking of the Green Cinema, on the far corner, gone now, where they'd had phones in the seats so the deaf could hear the picture. How many deaf patrons would they get, Billy Drury wondered? Maybe the kids from the School for the Deaf along the Royal Canal, hard by Mountjoy Jail, were regulars. Hearing, not hearing. The girl at the interval bringing her beauty and candyfloss to stand under the blank screen. Seeing, not seeing. Standing there under the gaze of the afternoon audience, turning on her little light. Billy glancing at him in dumbshow in a gesture that meant: Ice cream? Tom thinking, I'd marry that girl if she'd have me. I surely would. The starched blouse making him stiff in his work trousers. Some ould cowboy then on the screen, double bill always. Two shite films for the price of one, said Billy Drury. No, but they loved the cowboy films. Oh, Jesus, they did. *The Searchers*. They saw *The Quiet Man* there, obviously not a cowboy, but John Ford anyway, the cinema packed to the rafters, surging with laughter and tears. *The Guns of Navarone*. Good bit later, same routine. Then clumping back up for the night shift, the moil of trouble always just there in York Street, a breeding ground for gangsters, in the myriad dank rooms of tenements. But him and Billy, youth in their veins, a different planet altogether. Punch-ups, bottles, knives, but never a gun. And all before June: not BC and AD but BJ and AJ.

Now he was a dodgy old duffer climbing the familiar steps. Nothing much he could do about that. Could still be helpful maybe.

The telephonist was at her station in a blaze of silver hair.

'Good morning, Dymphna.'

'Detective, haven't seen *you* for a while.'

'They gave me the bum's rush – but here I am. Fleming about?'

'They're all in the incident room.'

'How's the hubby – Jim, isn't it? Is he getting it handy?'

'Handy-out,' said Dymphna, who was a Wicklow woman. Her perm had survived into the nineties. In 1980, if he remembered rightly, she'd won the Olivia Newton-John lookalike contest in her local. The hair had clinched it. She was a portly lady these days, but full of Grafton Street style. Silk scarf at the neck, though she was in uniform. There was no desk sergeant because it wasn't a proper nick. You couldn't just walk in. She was queen of the entrance hall, probably trained in firearms. In fact, he knew she was. Shoot you dead, then give her hair another blast of the aerosol. He headed for the stairs, built solid and wide for ancient grandees.

'Have fun, sir,' she said.

'The "sir" is a thing of the past, though I do like to hear it.'

'Sure why wouldn't you? Aren't you the heart of the rowl?'

'Ah, Janey, only on a Monday between nine and nine thirty.'

'You're a caution, Mr Kettle,' she said.

'Oh, the Dave Allen of Harcourt Street,' he said, going up the wide old stairway.

'It's really good to see you,' she said, laughing.

When he got as far as the incident room along the familiar corridor, there was no one there. There was plenty of stuff laid out on the tables, and if he was not mistaken he could see those damned reports he had managed to avoid, amid the seeming debris. There were also photographs he could half make out that gave him pause. Secured by Sellotape and Blu-Tack. Snaps and portraits from long ago, from the foreign country of the sixties. Even one of himself and Billy Drury. And who were those bloody clerics? Oh, he knew them. He did. Father Byrne and Father Matthews. Coolmine Parish. Tolka Basin and the painful past. He knew them like he had known his own face in the photo, younger and thinner. What age does to faces should be forbidden by statute. But these were posed jobs, probably in the parish yearbook. These things we have accomplished. He walked over slowly despite himself, to have a closer look. Fucking Father Joseph Byrne alright, and given he hadn't seen the man since, it was just like this that he floated in his memory. A gentle look to him alright, meek and neutral. Like a thousand other faces – but Tom knew it. He somehow wasn't surprised to see it, but he was not happy. And the other fella, the other fella, oh, ye gods, he knew him. The roast-beef skin, the mild set of him. The housewife's darling. Would be bishop one day, except . . . In other ages, might have been bishop anyhow. Only that in this age, or that age, lost age of the sixties, he was killed. He was killed. In the sixties. Vietnam was June's war. What war was theirs, these priests without conscience?

He was thankful to his instincts that he had rejected Wilson and O'Casey's overtures. But this was almost worse. He could hear voices at the end of the corridor, where the little room was, where they brewed their tea or coffee. Eternally forgot to wash and put away their cups. Maybe things had changed in the nine months he'd been away, but he doubted it. They'd get memos on their desks about it. Clean your f—king cups! Drove Fleming to distraction. One of his hobby horses. Bugbears that get you through the day – through a life. He could hear them, talking loudly and laughing, and he thought he could also detect a woman's voice. He had heard that a woman detective had replaced him. First of her kind. Good for her. June would have made a good detective, she had a brain like Sherlock Holmes. Looked deeply into things, the misdemeanours of her children, of her husband, idle conversations heard on the wing, she was taking notes without need of a notebook. He wasn't happy, he wasn't happy. In fact a deep lurch of panic was in him, somewhere in his belly, or deeper, as if his body in fact also went down though the floorboards and into the secret places of the station. Into the basements, into the ancient ground of the city, where the devils lived in echoing caves, no doubt. The devils of human affairs. He wasn't happy, he wasn't happy.

Now Fleming, Wilson, O'Casey and, yes, a lady detective trooped in, crowding the doorway and laughing, bearing their steaming cups, in a complicated dance of 'After you', 'Go on, then.'

'Oh my Jesus, you made it,' said Fleming. 'I nearly thought you weren't coming.'

'Ah sure,' said Tom.

'Thank you for coming, Tom, thank you. Jaysus, we might make headway now. This is DS Scally, Tom – Maureen, say how do you do.'

She gripped his proffered hand firmly in both of hers. Nice. Handsome girl, about thirty-five. A career behind her, and plenty of years ahead. He liked her, the honest face of her, and the blonde hair, he couldn't help but like that. And not a bit mousey, not a bit.

'Do you know,' she said, 'the boss just talks about you all the time.'

'Far too much,' said Wilson, laughing.

'How are you both?' said Tom to Wilson and O'Casey. He was trying to remember if he had picked up their first names, but he didn't think he had.

'All the better for our hollier in Dalkey,' said Wilson. 'By Christ, Maureen, the Welsh rarebit was only the biz.'

'So you keep saying,' she said.

'I'll be honest and say I did enjoy the evening, I really did,' said Tom. He was trying to say it lightly, and cause no embarrassment. Was liking something embarrassing? Probably.

'You see, O'Casey, I told you. And you were saying we had him driv mad,' said Wilson, theatrically.

'Not a bit,' said Tom, and now O'Casey was laughing too.

'And the great storm raging, 'twas like a scene from *Nosferatu*,' said Wilson.

'So who played the vampire?' said DS Scally.

'He was outside hanging on the castle wall, or being blown about Dalkey, probably,' said Wilson, for fear of Tom thinking she was playfully referring to him. Tom was no Klaus Kinski anyhow, with his tubular, stocky shape.

'Rightyo, ladies and gentlemen, girls and boys,' said Fleming, pulling out a chair, 'let's be getting to it.'

Oh, but suddenly, or gradually, or in a blur, clearing slowly, or was it quickly, there was no chair. There was no Fleming. Tom was waking – well, he assumed he was waking, but was it normal waking? – he was engaged in some activity, let us say, kin to waking. On one of the benches in St Stephen's Green, not a stone's throw from the busy gardeners. He must have sat down a moment and fallen asleep. He remembered neither action. He felt hot in his dark suit, the spring sunlight, which seemed to have followed him from Dalkey, all the hotter for being confined in the great dish of the Green, of the city itself. Of course, when he woke now, he realised the weirdness of his fading dream. His old nick was a functional building on Harcourt Street. Not a Georgian mansion. He would be surprised if the telephonist existed in the form he had imagined her. A colourful scarf from Brown Thomas's – no, not likely. What had hovered in his mind with the force of reality was now dropping away, growing vague, dim. The nick was always a crowded place, there might be two hundred detectives in the building, and a jostling cohort of clerical staff. The deserted nature of the corridor upstairs should have alerted him – but to what? There would be no incident room, just Fleming, and maybe Wilson and O'Casey, as the investigating officers. He was clearly going mad. But he had read somewhere that the truly mad would never know they were mad. He knew he was mad. Was that a proof of sanity?

He certainly felt demented as he rose. It was as if he had been on an all-night drunk, and he never had been drunk his whole life. His legs were trembling and his eyes were sore in the sun. How long had he sat there, maybe snoring and snorting? The gardeners were settled in their two electric buggies now, drinking tea and chatting. Elevenses. He would look at his watch but he couldn't locate his glasses just this minute. It was always good to have a structure to the day's work. Fleming would say that to young recruits. Take your breaks, lads, they're there for a purpose. What was to prevent this little run of events going the same way as the last? He had no idea. As a desperate attempt to establish the reality of these moments, he slapped his own face. That was sore enough. Very sore. Some kids in red blazers going by were looking at him. CUS. The old might be invisible, but not the demented. He fixed them with a glassy stare.

'Why aren't ye at school, why aren't ye at school?' Now the madman was a shouting madman. Jesus, what was he like? Disgusting. Frightening the young lads. Turning about, as if more or less rejecting himself, he pushed on to Harcourt Street, or hoped that was what he was doing.

Chapter Eight

'You're bloody good to come in to us,' said Fleming, in a version of what he had already said in Tom's dream. They were in Fleming's office, himself, Wilson and O'Casey. Wilson and O'Casey said nothing about the long visit in the storm, nothing. They were official-like, calm, neither friendly nor unfriendly.

'We have it all spread out before us,' said Fleming, indicating the little pile of papers and notes, the folders that had menaced Tom in Dalkey. It was a bleak, bare room and Tom loved being back in it. 'You had a chance to look at the case notes?'

'No, no,' said Tom, guiltily, 'sure I didn't.'

'The lads weren't sure. But sure you'd know most of it already. We're trying to respond to new info, but most of the stuff is from long ago, in William Drury's hand, God rest him. He was an excellent writer of the case files, Jesus, he was. Only O'Casey here would be a match for him. So these two lads are the investigating officers, as you will know, but – what are they investigating? What are they able to achieve? We have good reason to bring this further, but, Tom, I won't lie to you, the assistant commissioner is not keen. He's very troubled by our efforts. Good old-fashioned Catholic, and we're fairly God-fearing ourselves. When we were young policemen, think about it, would we ever have said boo to a priest? Never. Sure they were the leaders of our solidarity. They were our guides. They comforted men when they were wounded in the line of duty. When they were shocked by the iniquities of life.'

'That's true, you know,' said Tom, looking at Wilson and O'Casey.

'Yes, yes,' said Fleming. 'But the priests have brought this on themselves. They've cooked the devil's stew for themselves. And now they must sup. All these revelations, and the Smythe case, and so on. You just can't leave it now. But the AC is not keen, all the same. So I must go along softly. Hence I'm asking you. You were there on the ground, the first time Byrne showed up on the radar. And how did that happen? He was living with a Father Matthews, now deceased?'

'Byrne was a curate in Coolmine, where Matthews was parish priest – he was older. Forty-five maybe. Byrne was about thirty. They lived in the presbytery together, with a housekeeper, I don't remember her name, it must be in the file. Byrne came up because there was a tip-off from Scotland Yard, I'm sure you've read the file, but this was very rare. Something he had done had somehow registered with them, wasn't it something to do with photographs being developed in England, the eejit had sent them there, pictures of little boys, not a stitch on them, and Scotland Yard contacted the chief commissioner of the time, what the hell was his name, it's all there in the file, I am sure, sure Billy Drury was an ace at all that, wasn't he, you won't have any trouble following it, clear accounts of things, like a mother telling a bedtime story to a child. Anyhow, we were young enough, about your ages, boys,' he said, nodding to Wilson and O'Casey, 'and young enough not to like this at all, and we were keen to do something about it, and intended to, and we wanted to go over to Coolmine to have a little chat with Byrne—'

'Just ye two?' said Wilson.

'Of course, yes, me and Billy, wanted to go over, see what Byrne would say. But the chief commissioner, he had – well, he talked to our chief, you remember old Garvey, that's why we knew about it, and were ready to respond, but then he seemed to change tack altogether, and gave whatever he had, I mean, the photographs too, to the fucking archbishop, and said, you know, you can have these, your grace, and do whatever you see fit, that's the end of our involvement, unless you wish it to go further. Oh, thank you, thank you, my son, of course I will see to it, worry not.'

'And how did you feel about that, you and Drury?' said Fleming.

'Sure you know how we felt, Jack, we talked about this in the seventies, if I remember rightly.'

'No, we did, we did, I remember. But how did you feel, I mean, looking back, at the time?'

'We were fucking furious. We thought the man should be questioned at the very least. My own babies were small at the time. I couldn't credit the whole thing. The fact that a priest would be interested in making photos like them, and the fact that the chief commissioner wouldn't care beyond giving the photos to McQuaid.'

'Ah, you see, McQuaid, McQuaid,' said O'Casey with some wisdom, 'the king of this fuck-up.'

'Well, you're right,' said Tom. 'I never met the man. But the fecker did nothing. Not a thing. The chief commissioner. I doubt if he ever thought about it again. We were angry, but what were we, a couple of young detectives. I had only passed the exam the month before, June was delighted. A few more bob, you know. June was my wife,' he added, for the benefit of Wilson and O'Casey.

'He would have been well advised to follow it up,' said Fleming. 'This boy Byrne has been busy. Built himself a swimming pool back of his house. It's been a magnet for children, as I am sure you appreciate. So now Wilson and O'Casey are you and Drury. How should they approach it, in your opinion?'

'Get evidence for themselves, and don't run it past higher-ups till it's all written in. Talk to the witnesses or victims, whatever you have, write it all up. Get it down in black and white. Verbatim, recordings if you can get them. Photographs, ages, precise details. God knows what he was doing out there in the Tolka Basin all those years ago. And let me tell you, Matthews was another one. I knew of him from someone else, so I did, Father Thaddeus Matthews. So there were two of them in it, maybe Matthews set Byrne on his path, or they found each other. If you can do this work now without interference, without it all being buried again, I'll be a happy man to hear it. And good fucking luck to you. I mean it.'

Tom's voice had altered a little, there was emotion in it, making a tiny assault on his vocal cords.

'Where is he based anyhow, Byrne, these days? Not Coolmine, I'll be bound. They were always moving them around. You'd get parents come raging into the school or whatever. It wasn't just photos. I did manage to pursue it a little.'

'You pursued it?' said Fleming.

'I did. On my own time. And he was doing things to boys in the confessional. Imagine that? In the fucking confessional. No, he was a bad one. And he's still at it, you say. You know what that is, almost thirty years. Thirty years. How many children is that? Do you think it does them any good? I tell you, I tell you, lads, there's nothing you can do to a child more destructive, nothing.'

There was a silence now as the four of them sat there in Fleming's dingy office. All thinking about this in their different ways, Tom supposed – but like sitting in a general fog. Polluted fog.

'I thought it might be key for Wilson and O'Casey to get your views. I think I was right, Tom. Thank you.'

'If the high-ups let you, you'll get him,' said Tom. 'And when you have prosecuted one, you'll be all the better for the next one. Like those lads that hunt Nazis. Yes, indeed.'

'Wiesenthal,' said O'Casey, quite proud of his knowledge.

'So,' said Fleming, 'this other priest, Matthews, died. What do you remember about that?'

'Matthews?'

'Yes, Matthews.'

'Well, I never heard much about him after, no. I heard nothing, really. About either of them.'

'We've been thinking of opening that case again, you see, Tommo,' said Fleming. 'It's a kind of related thing, really. Cold-case file of a sort. There is quite a bit of evidence still in bags and boxes in Store Street, apparently. Not always the way of things. Billy Drury again, meticulous and thorough. What a loss he was. These days we might get DNA, it might not be too late. There's bloodstains and all sorts, I'm told. There might be some hope of that. But I only asked you about it because I see you were the investigating officer on that, you know, when he was found. In the Dublin Mountains it was, wasn't it? But I can see this has slipped your mind, and I don't blame you, it was so long ago.'

Tom looked up at Fleming and could feel his face opening and closing like a sea creature. It was a very strange feeling.

'I was the investigating officer?'

'Yes, with Billy Drury, according to the reports here that we have. That's why I wanted you to read them, not just because of Byrne.'

It was the pain of trying to remember that coiled about his throat, or he thought it must be, because Tom was struggling to breathe easily. The shock of being told something he did not remember, but instantly did as soon as it was put to him. It was the most extraordinary out-of-body experience.

'I did not remember that. All those years, I did not remember. I really think—' And now Tom felt truly faint, and was looking about for water. The office had nothing in it but two filing cabinets and the desk and the chairs and the men, so he didn't know why he was bothering. There was no water in the room, unless it was the stuff running down his back. He truly felt bad. He felt dreadful. Ambulance? Medics? There was a chief medic somewhere in this very building. What was wrong with his head? Had he always been so? He'd never felt right after June died, but she died twenty years after this forgotten business. And then Winnie, oh Winnie, and Joe as the finishing blow. But no, it was coming back to him. Of course he had investigated that. It was a murder in the mountains, on the way up Lugnaquilla, the body, multiple injuries, had been thrown down a ravine, but also, many marks from other injuries, deep deep knife wounds, no rocks could do that, as the coroner pointed out, and he had investigated that, of course he had, oh June, June, forgive me, forgive me, for that, for that, and all that came after.

'We're going to go through everything anyhow,' said Fleming. Wilson and O'Casey maintained their silence. Monks in an enclosed order now. 'I have to gather a few things. I told them I'd get a sample from you, Tom, and Wilson was supposed to ask you the other night, but it was alright, and they didn't want to wake you the following morning, they had to go off so early, so they took your toothbrush, I do hope that was alright.'

Tom blinking now, like an old owl on the very edge of life.

'You're not annoyed with me?' said Fleming, his words infected with friendship.

'No, not a bit. I got a new one, sure. Pink.'

'Pink?' said Wilson. 'Fancy.'

"Twas all they had.'

'This has been so helpful,' said Fleming, standing now, like a floating man. You couldn't see his boots for shadows.

Tom said goodbye to the two young detectives. Strange to think that just a few days ago he had thought they might be Mormons, framed by the radiant rhododendron. He had a sort of nostalgia for that more innocent self. Idly thinking things like that. Fleming walked him down through the throngs, there were many that had known him along the way. Howayadoing, arra Tom, looking well, how's it hanging? Outside the glum building Fleming shook his old colleague's hand.

'We'll be in touch,' said Fleming. 'I'll ring you.'

'Anything I can do to help, just say.'

'Arra, yes.'

He was just about to turn to go when a thought struck him, two thoughts.

'Who is Bríd, Jack – you mentioned her the other day. I've been racking my brains.'

'Oh, the old Labrador!' said Fleming. 'Maybe you never met her?'

'Right. Okay.' And he was laughing. 'And tell me,' said Tom lightly, 'do you have a DS Scally?'

'Killed in Clondalkin. Earlier this year. Did you know her, Tom?'

'I honestly couldn't tell you,' said Tom, with a mysterious measure of sorrow. 'Old age, old age.'

They stood there a few moments. There was an awkwardness. Oh, but they bestirred themselves, they gathered their forces anew. And then they were laughing again like the old friends they were. Through many a thicket of brambles, through many a muddy mire.

When he got back to the castle he read the riot act to the sweating hash. Heat coaxed it back to life, he opened a can of mushy peas and Bob's your uncle, he had his supper. He moved around the annexe as if he wasn't there. His mind was elsewhere, minute by minute, but the known tasks, the vampire hash rising from its darkness, soothed him, and the wicker chair beckoned with something of its past powers. He had no inclination or need to turn on any lights, he was content to be a barely discernible shadow. There was no one to discern him anyway. He was appalled by his visit to the nick, but at the same time he knew that deep within there was a pride in him, a pride in something that had only seemed terrible and mayhemic long ago. Now it felt like some kind of epic thing scribed on his heart with a tattooing needle. Like those strips of indecipherable Tibetan script on a flag. He couldn't read the words and symbols but he felt they spoke of things that were just, and integral, and right. Random stones that the stonemason of the heavens had matched to each other, seam to seam, so no light showed though the intricate lines where they joined. An Incan wall.

He was so strangely excited that he finished off his hash as quickly as he could, as a mere service to his body and ongoing life. Then he went over and stood at the window and looked down into the garden. The sheltering hedge shifted in the breeze, so animal-like you could expect to hear it snort and whinny, the darker green of the yew trees, or were they just mere leylandii, in clear definition against the spring grasses. He fancied his new friend Mr Tomelty had been out with his mower, a machine of some magnificence that combed the grass one way and the other as he went to and fro. The light from the other flats was laid out on the lawn like modern paintings. The grass pressed this way, that way, precise, expert. It was a memory of the hour Mr

Tomelty had spent there when Tom was elsewhere.

It was only about six but he was surprised to see the little boy running through these different patches of light. There was an older girl with him, or at least taller, so maybe she was in the act of minding him. This must be the invisible sister. They were laughing and talking, and sort of hoo-hooing, and even shouting, and they went down the granite steps towards the old sea wall and through the arched gate there, and out onto the concrete jetty. It was broad and dark, and the wastepipe jutted out from the edge like it was its offspring, itself encased in concrete against the storms. Now the girl was twirling her arms, and the boy started to as well, and they swirled and danced about the jetty as if there were no tomorrow. The girl seemed to position the boy then, stilling him, as close to the sea as she could get him, the water probably three feet below. Then she swung her arm in a vigorous arc so that it struck the boy on the chest, making him fly into the sea. Tom's whole body stiffened. He couldn't believe his eyes. He called out to no one in particular, and turned about and raced through his flat, pulling the front door open with great force, and ran round the perimeter of the castle, passing Mr Tomelty's nice car, and the metal bins, and crossed the otherworldly lawn, past the square of hedges, and took the steps two at a time, in a motion of agility he had not attempted for some years. He found he was as fleet as a pony. He came to the arched gate and stopped. He was fully ready to jump into the water – should he take off his shoes, he wondered, as quick as he could, in case the current took him to Davy Jones's Locker, along with the boy? But there was no one there.

He hurried to the lip of the jetty and gazed in. Nothing. He could see through the water to the dim seaweed and rocks below, despite the darkness. From the jetty to the island far across the moving sheet of the channel, a dismal radiance danced on the million tiny waves. There was a low moaning of wind and somewhere along the shore metal clanked on metal, but otherwise it was eerie and silent. The gulls and the cormorants had shut up for the night. He had no coat and the air was cold on his pate and chilled his breast. He scanned the channel again, sure he would see the boy's body floating, and though there were a hundred bodies floating, they were only the dips and hollows of darker water. Was that him there? Should he throw himself in? The current may be lethal. He felt in that moment a ridiculous responsibility for this child he had never met. Images from Stevenson passed freely through his mind, of Long John Silver, and galleons, and gold, and Blind Pew coming to just such a village as Dalkey with the black spot in his pocket to give to Billy Bones. And Joseph his son as a little boy, more precious to him than any buried treasure. Who used to stand even in a room as if poised for flight, a small chap of six with arms ready to propel him, though in truth he was completely at rest. An attitude of permanent readiness. The last book he read to Winnie was *Treasure Island*, wasn't it, and they had stopped at the chapter where the story passes from Jim to the doctor, and neither he nor Winnie could tolerate the change, and so he stopped, and closed the book. And it just coincided with her growing too old for a bedtime story – the alteration of a single night, it seemed – so the book was never finished, and gathered dust on her bedside table for a few years, and then disappeared, who knew where. The ghostly wind carried new ghostly sounds now, and started to whip at the surface of the water, whip and whip, a rodeo of miniature stallions. Frantically he headed back to the front of the castle and went in through the main door, and instead of going left to the Tomeltys' took the stairs, where he had seen the unknown old gent descend, two steps at a time.

Chapter Nine

He would have had to make a guess at the door, only Mr Tomelty had helpfully attached *Turret* to it, using those shop-bought metal letters. He understood full well that he was drenched in sweat from his swift run, and panting like a harassed dog, but he knocked on the door, trying to tone down what he thought of as his 'policeman's knock'. With surprising promptness the door was opened, and a preternaturally young-looking woman appeared. If she was the mother of two children it was a victory over nature, because she was twig-thin and so girlish he thought she might be the childminder. Which she was not doing a great job of, in the circumstances. Behind her he could see one of the windows that looked down on the front of the castle. He had the unnecessary thought that it might be nice to be higher up like this – a better view of the Muglins, anyhow.

'I'm really sorry to bother you,' he said. 'My name is Thomas Kettle. I live in the Annexe Flat.'

'Oh,' she said, 'you're the policeman.'

'Retired,' he said. 'Look it, I was looking out my window and I saw two children . . . Are you the mother of, of . . . I mean, de facto . . . ?' he asked quickly, what an official phrase, just in case he was about to traumatise the babysitter.

'I am, yeah,' she said. 'I am.'

'I saw, I think I saw, your little boy pushed into the water, and I went down to check he was okay, but there's no sign of him.'

'Oh,' she said, 'I don't think so. I just put him to bed. Jesse? Yeah, I just put him to bed this minute. I could check, I suppose,' she said, vaguely enough.

'Could you? Sorry about—' And he indicated the disarray he was in.

She laughed lightly. 'Hold on,' she said, and strode back into the room. The entrance was in a sort of crook in the building, so he couldn't see in very far. He stayed where he was. He heard in the new silence the strains of his neighbour's cello seeping through the Victorian walls. He didn't think it was Bach. He didn't know what it was. Then her handsome face, and the dark black hair framing it, and her neat blouse, popped back into his view.

'Nope,' she said. 'All's well, he's asleep already. As soon as he hits that lilo, boom.'

'And your little girl?'

'It must have been some children from the neighbouring garden,' she said, nodding her head, or was it shaking.

'It wouldn't have been your little girl?'

'My little girl is dead,' she said brightly.

'Oh,' he said. But Mrs Tomelty had said . . . 'Oh,' he said, 'I'm really sorry. Jesus, Mary and St Joseph. Forgive me, Mrs . . . Mrs . . .'

'I've gone back to my maiden name,' she said. 'McNulty. I don't know if I'm a Mrs or a Miss now, really.'

'Is your . . .' This was very tricky, he thought. He wanted to say *husband*. But it was the modern age and maybe that was just not right. Partner? He was beginning to talk to her like a detective. He was a detective. Retired.

'Could you come in for a moment, Mr Kettle?'

'Come in? Me?'

'Yes,' she said, laughing again. 'Mr Tomelty told me who you were. I need to talk to you. I really do.'

'Oh, I can. No bother,' he said. 'Heavens.'

So he followed her in. Now the room opened out and there were the two windows looking out on the sea, as he'd half expected. It wasn't really part of the turret, he adjudged – the turret began at the back of the room, if he was not mistaken. This was a part of the main castle, over the Tomeltys below.

'You sit down. You sit down there,' she said, indicating a plump becushioned armchair. Beside it on a little side table was a pipe and a bag of tobacco. He didn't think it was hers.

'The gentleman who lives here,' he said – maybe that was the best tack – 'he's not about?'

'Who do you mean? Oh, my father?'

'Oh, that's your father,' he said, like a solver of mysteries.

'Did Mr Tomelty not tell you?'

'He didn't seem to know. Well, he . . . I'm sorry, it's an old habit, asking too many questions.'

'Oh Lordy, well, maybe I didn't say it to him! Jesus, he must be . . . Stupid me. No, Daddy's in town. But that's exactly why I need to talk to you.'

'Why so?'

'Because you ask questions. Because you're a policeman.'

She was a lively, pretty sort of woman and she didn't seem to have side to her. No edge. She presented herself like an open book, and he was diligently reading her. Her way of talking was open and plain. Did he catch a faint vestige of a Sligo accent? Now that he was looking at her in the better light of the overhead bulb, she must be about thirty, thirty-five. Something of the lady on the banknotes about her. *My Dark Rosaleen, do not sigh, do not weep!* He wondered was she any good of an actress? Maybe, looking like this, she didn't need to be.

'You're an actress?' he said.

'Act*or*,' she said, without a trace of animosity. He didn't know what she meant immediately, but he knew he was being gently corrected. Gently improved. She reminded him of Winnie and her project of modernising him. He really liked her, this Mrs or Miss McNulty. Who could have resisted her? He was suddenly happy to be in the room, despite the dreadful news about her daughter. He felt at home, weirdly, as if *he* was the father, just returned from town, from what task he didn't know.

He was content enough with the situation to wait in silence while she made coffee in the little kitchen dock. She was right there in front of him, but she acted as if she were in another room. He would have greatly preferred tea, but she hadn't offered him any. She went to all the trouble of a tall aluminium pot, with various stages, unscrewing this and screwing that, and spooning in the coffee, and it took a while. Meanwhile the night grew older in the windows, as was its wont. Or the day grew older maybe. No, the day was dead. Things were dead. Her little girl. His little girl. Things were dead. The lonesome cellist next door was still sawing away distantly. What was his name – Delany? No. Now, you'd think a policeman would remember. He had only spoken to him once or twice, and he had been very interested to try and see the make of gun the cellist used. The only thing he had been good for in his brief sojourn in the army was sniping. He had just had a steady eye, so, unlike many serving soldiers, he had killed a fair number of the enemy. He wished he hadn't. He wondered now about those lives he had ended. Mostly local men among the Malayan rebels. They had given him an honourable discharge after a year of that. He had begun to be sleepless, and to have nightmares when he did sleep. The army doctor had called it 'gross stress reaction'. Doctors had to give even terror a name, he supposed. The effects of Malaya had been like a series of aftershocks in the body – he was just a wreck when he came home. As soon as he hit Irish soil, though, mercifully, wonderfully, his symptoms slowly began to subside, slowly, and then he had a notion to try the police. He didn't know if they would take him because of his wretched background. Orphans were held in low regard. Not that he was an orphan, but he was tarred with the same brush. But they took him. They liked his rifle skills, and the recruiter had a great regard for the army. Lucky Tom. He must stop his mind wandering now, he was growing too comfortable. On another table was a bunch of African knick-knacks – now his mind had strayed to Africa – of the kind soldiers used to bring home to their wives and children. Congo. Elephants in ivory, and various little gods. Maybe the father was an old Africa hand. He couldn't shake the feeling of having been here before, in this room. But then the blank panes inked over by night, that was so familiar, and the strains of the cello, and the sea and the sea wind offering their own poignant music.

'We're so lucky to live here,' she said, as if reading his mind, and as if the 'we' was herself and himself. She gave him his cup of unwanted coffee. His hardened old 'asbestos hands', as Winnie called them, weren't much bothered by the heat.

'My story is a very hard one,' she said, 'and I don't think I could tell it to anyone except someone like you. I haven't told Mr Tomelty. I came at Christmastime. My father was still in Africa, and he couldn't join me immediately. I was—'

Now suddenly, despite the admirable calm in her voice, she stopped, because tears were assailing her. For many minutes she wept in front of him, without moving, as if she had been instructed not to by an unseen presence. When she spoke again she made no apology for the tears, as people did, which Tom admired. 'I was running, running with Jesse, trying to get the hell away from London. I can't tell you,' she said, but then did tell him. 'My husband . . .'

Tom knew when not to ask a question. He just sat with her, like you might sit with a nervous horse, to give it comfort. Waiting without haste. Time suspended. There were many terrible stories in the world, and he had heard most of them. It was his business, terrible stories. An impossible profession. Milkmen just had to think about their float and the safety of the bottles. Even a doctor, unless it was a police doctor, was safe, in comparison, from this realm of suffering. People endured horrors, and then they couldn't talk about them. The real stories of the world were bedded in silence. The mortar was silence and the walls were sometimes impregnable. But this young woman was open, which in itself was unusual. He didn't think she needed any prompting. She knew her lines.

'Can I be honest with you?' she said, again as if she had access to his thoughts. 'I need to say things that haven't been proved in any court of law. I mean, things denied and—'

She gathered herself.

'I don't know if you have ever been the custodian of a story that no one else believed?'

'Oh yes,' he said.

'You have?'

'Yes,' he said.

'Then I can tell you.' She placed her hands palms-down on her thighs and tapped at the floor for a moment with the heels of her shoes. They were nice, patent-leather pumps, which even he knew were the height of fashion. Everything else in the flat, it struck him, seemed to belong to the sixties more than the nineties, probably because the stuff was all her father's. Even the plates in the galley kitchen were an old black-and-white design that he recognised from his and June's early days. It was like a set dressed for the wrong decade. So it was pleasing in an odd way.

'Oh dear,' she said. 'It's very difficult just to say this. I haven't even told my father. And I've just met you. So why am I telling you? I swear to God, I feel like I know you, Mr Kettle. But we haven't met, have we?'

'I don't think I have even seen you till now. I have seen your little boy, playing in the garden. With his cane.'

'That bloody cane,' she said. 'What a swizz. He sent away the back of a cornflakes packet, the prize was a Brownie camera, and didn't that cane come instead, a cheap plastic thing worth about a farthing.'

Tom laughed sympathetically.

'The modern world,' she said. 'Okay. I'm talking to you now because I really need your advice. I'm in desperate need of advice. I am absolutely terrified my husband will turn up here, and I need to know what to do. My father says he will kill him if he does show his face, and my father is ex-army so he might well be able to. But.'

'Does he know where you are?' said Tom, noting the ex-army. Irish, British, he wondered?

'I don't think so,' she said, with a little rat of doubt sitting up in the words.

Then she told him what had happened to her daughter. As he listened, Tom was trying to itemise the information in a professional way. But the story was shockingly familiar to him, not a familiarity he welcomed. First she had noticed problems with her daughter's body. She had brought her to the doctor in London because there was blood in her rectum – the child was only a little girl of six, and she had no idea what was wrong. The only thing she could think of was colitis, something like that. The doctor was in his fifties and not very concerned, and indeed the bleeding stopped for a good long while. But after she'd been away in Ireland working for a few weeks down in Cork, she discovered the bleeding again when she came back. She had not the slightest clue what was causing it, and she didn't think the doctor did either, except that he wanted to refer the child to child protection services. Even then she didn't understand. Her husband professed himself entirely in the dark. He had minded the kids while she was away and she had only the greatest admiration for him – two children were like a double tornado, God knew. But the obvious conclusion, not obvious at all to her, was being reached by the doctor, and then, before anything else was done, her little girl grew sicker and sicker, and died, right in front of her, she died, and something had been ruptured in her that didn't have a remedy, and she died. She just died. And the post-mortem said she had been abused, wasn't that the word, most likely with a big hard object, her own little girl, and the social worker or whatever she was questioned her husband and he made a complete denial, and why on earth did they believe him, just like that, she wanted to know, and she was absolutely terrified, terrified, Mr Kettle, and *she* didn't believe him, and she just made a run for it, packed a suitcase in the small hours and crept away with Jesse, weeping like a banshee, she said, in the dark taxi, and poor Jesse already asleep, he could sleep on a bronco, and the advice I need, the advice I need, Mr Kettle, is how do I protect him from my husband?

This young woman was stirring at memories so deeply set that he didn't know if they were his or June's. They were like a waterfall at the back of his head, falling glimmeringly from a height. Of babies strapped onto their potties, all day, some of them tilting over, in that curious silence that fell on all the poor babies, and at teatime the older children unfastened them, and placed them in their cots, the thing he remembered, or was it something that June had told him, because he couldn't remember, the thing he remembered, or maybe not, was the little rectums hanging out of the babies, little red rectums hanging out of the babies. But. He was an old sick man. He must be staunch, though, now.

'Has he threatened you?' said Tom.

'I asked him to tell me the truth, and I don't know what the truth is, you know, he could even be innocent in some way I can't imagine, but, I don't think he is, that's my feeling, but why didn't the child protection services protect us, protect my little girl, who's dead. Do you know how absolute being dead is? Is that a crazy question? I've lost a child, she is absolutely dead, I am heartbroken, I will never be right again, but I am going to protect Jesse, I so dearly want to, everything can be taken away in a second, I can't understand why he wasn't at least questioned by the police. Mr Kettle, what should I do? I am so so sorry for bothering you with this, my poor neighbour, and you haven't even touched your coffee. Oh, it is all too terrible. At the graveyard he said if I ever caused trouble for him again he would settle my hash. At the graveyard. As we buried her.'

'Sometimes the police are slow to move. It's just – I've seen it a thousand times. It's better these days, but it's not perfect. We always have this problem, if your husband, say he comes here, if he doesn't break the law, if no law is broken, then nothing can be done.'

'So if he kills me, the police can do something?'

'Do you think he wants to kill you?'

'Well, he won't be happy I fled in the night, I can tell you that. And he won't be happy that I'm sitting here telling you all this. He will be very, very, very angry, and I'm terrified.'

'But he will never know that,' said Tom. 'Listen, you can go to the Garda station in Dalkey and see if you can't get a barring order. Your solicitor will guide you through all that. In the meantime, I'm in the Annexe Flat, and I see when people come in and out, and I'll keep an eye out. And if you hear of anything, you tell me. And your father? He'll help you?'

'He's a bit useless but I suppose he'll try.'

'You might be reassured to know that I was a firearms specialist in the army, and I still have two guns in my flat. They're thirty years old but I keep them oiled. They can kill a man from a mile away. Well, when my eyesight was in better nick.'

She laughed. It was just impromptu laughter, meaningless. Why am I talking about killing? he thought. Enough killing.

'I'm sorry I've burdened you with this,' she said. 'When Mr Tomelty said you were a policeman, I don't know – desperate remedies for desperate times. Thank you for listening to me.'

'You know, if you're a well-known person, that might help you, in a way,' he said, fearful she would feel he was letting her down.

'I don't know if doing a few small films and a few auld plays at the Abbey adds up to much. Maybe.'

As she spoke, he saw the little boy now, standing in the gloomy doorway, which led into the turret proper. He was wearing a miniature version of his own pyjamas, the traditional ones with a blue stripe. He was smiling, and raised a sleepy arm, as if in greeting. Or actually in greeting.

Chapter Ten

He needed a good lie-down.

He hadn't eaten and he wasn't hungry, but he reckoned that, like an old wintering bear, he could get by on his fat for a night. He was longing for sleep, he was longing for – what, peace? But there was no peace now and maybe rightly. The nine months alone *had* been like a pregnancy, and it had given birth to new thoughts, and new light on old thoughts, and this time now was going to be the time when he reared those thoughts. Wiped their arses, stuck plasters on their grazes, and sent them to school. He felt there was a great reckoning coming but he didn't know what it was exactly. What face it would have, or the carriage that would bring it up the lane. There was emergency and difficulty everywhere, and he was no doubt terrorised by it, but with emergency and terror comes a test. He wondered could he pass it?

They had taken his toothbrush. Of course, in a real case of law, they couldn't do that, it wouldn't be admissible. How could you prove he alone used it? What about Winnie? But he mustn't keep invoking Winnie. *Inadmissible*, the file-writer's dreaded word. What Billy Drury was so good at avoiding, and probably O'Casey too as he drew up his files now. Somewhere, somewhere, he was drawing up his files. Putting everything in, just so, carefully framing, but not altering, oh no, too risky, composing the evidence, the interviews, so that no lawyer could get a hold of it, like a bloody puppy with your slipper, and make shreds of it. But among friends, among colleagues, just for the sake of *elimination*, to have taken his toothbrush without permission, should some old DNA survive in Billy Drury's beautifully preserved evidence bags, in the far-away sixties, that was alright. He knew that. If they had asked him to pop over to forensics, in that wrecked little building they occupied, he would have had to say yes, no bother. And it was no bother. No bother.

The eternal fight in the solar system between night and day was being waged above him, he supposed, and it was dark as dark could be now, night was winning, but still, it was ridiculously early to be abed. Winnie would obey the weird notions of Mrs Carr, and trot off to bed at six, but Joseph – June called him Jo-Jo, but he couldn't ever use that – always kicked up hell. He was one of those hellish children that came good in the end. No, that wasn't fair, not hellish – hectic, he meant. Sometimes. June laboured at the rock face of his character and gathered something pretty good from it. The second he saw him after he was born, Tom thought: Uh-oh, trouble. It was just a voice in his head. June in the room beyond, panting and bloody, and the nurse ferrying this stocky baby down to the nurses' station to be fed. And him going with them, not that he was invited, and asking if he could be the first to put a bottle to his boy's lips. Would you ever be so kind? And the rough face of the nurse, the *entirety* of a country woman, frightening, bred for troublesome husbands, being disarmed by the sheer ludicrousness of Thomas Kettle, wanting to do a thing like that. 'Arra, here,' she said, 'what harm, don't choke the child, go easy.' And Joseph – he would go as far as saying Joe, but you could keep your Jo-Jo, that was no name for a Christian – latched on to the nipple on the bottle like his life depended on it, which of course it did, as it had done with babies since time immemorial. Which seemed to Tom like a very fine thing. If the baby was going to be trouble, he was going to love him anyway. And there was plenty to love, in the up-shot. After a while. One time on holiday in Bundoran, in the arrows, the piercing bullets of the Donegal rain, when everyone had fled the swimming pool, yet again, they left Joseph behind with another little child, a girl, the pair of them no more than seven. And ten minutes later, in comes the mother of the little girl into their chalet, screaming blue murder, with some justification, as Joseph had pushed her little girl into the swimming pool, though she couldn't swim for toffee, and but that the mother, with better instincts than he himself had shown, had almost immediately missed her child, and gone back, and witnessed this act of pure devilry – she was screaming that, *your devil child* – Joseph might have been a murderer at seven years of age. Which would have been a heavy thing to carry, leave alone the sorrow and ruin of a little girl's drowning. And he had brought Joseph silently into one of the nasty bedrooms – sheets so full of nylon they were like an electric storm over Switzerland – silently, in an asphyxiating fury, and smacked him on the bum, wanting, oh wanting so desperately, Joseph never to forget, and never to be going drowning little children again. The only time he ever struck the boy, a blow that cost him a quarter of his own soul's worth. Since there was one thing he had sworn to himself and to June, which was that they would never strike a child like they had been struck, like she had, like he had, the both of them, in their separate places of dread exile, nuns and priests and Brothers, flailing them alive, or was it dead, as the supposed spawn of the devil. Better to have been born dead, the Brother used to shout, than be the filthy melt of a prostitute. His very words. But Tom had hit Joseph that time.

And he was thinking all this, and before he knew it he was waking, not really registering the boundary between thought and sleep, waking, groggily, like he had drunk a barrel of whiskey, not that he ever had, nor even a glass. It was still very much night, and he fumbled on the bedside table for his old wristwatch, and peered at it in the unenthusiastic light from the bathroom. Only midnight. He felt a weariness weighing him down. He felt as empty as the empty chair at his bedside. Bloody midnight, when the witches would be abroad. Seconds later, his conversation with Miss McNulty flooded back into his brain. Jesus, Mary and St Joseph, the poor woman. All the dead children. A cold hand closed on his heart. It squeezed it, coldly. Perhaps he was to be delivered up now to death. It certainly felt like a strong weakness, as Mrs Carr might say. He did have a great curiosity often about it, of course he did – didn't everyone? He could picture in his mind's eye St Peter's gate. It looked very real there, at least, if not surrounded by anything else. And St Peter, a venerable type in his middle age, miraculously speaking every language under the sun, asking questions, and you would hope without any obvious edge to his voice. And wearing one of those white robes like a job lot from a Hollywood costumier's. Could such a thing ever be possible? Of course not. But those childish visions – how, in his iron bed among the rows and rows of iron beds, he had pressed his knuckles so hard against his eyes, insisting, insisting on seeing heaven, despite all – still lingered. Powerfully, ineradicably. Stupid, but true. Mercy, but he might well have been having a turn of some sort. There was an evil pain in his middle back, he was on the verge of retching, like he had eaten deadly nightshade, supped on it like a salad, oh dear God. Now his whole stomach area seemed to be going to be ripped apart, and he sat up in bed to try and relieve it, he *shot bolt upright* was the phrase, he thought, should he even call an ambulance, did he even want to, but to die like this, in the most extreme and sickening pain, it didn't seem desirable at all, and he swung his shrivelling legs from the mattress, and staggered from the sticky bed, and clutched at the nice Victorian hook on the door, where his dressing gown hung defeatedly, and let out a huge and unmerciful – since he was begging for mercy, maybe merciful after all – blast of wind, not just from his exploding anus but his very mouth, as if what Miss McNulty had told him was only something to be vomited up. Somewhere in that violent and inelegant fart were all his own sorrows and losses. It was it seemed to him an effort to emit, to *emit* what could not be emitted, God help him. God help him.

But no human can be ungrateful after the passing of pain, and he was grateful. He hung there gingerly a while, in case this volcanic tempest gathered again, but it did not. He wished he was still young, and the two babies in their beds, and June in their own. He wished Joseph, and he would call him Jo-Jo, of course he would if June wanted him to, and he could go back and be that Tom Kettle again, he wished Joseph would come in like he had a thousand times and tell him he was afraid, 'Dada, I am afraid of the dark, there's a witch under my bed', and he would march him back to his own room, and hoist him into bed, protests and punches all the while, small fists flailing, and stick his own clumsy body on the covers beside his son, the little body now caught in the clamp of the sheets, and turn on the shaky light, there by the child's bed, and read to him, Peter Rabbit or Mrs Tiggy-Winkle, with Mr McGregor and Sally Henny-Penny, all still there, present and correct on their allotted pages, till Joseph sank into the pit of sleep, sank away like a body in water, and he brought himself back on quiet pads to bed, and inserted himself in beside June, half asleep, 'Did you get him back to bed?', 'I did', 'Oh good, Tom, that's marvellous. He'll grow out of that, you'll see.' 'He will, but will I live to see it?' Tom would be thinking of the early rise in the morning to get out to the bus, and the long trek into town, head nodding from the broken sleep, and the passing from his character as father and husband into his character as policeman and colleague, a curious transition that in the evening would be reversed, in the eternal see-saw of his life, of everyone's life. The only thing being missed by him in those moments being the absolute luck of his life, the unrepeatable nature of it, and the terminus to that happiness that was being hidden from him in the unconsidered future.

So that when Joseph was going, the last time, it was the gap between little things like that, the bedtime stories, the attempted 'murder', which became the very myths of his childhood and Winnie's, all turned into something good, the good gold of memories retrieved in a certain way, mostly for their quotient of humour, laughing like drains the four of them, when adulthood was reached, or nearly, and you could anecdotalise even old frights, the gap between them and that *new* new moment, in Dublin Airport, just the two of them, himself and his son, sitting on the plastic chairs, waiting for the flight announcement. The flight that would take him to – was it Dallas first that time, then Santa Fe, then Albuquerque, then home to his dispensary in the desert? Well, his flat in Albuquerque, wasn't it, and then the dispensary. Where 'I am never lonely, Da' was his oft-uttered tune, 'because the desert is so beautiful. The desert is like a young girl, a million young girls, all perfect in their beauty.' Or something along those lines. Just to express to his father that he was not lonely. Although it wasn't a girl he wanted to fall in love with but a boy, as Tom well knew, though that wasn't something he could talk about as well as he should have been able. 'There's no harm in it,' said June. 'It's just the same as Winnie liking a man, it's exactly the same.' It didn't seem the same to Tom but he was understanding it all better as time went on, till time was taken from him. There was no point thinking of the Brother that used to use him as a little boy, because it just wasn't the same. June said it wasn't the same. It was the soul that loved, she said – his soul is looking for its soulmate. 'Don't you get that, Tom?' 'I do,' he would say, but not really, truly, absolutely getting it. His boy kissing another boy. That hadn't been a good thing at the orphanage, it had been a bad thing, a bad thing on top of many other bad things. 'But, Tom, no, this is different, this is like David Bowie in the make-up, and boys liking his music, it's just entirely different. And Jo-Jo needs you to see that, you old dinosaur, Tom.' But Tom still couldn't quite 'get there', as June put it in her American hippy way, as if it were a train station somewhere down the country, he couldn't find a ticket and the line seemed to be disused. But that evening, sitting on the plastic chairs, with the electric lights fizzing and humming in the refurbished airport lounge – didn't he remember well the old airport, a scimitar of concrete as graceful as a cruise ship, where all sorts had arrived in vanished days, The Beatles, The Rolling Stones, Ronnie Delany after the Olympics – that evening it wasn't important if he had got there or not, because his son, which was his destination really, was going back to New Mexico to work, and he, old Tom Kettle, detective sergeant extraordinaire, as in, never promoted beyond that rank, but still valued – he hoped – he was to be left behind. It wasn't as if his son was going, but as if he himself were going. The world would continue to form around Joseph, and retreat from him. Joseph would drink his fizzy water on the flight, and look out the darkening and brightening porthole, at new cloud-lands and land-lands, maybe drop by drop, bit by bit, not forgetting his father exactly, but sort of losing him. Misplacing him in the great aether of the earth. As if his father were going away, further and further, and at length beyond retrieval. They sat there, on the ugly plastic seats, the swarm of lives coming and going around them, and Tom wanted to take his son's head in his hands and kiss him, kiss him so sweetly his son would never forget him, carrying for ever that proof of his love, like the faint mark of ash on an Irish person's forehead on Ash Wednesday. 'You understand why I have to go, Dad?' he said, even though he wasn't going for the first time, it had in fact been his first visit home, and Tom himself had been to see him in Santa Fe, and they had toured the pueblos together in a smart blue Buick, he remembered that, coming into Zuni pueblo finally and the pride in Joseph to show him the dispensary at the edge of the little town. And how clear it was to Tom how loved his son was there, the other young doctor, a Native person himself, revelling mysteriously in the name Sean, easy and friendly with the strange old Irishman. And he could see Joseph had found his home place without a doubt, and Tom didn't have an address in it. It was Tom then at the airport in Albuquerque, astounded in a way by his son, his magnificent son, and what he had achieved. The long years of medicine, and the sense of the world and of himself that had inspired him to travel out so far. So far. And they had eaten a meal in Santa Fe the day before his departure with the hottest chillies in it known to humankind, and nearly expelled the lining of their tongues onto the plates, you might think, and the two of them with burning mouths laughing and laughing. And the truth was when Joseph rose at last to go, neither reluctantly or precipitately, to go back and yet go nowhere, bringing the world with him, and leaving his father, and all that spoiled cargo of truths, Tom had the presence of mind, *Deo gratias*, with the old words of June in his ears, in his head, to embrace his good son. And if he didn't kiss his forehead he did in kind, in that he touched the back of his son's head with his right hand, and held it lightly there, like a holy covenant, and said that no matter what happened in the future, or what had happened in the past, he would always be his father, remember that, Joseph, I will always be your father, a tie that cannot be broken, and I will always love you.

A person might be forgiven for not sleeping after thinking of these things, but Tom felt himself dropping away into a shallow slumber. That deepened into a dark pool of dreams. That seemed so real they were real.

For the next few weeks the world appeared to leave him severely alone. He almost gained a simulacrum of the old times. He was the citizen again of his wicker chair. His appetite returned and he didn't spare himself the magnificent Clonakilty sausages as championed by Mr Prendergast in the village. He was the agent also for Clover Meats, which put a spring in the step of any sort of hash. At the orphanage the Brother had been a great user of Erinox Cubes, which, while he was infusing them, rendered a saving calm into him, so that that violent man waxed lyrical and almost kind. 'Made in the townland of Christendom, in the county of Waterford, don't you know?' he would say, almost piously. Tom supposed there really was a townland called Christendom, though he never dared to ask, nor had ever heard of it since. Now was the time of year when a man might be thinking of the new Wexford potatoes that would be ready in June, burst out of their hidey-holes in the soil like the white heads of dolls. Your mouth could water thinking of that, and the miniature gravestones of butter laid across them. Mr Tomelty's daffodils had taken over the scutty ground under the shelter trees. He had returned to his persona as some old Roman god, in his disguise of rags, and moved about the garden with military intent. The old growth from his taller perennials was now chopped away, like the silenced song of the fled year, and Tom reckoned that in Mr Tomelty's imagination the fresh spurts of shoots that his cutting-away revealed were already flowering, already piercingly yellow and red and blue in the high summer yet to come. Although they had not spoken again, he was deeply content with his landlord. The exchange of words had mysteriously conferred on Tom a deeper sense of being at home. The sprightly Mrs Tomelty never came into the garden, which was maybe the point, Tom didn't know. Soon Mr Tomelty would have to fire up his mower with the handsome, high Briggs & Stratton motor, and the levers and gears like the ears and whiskers of some exotic animal in the zoo, or the curious shooting ears of the wild Irish hare. God knew what comfort Mr Tomelty would receive from the low growling of the machine. There was a wide flower bed under the wall of the house that Tom could only see if he went to the window and craned his neck. This was the canvas for Mr Tomelty's annuals, the big-headed daisies, the violets, and best of all the blue lupins that grew wild on the high plains of the American west. African lilies went their own way on the far side of the garden, and he could see the ancient carnage site of the gunnera – collapsed in the winter into a great circle of rotting stalks – begin to stir again, with the promise of those leaves as pleasing as the ears of elephants. When Tom had married June he didn't know the name of a single flower, unless it was a dandelion or a common daisy. In their little back garden she had fashioned a secret paradise. With a suntrap and a painted seat to boot. It was when she began to neglect her garden that the old alarm bells had started to sound for Tom. She had done so well for twenty years, tucking all troubles under her oxter, keeping the light off the filthy weeds of things so they couldn't flourish. But weeds will have their way, he supposed.

The peril of pleasant thoughts. Sometimes his head was like a wild horse, without bit or rein. He couldn't leave it to its own devices. He must be talking to himself, give himself good orders like an officer of a higher rank. A state of mind he had beheld in so many men in the army who had been in orphanages and industrial schools. They had been incarcerated among gradual and impossible torments. Yet oftentimes as a bewildered boy walked out the gates at sixteen, he might shed a different kind of tear, with the new fright of the unknown world before him. Up early, get your grub, obey your commands – the army was something of a tonic, and no war ever seemed to compare with what they had already endured. Nothing again as terrifying as the shadow of a dark-soutaned Brother by your bed, in the deep night, to drag you out either to lather you or fuck you. No Malayan fighter, magnificent, fearsome and dark, ever as terrifying as the small shopkeeper's son in his measly garb, given a coward's power over you by virtue of being at least a grown man. No wonder they released the boys, like knackered greyhounds from the cage, at sixteen, before they gained the muscles and the strength to fell the Brothers with righteous and merciless blows.

And just the same for the girleens. Not the army, but little domestic jobs for those illiterate angels. Or a bit of regrettable streetwalking in the dank back alleys of northern English towns. A plethora of disagreeable futures. Or a poor job in a mere café, like his June. June, a woman named for the summer.

Before the commissioner pulled the plug. That was the big thing. Father Joseph Byrne and Father Thaddeus Matthews, two jackals in a coop devouring little chickens. Filthy, relentless, feckless men who never paused a moment in their evil. Oh, he had known what was to be found there, in that pristine presbytery. Jackals, snakes, scorpions, monsters. And the fury he felt when the commissioner did that. Which he did not really express to Jack Fleming and the boys, because – because it was not a fury that had a name or a nature. It wasn't in the dictionary of furies. It had no gradation, it was limitless and pure, even. And their old chief, what's more, Detective Superintendent Garvey, had no idea about this fury that possessed Tom Kettle, because old Garvey had been raised up nicely on a decent farm in Leitrim, he knew nothing of such dark things. If you hadn't seen such subtle, glooming sights, you knew nothing about them. But the fury turned to something else when he brought this hard news home with him. When he gave an account of it to June, something he so rarely did, trying to leave his work at the doorstep, but this, but this. And seeing her face as he spoke, and her jaw literally drop, going slack at what he was saying, himself muttering and growling low so that his own little children, his own precious little children, wouldn't hear it, though they were too young to have a clue what he was talking about. And he had supposed it was from his own disasters he was speaking, and that she would respond like that, with her beautiful and usual words, well placed, expert in her mouth because she had experienced similar things, and worse, he always thought, far worse. But the peroration he was offering seemed to veer into a steep curve, his words seemed to gather a dangerous speed, Father Joseph Byrne and Father Thaddeus Matthews, this and that, and the bloody commissioner, and she said, Tom, Tom, Father Thaddeus, you say, and what age would that priest be, and Tom said, I'd say mid-forties, that sort of age, mid-forties, she said, and such a rare name, and is he a dark sort of man, a big sort of man, with a belly and his red hands, does he look like a butcher that has washed his hands all day, his face like the lump of ham on the side that's not yet sliced, where the iron spikes are stuck in, oh, he does, said Tom, he does, I do not doubt, and she cried out, forgetting to shield her distress from her babies, but no matter, they did not hear, that's the man, the man that hurt me, that's the man, Tom.

Talk to yourself, Tom, talk to yourself, calm your heart. Hold on by your fingernails. Something was coming, something was coming, but not yet. He was king over time in the wicker chair. Preserving the beneficence of the present. Not smoking, true, his old cigarillos, heeding at last the intimations of his old doctor. For in a very curious way he wanted to live. He wanted to live long enough to get through the dark forest, like a medieval *childe* in the old stories. To get through the tall, dense trees and the dark light that barely merited the name of light. Along the ancient road with its carpeting of the leaves of a thousand autumns. To see at last the sparkle begin in the distance, the diamonds and fires of the sunlight, where the forest would end.

Oh, Mr Tomelty raked and dug, insisting on his own version of paradise. He raked and dug. And Tom was grateful to witness this old ritual and dance of a gardener. And there seemed to be a sort of gratitude even in the sea, with its coat of many colours, streaming as may be between the difficult land and the lonesome island. The way the wind raked at it betimes, and the overwhelming cascades of spring rain, nearly stiff you would think as iron nails, dressing the surface like some celestial mason with his hammer and pointed chisel. Everything busy, accurate, mysterious, ongoing, unstoppable, tending not to car crash and disaster but beauty, recompense and happiness.

Chapter Eleven

'A very violent death, suggestive of fury and frenzy.' It was Fleming talking. He was reading from Billy Drury's notes from long ago. He had arrived to break Tom's run of peace, but Tom didn't mind, in the sense that he didn't mind Jack Fleming. He just liked the big lump of a gossoon. He had brought him inside this time, since he had given the flat the bit of a going-over at last, the long-awaited rinse-out, the spring clean deferred. He wasn't one of nature's housekeepers, that was for sure. The little bag of cleaning things must have abandoned all hope in the darkness of the kitchen cupboard. He hadn't, unbeknownst to himself, gone so far as to disturb the spider in her station on top of the cupboard, though the fresh spring weather had woken the butterflies, and they were gone for another year. Tom had found them fluttering against the windowpanes and had delicately helped them out in cupped hands. Off they had flown, as fit as tiny fiddles, without a glance back or a second thought, leaving their winter refuge for ever. 'So long,' Tom said to their disappearing backs as they merged themselves into the myriad flying colours of the coast, with more than a touch of John Wayne. 'So long, amigos. Thanks for the company in the long nights.' And Fleming had begun by thanking him for coming in the few weeks back, and how helpful O'Casey and Wilson had found all that he had had to say.

'Well, it wasn't much,' said Tom.

''Twas a deal more than they had, the craturs,' said Fleming.

And he said he didn't think the assistant commissioner would stand in their way now, and that Wilson and O'Casey had been to talk to Father Joseph Byrne. There were so many witnesses, and Fleming said his arrest was only a matter of time. But that there were a few things that had arisen and needed a bit of sorting out.

'And did you get anything off of the evidence that Billy kept, from the sixties?' asked Tom, perhaps unwisely, he didn't really know.

'Nary a bit of DNA. Of course, I don't think anyone thought there would be. Forensics ladies were sceptical at best. Worth a try. They said to tell you sorry about the toothbrush, they wrecked it.' And Fleming laughed, enjoying their forensics humour. 'There was plenty of old dried blood, a gallon of it must have been spilled. The black soutane, you know, stiff with black blood. Sure, all too old, and dead as doornails, DNA-wise. But there are two blood types. A whole sea of one, probably off Matthews, and then a nice little sample of another.'

Now Fleming went silent for a bit. He didn't look about the room – he was in Wilson's old chair, as it happened – but stared down at the bare floorboards. Tom was still hoping to pick up a cheap Persian carpet at Slowey's, if he ever got over that way, Bachelors Walk. Was Slowey's still there, even? Tom was travelling with his eyes along the nice stitching of Fleming's suit. Like a tiny train track, thought Tom. It was a pity that eejit minister in the sixties had decommissioned all the little branch lines of Ireland. Not profitable. But beautiful. Not that Irish governments concerned themselves much with beauty. Stopping the blood flow of visitors to a thousand towns. Machine-stitched or hand – how could he tell? He could ask, but he wasn't in the mood for asking. The stitching travelled up his friend's lapel, and vanished at his throat. Fleming had shaved that morning, but he had a thick grey growth of hair on his lower neck, which Tom supposed went on down into his vest. Probably a hairy chest enough. Had he ever seen Fleming naked? Hadn't they been swimming one time at the Half Moon Swimming Club on the Great South Wall? Or was that himself and Billy Drury? The deep ruined water of the Liffey river, widening and widening between the old Georgian sea walls. And on the other side of the old bulwark – the long butter-coloured stones laid by convict labour no less, useful criminals, long ago, infinitely heavy in the sunlight of that vanished day – on the other side, the expanse of Dollymount Strand, like a wet desert, away to the distant shimmer of the west pier at Dunleary, where he had walked with June. Before June or after June. BJ or AJ? He couldn't remember. He could remember that they had cycled down at the wrong time of day, as it turned out, past the sewerage plant, the Tide Hotel, the potholed road behind the power station wall, the city kids in their nicks at the Shelly Banks, all the city families in their lambent aspect, like walruses the fathers, dainty seals the mothers, the children stitching the air with happy screams and shouts. Only to laugh at each other for their foolishness: not a trace of the tide at the Half Moon! 'You can't dive into nothing,' said Billy Drury, or was it Jack Fleming. So they had gone back the way to the sharp-shelled beach, and swum contentedly enough with the families, the water curiously warm for an Irish seaside place. 'It's the kids pissing in it,' said Billy, and yes, he did think it was Billy now, not Fleming, so he was none the wiser about the chest hair.

'Now, you and DS Drury were the men at the scene – it was in the Dublin Mountains, wasn't it?'

'Well, the Wicklow.'

'Wicklow, right. I was wondering did you get an analysis of the blood at the time? There's no contemporaneous sample from Byrne, for instance. We can easily get one now. Did you? Or was that all lost maybe? You didn't collect blood samples from suspects or the like?'

Tom felt a tug at his professional heart. The answer was clearly no. He sensed Fleming would find almost any answer lame. But he had given him a little door out. Things did get lost. Weren't preserved properly in the first place. But at the same time Billy had been renowned for his evidentiary prowess. Reliable. Thorough. Not doing it all quickly in order to get the hell home. Labels falling off because the glue was badly mixed, stuff thrown in willy-nilly, making good evidence into bad. That had never been Billy's way. He didn't know what to say. He was so proud of most of what he had done over the long years. But he felt a flood of almost liquid embarrassment course through him.

'Billy used to collect blood samples on these cards,' said Tom. 'Just a pinprick, there'd be a pack of them, like a deck of playing cards.'

'Oh yeah?' said Fleming, neutrally.

'Indeed, yes. We often did the same together, you and me, Jack. For other murders.'

'Ah, yeah. Of course. As may be.'

Jack Fleming wasn't doing a great job of hiding his disappointment. Tom didn't know if he was disappointed in his lousy answer or in the general failure to preserve evidence from the sixties. There must be items at this very moment stuck in obscure drawers and cupboards in a thousand Garda stations. There was never any central place where you could deposit evidence. And clerical staff and station sergeants died, and the stuff would become as hidden and forgotten as Tutankhamen's tomb.

'Well, sure,' said Fleming, 'the best we can do is take a sample from you. We can hardly dig up Billy Drury.'

'He was cremated,' said Tom, with an attempt to lighten the atmosphere.

'Lord rest him,' said Fleming.

'He thought Byrne might have done it, but he didn't know.'

'Byrne? I suppose. Maybe. That would be something. Jesus, a murderer and a child molester. You remember nothing about the blood on the soutane? You didn't take a sample from Byrne?' said Fleming for the second time, sharp as sharp. Not for nothing promoted. He just wanted an answer, aloud, in words.

'Oh, I suppose so. Matched Matthews to Matthews? What does the file say? Jesus, I don't remember. We didn't get a match for Byrne, I'm fairly sure, or we'd have charged him straight away.'

'We can check it, we can check it,' said Fleming, and he

joined his two hands together in almost a praying gesture. 'When O'Casey and Wilson went to see Byrne, he said nothing about the swimming pool and the kids, wouldn't answer anything about that. Said he would need his solicitor present. So they asked him about the Matthews cold case. Just to warm him up. Wilson is so clever. And Byrne said, much to Wilson's surprise, he thinks he saw the murderer on the mountain earlier. Said nothing at the time. Had his reasons, he said. Secrecy, his own fucking crimes, I say. Byrne was walking far behind Matthews, who was gone ahead like a mountain goat. This is just what he told the boys. But he saw a man right enough, yes, and some while later, he said, but away in the distance, so he couldn't be sure, the blur and ruckus of a struggle. And heard Matthews cry out, again and again. Oh, he did. Byrne was scared shitless. He didn't even go up to the scene, he said. He just knew it was bad, bad. Thought maybe an irate father, you know . . . And when he went down to the car park to get away, a walk of some two miles, stumbling along on the heather, he found what he thought was the same man he had seen on the mountain, in the car park, and he was very surprised that the man came straight over and said he was a Garda. What was he doing there? On his fucking Sunday walk? He had no idea. He was absolutely terrified, was sure he was next for the chop. Molesters are cowards, Tom. The bloody same man he had seen on the mountain above, he was nearly certain, so what was going on? His head was swirling. So he didn't know what to do, but he told the policeman his colleague had fallen on the mountain. And at a farmhouse this detective telephoned for back-up, Byrne had to go along with him, a priest of the cloth, respectable, admired, and an hour later, as the light was failing, the car arrived, with two men, including I suppose Drury. And who was that man he said he saw on the mountain? Who was that detective? Well, I don't need to tell you, Tom.'

'He never said anything about that at the time,' said Tom, helplessly, like a cretin. 'He couldn't have been surprised to see me. I mean, the man on the mountain, this supposed killer, and him coming over and saying he was a guard. Because he knew me. Me and Billy were over at his house.'

'It doesn't say that in Billy's notes. You went over to their place to interview them?'

'I thought you just said we did.'

'No, I said Wilson and O'Casey went over to his present gaff.'

'Oh, Wilson and O'Casey.' Well, not the same thing at all.

'Are you alright, Tom?'

'No, I'm not, really,' he said. 'Not really. What do Billy's notes say about the call to the guards?'

'They back up what you've always told me, but Billy was your partner, Tom, Billy would have walked across Death Valley for you, with a three-piece suit on and an overcoat.'

'Ah, Janey. He wouldn't have covered up a murder for me. No way. And Byrne would have spoken up long since. He would have said something at the time. I remember him, a smarmy little lad with a posh Midlands accent.'

'He wasn't going to rock that boat maybe. Too dedicated to his pastime. And didn't he get another twenty years of it? Whatever you say, say nothing. But he wants to rock it now, because he knows the game is up. He knows it.'

'That's exactly it. Tactics. Obfuscation. They'd better put him in Arbour Hill, because in the Joy they'll have his guts for garters.'

There was another silence. The voices of children playing rose up to them from the gardens.

'Do you mind if I ask you, did you kill that priest?' said Fleming.

'I didn't kill no priest,' he said. There was a faint hint of humour in his answer, echoing the double negative that priests were supposed to have offered during penal times when they were captured, to avoid the sin of a lie – 'I'm not no priest.' If Fleming caught the joke, he gave no sign of it. A little more air went out of Tom. 'I wasn't even there when it happened. Byrne called nine-nine-nine, and the dispatch recognised his name because she was a mate of Billy's – not a girlfriend, because he had no girlfriends – and she knew how angry Billy and me were about the chief commissioner stopping the investigation, a lot of young guards were angry. So she put through the call to us, and that was the first time I was on that mountain, I drove Billy myself, and then we met Byrne in the car park, he was waiting in great distress, and the daylight going, and he brought us up to the ravine, he was prattling like a turkey, and we both climbed down to the body, me and Billy, and right enough it was a mess. Carnage. Because the rocks were sharp as bread knives and cut him all over. He probably lay there for a good long time and died a slow death. And why didn't Byrne go down to him in the first place, and see if he could help him? His fucking co-conspirator. The coward. And there were brambles and nettles and all sorts to contend with, but we climbed down, and I am sure we were cut a few times, the both of us, so if my blood or Billy's blood is on that soutane I wouldn't be surprised. No one thought I had murdered him, it's ridiculous. Was he even murdered? He might just have slipped and fallen.'

'Byrne heard the struggle, saw it. *He* says it was murder. *He* says he thinks it was you. Why would he even say that? What would put that in his head? That's the bit that worries me. Call it a copper's instinct. Billy's notes here, they all point towards murder. He calls it a frenzied attack. He says quite clearly there were knife wounds, and even in the sixties the Garda doctor confirmed it. It's all in the notes. Unsolved murder.'

'Well, maybe so. I don't know why Byrne accuses me. Haven't a clue. Because he's trying to throw Wilson and O'Casey off their game? Get them off the present day and back to the sixties? Where he's on happier ground? That man is guilty of terrible things, and Thaddeus Matthews was an evil man that caused great hurt to people. To little girls. To their families. It's still a great surprise to me to hear of a priest lying. I don't know why.'

'And you'd no prior connection to Thaddeus Matthews?'

'What do the notes say?'

'Not a thing.'

'There you are. Billy Drury's notes will bear me out. You've read them already, so you know. It wasn't me. Why would I kill Matthews? I was angry about the commissioner but I wasn't that angry. Pervert the course of justice? No. And I wasn't crazy. If I had done something like that, I'd be in Dundrum to this day. Jesus, Jack.'

'I know you've had a hard few years, and these past times haven't been kind to you, Tom. I know. But when a bastard like that says something like that, I have to follow up. You give us the blood sample, come in at your leisure, and sure we'll take it from there.'

This was worse than retirement – it was Purgatory. It was the ten pains of death, it was the seventh circle of hell.

'Sure I will,' said Tom, as easily, as smoothly as he could manage. 'No problem at all.'

Fleming went off then, managing to do so with great bonhomie, in spite of all. Goodbye, goodbye. See you in a few days. Certainly, certainly. Blood sample, blood sample. We'll get that priest now, whatever happens. World a better place without him. Nick him for sure. You'll see, Tom. Goodnight, goodnight. Devious bastard. Throw away the key.

He thought of Fleming getting into his nice car after an encounter like that. He wondered what he was thinking. What a thing to bring to your old friend's door. A new peril of cold cases that he had never foreseen. Enough time goes by and it is as if old things never happened. Things once fresh, immediate, terrible, receding away into old God's time, like the walkers walking so far along Killiney Strand that, as you watch them, there is a moment when they are only a black speck, and then they're gone. Maybe old God's time longs for the time when it was only time, the stuff of the clockface and the wristwatch. But that didn't mean it could be summoned back, or should be. He had been asked to reach back into memory, as if a person could truly do that. Could he ever truly tell Jack Fleming what had happened on that mountain? His embarrassment had partly been because he didn't know, but must once have known, and might never know again, the gospel according to Father Joseph Byrne. It was something that belonged, was locked in, was fatally preserved, in the long-ago, which was now neither true nor false. The real answers to Fleming's questions were not in his cranium, they existed elsewhere, in the great cloud of unknowing where all human stories congregate. An average life was half a million hours, and so what was the sum of every hour lived by every human person since the dawn of human time? And which of the lost stories was important above all the others? He could have little suspicions about the veracity of every thought he had, every thought. He knew, when he looked at it forensically, like the denizens of the forensics department, in their terrible old office building at the back of Harcourt Street, that the memory of the baby strapped to his potty with his arse hanging out must be a memory not of another child, another suffering baby, but of himself, no longer recorded inside his brain as his own. Something he was now looking at from outside, in order to render it down, defuse it, like a bomb disposal expert might a dangerous bomb, to take himself out of the picture, and allow the tragic child a kind of mercy, an anonymity, where he would be released from pain, and gone, and past.

He knew exactly what had happened, but he couldn't tell Fleming any of it. Beyond the ken of Fleming. Beyond his own, really. Not because it was incriminating but rather beyond belief – beyond Fleming's belief. More things in heaven and earth. When June had let out her wail of anguish, she begged Tom to bring her to where she could get a sight of

Matthews. She begged him. Her immense distress was not just for the past rushing back to her, all teeth bared, incisors gleaming. But also because the commissioner had stopped the investigation. For years and years he had been the viper in the tall grasses of herself. Then her marriage to Tom, then the children, nearly assuaging everything. Nearly. Like a healing compensation. Not completely, but nearly, nearly. Didn't she have a gift for ordinary things, the common matters of lives? She saw the use in everything, how the smallest things, the making of scones on a Sunday morning, the onion buns she would often commission him to buy in the Jewish bakery in Portobello, were in the upshot the biggest things. 'Don't come home without them buns, sure you won't, Tom? Or my heart will be broken.' Stray things, the small events of a human day, the mobilisation of care for the kids, their bumps and bruises, their mysterious aches. The time Tom and herself ferried Winnie down to St Michael's in Dunleary, Tom with the child in his arms, fearing the little girl might have meningitis, which had popped up in her kindergarten. The pair of them then, banished from the action by the nurse, but managing to look in through a gap in the door as the nurses held Winnie down on a bed, and the doctor did the lumbar puncture. Her tiny form, and the huge doctor, and the huge needle, and the otherworldly white fluid drawn from the spine, the whole discouraging scene backlit by a big metal window in the spartan ward. Merciful God. But the importance of these matters, all strung in a row of time, the precious necklace of the events of their days. Now this old name, Thaddeus Matthews, this old demon, in the person of a forty-five-year-old priest, still in ministry, as invulnerable as you like, roaring up the years to June, breaking something, severing something, like a madman taking a scissors to the Bayeux tapestry and cutting it in two. And he had their address there in the Tolka Basin, their big neat presbytery where they schemed their schemes, seemingly in dark cahoots with each other now, Matthews no longer a solo hunter. With another non-priest priest to advance his ambitions. 'Let's drive out there and just have a dekko,' she said, and it was a Tuesday, well, he had to work, of course, so he said they could do it on Saturday, if she really wanted to, if she still wanted to.

He didn't remember her moving much again in the time from that Tuesday till the Saturday. She sat in the living room like a bold child told to sit, or a child waiting for someone to come to take her out. An orphan look. He had absolutely no memory himself of any mother or father, but when he was three or so, coming to consciousness as it were, he noticed that not every child where he was was an orphan. Sometimes a mother did come to see a boy, sometimes even a father. Or an aunt, or an uncle. He saw this with his three-year-old eyes, and he started to wait, he started to wait himself for someone to come for him. He waited and he waited, sometimes sitting still just as June did now. Sitting still and waiting. After he gave up waiting he was still waiting, somewhere deep inside himself. Mercy, he was waiting yet maybe. It was fish and chips, then, four nights in a row, brought home by him in the vinegary bags. Salt and vinegar? The bottle of vinegar poised, the big stainless-steel canister of salt. Yeah, yeah. On everything? Oh, everything. Thank you, Luigi. And home to June, as still as a salmon suspended in the current of the River Moy.

Saturday came, and they drove out in their Ford Escort, rare two-door version, to the region where he knew the priests lived. With careful light-hearted questioning of people on the pavements he was directed to the house, winding down the window, asking, winding it up again. Because it was a summer's day but cold enough. One of that legion of Irish summer days that let you down after the promise of morning, like betting on favourites at the races. He had no idea what to do, this wasn't policemen's work, but he contented himself, when he identified the right building, to park in the quiet street, and gaze over at the blank windows.

As it happened they didn't have long to wait. It was about eleven o'clock when the front door opened and two priests ventured out onto the semicircle of granite at the top of the steps. June's head went forward, like a runner before the gun, poised you might think for flight, to make a missile of herself somehow. Tom looked hard at her face, because she said nothing, and he needed to read her intention. The two priests came down the steps, dressed in their black soutanes, but with see-through plastic rain gear over them, and, if he wasn't mistaken, it was hard to see down under the soutanes, sturdy black boots. He saw them when they lifted their skirts daintily to descend, like little girls playing queens. If they did ever meet the English queen, would they bow or curtsy? They walked down their weedless gravel drive, just as carefree as you'd please, and with half-heard talk and laughter climbed into their three-wheel bubble car, and away with them.

'Do you recognise him, June?'

'Tom, Tom, follow them, follow them.'

He supposed that was a yes.

'But, June, do you think so? We don't know where they're headed. They might just be going to the shops.' He was being poisoned now, poisoned by panic.

'You think they do their own fucking shopping? Follow them, follow them. Quick. They're getting away . . . Come on, come on.'

He nosed his leaf-green car out onto the blithe, sun-washed road, and after them. It was no bother to keep a tail on them. Sure he was well used to it. For some reason he wondered if his Smith & Wesson was in the boot, where he had a bad habit of keeping it. As in, against regulations. But still. And anyway, he would hardly need it. But otherwise his mind was strangely blank, like a window at the wrong angle to the daylight. This is for June, he kept repeating, muttering, muttering, like a Buddhist mantra, this is for June. And that fucker there, whose head I can see bobbing about as he drives that stupid little car, he looks like the black dot in a bubble of frogspawn, that creature there, indicating right, and left, and right, little flashing lights, on stalks springing open, retracted, heading to the back of the city now and up onto higher ground, motoring towards the mountains seemingly, is the lousy, filthy, fucking cruel, vicious shite of a man that well-nigh destroyed her, tore through her, a little girl without defences, week after week, his possession and his plaything. Something of the wolf came into him now, he was driving with an altering intent, hunched into the plastic seat, something of the leopard, keeping his expert distance, they wouldn't have an inkling he was on their trail. How casually he had done this, a hundred times, keeping tabs on the movements of villains, druggies and thieves, but of course this was a different thing altogether. Apart from anything else, he was not used to June being near his work. Always that seven miles that separated Deansgrange and Dublin, between her and the dangers he risked every day. Didn't bother him much. Ex-army man, he had seen slaughter aplenty. Sticking his neck out for some principle of guardianship, some heartfelt but hard-to-find-words-for principle, but never with her, the heat and the shape of her, in the seat at his side. Nor even the car, for that matter – he never even took the bloody car. It was overwhelmingly strange, and in large part terrifying. Maybe perversely exhilarating too. Was this what shooting heroin felt like? Could she come to any harm? What was she intending? Was the gun in the boot? What did she want him to do?

Chapter Twelve

Next day, with due regard to the imperative demands of a policeman's schedule, even though he was on the wrong side of it, or this new queer side of it anyhow, he scooted into town again. If they wanted his blood they should have his blood. Now that he was experiencing life on the other side – the penumbral world of the suspect, more or less, or at least of someone to be eliminated, in the rather murderous terminology of these matters – he still felt the electrical charge of duty. Fleming had requested a sample, Fleming should get one. There might as well have been a button on Tom's shirt that Fleming could have pressed marked 'Do This Please Now'. *Alice in Wonderland*'s 'Drink Me' couldn't have exerted such a pull on him. As always the city with its great spokes and whorls and concealed wires of connection assailed him, memories assaulted him, he was walking along like a creature with a hundred eyes and ears. For the thousandth time he longed for the casual satiety of normal life, but then, when had his life been normal? Or was abnormality the measure of all lives? No doubt. He was nevertheless half adream. He wasn't absolutely sure of the health of that either. The city was lying under a huge dark belly of cloud, like a child reading his book under a blanket, except there was poor light enough for the city to read by. It was bang on midday, he could hear the bell of the Trinity campanile tolling twelve, he thought it must be that, or maybe he was catching on the windless air one of the other churches of Dublin, the Carmelite place the back of Grafton Street, or the old Protestant chapel on Dawson Street. There were more decommissioned churches now than pubs, nearly. They had had a grá for church-building, the ancient merchants of the city. Harder for the rich man to enter heaven than for a camel to pass through the eye of a needle. When he thought of that saying he always thought of Cleopatra's Needle in London, though it wasn't a needle, it had no discernible eye, anyhow. The toll of the bell entered the eye of his poor brain – ear, rather. But he wasn't quite there. What thing, what sight, what streetscape, had carried his mind back to Malaya? Maybe he was in need of heroic thoughts. He was going in to see the forensics crowd but he knew in his heart he couldn't satisfy them. They might get a match and it would be ambiguous in implication. They might not get a match and be disappointed, frustrated. Forensics people swarmed over crime scenes, then withdrew with their bounty to their private, still rooms. Of course they were housed in a dreary old office building that was little more than a shell of cinder blocks. It was cruel cold, they always said, when it wasn't cruel hot on the rare days of Irish sun. So he was inclined to feel sorry for them, separate in a way from everything, the legwork and the questions, the sudden flight of understanding. They were sober, quiet, scientific, oftentimes bursting with qualifications. But he wasn't really thinking about that, even as he approached them. He was walking through the streets and avenues and squares of his own city, thinking of Malaya, of the suspect war he had been part of in the long-ago. Nowhere more different than these granite streets, with the buds of spring crowding the sycamores and the oaks of St Stephen's Green. A pleasing rash of green appearing, mid-air, as some trees went ahead of others. Last would be the ash, he knew that. Ash was a late boy for the greening. Maybe it was the subtle green was tweaking at his brain. The huge leaves of Malaya, the sombre shadows of the forests, the stunned bungalows in the hammering heat. First you had your dress of sweat, only then your uniform. There was never a soldier didn't sweat in Malaya, there was no such creature. Herding all the Chinese into the new villages, dirt-poor men in the new wooden streets, them giving out yards at the foul imposition. It was to prevent the strange rebels of that war finding succour from them. Ghostly, fleeting men who would be growing hungry now in the margins. They'd be trying to creep in at dusk just to get a bowl of rice. His job was to position himself in a high tree, lifting himself up there by rope and pulley, and keep his rifle trained on the little roads leading in. Not a fecking Lee-Enfield, why had he said that, no, it was a Model 70 Winchester. A rifle as beautiful as an American car. As effective as a tinker's curse. When he saw someone — unknown, hesitant, looking around nervously — approach, he had to make a decision. To kill or not to kill. If he didn't look Chinese, it was bad news for that boyo. If he looked like one of those Malay rebels, it was in with the bolt, and bang, and four hundred yards that bullet would fly, and the casing ejected from the rifle like a James Bond villain out of James Bond's fancy car, looping up, brassy, its job done, the bullet crossing the distance in a fraction of a second, as flashy as a kingfisher, only God could keep his eye on it, and far away down at the village edge the rebel would no doubt hear the shot too late, since the bullet itself travelled that bit faster than the sound, and not in any fashion so as to save him. And all soundlessly, with an almost comic fall, the poor creature would go down, hardly bothering the hard earth, Tom's aim so good they called him Beady-Eye as a happy nickname. Beady-Eye Kettle. A talent that rescued him in his own country, the mercy of being allowed into the police. Oh yes. Killing rebels gave him his Irish life, away from the shames and shambles of his childhood.

There wasn't a man among the forensics girls that day. It was the easiest thing in the world for them to draw his blood. It was the easiest thing in the world to banter with them. Would the IRA keep the ceasefire, would they feck. Did he see *The Bridges of Madison County* yet? That seemed to be a tease. Did they have a cinema in Dalkey anyhow, what was the craic down there? If there was a cinema, he had never spotted it. Loads of pubs. More bloody castles than you could shake a stick at. One of the ladies, Attracta Geary, she said Dalkey was a great port one time, everything run into Ireland came through there. 'You'd want a rake of castles,' she said. 'I thought that was Howth,' said Tom. 'Sure there was never a big harbour at Howth.' 'Was it maybe Dunleary I mean?' he said. 'Ah sure look it,' said Attracta, 'the blind leading the blind.' Then she knocked his blood sample a little in the phial, and stuck a little label on it, and sort of sang to it, he thought, or hummed at it, as she brought it up closer to her eyes, as if indeed she were challenged in the eyes. But it was only her way of seeing into it. 'Well, you've very nice blood, Detective,' she said. 'It's not all the same, then, like they say?' he said. 'Some blood is very murky when you get it,' she said.

He headed back out, leaving the dilapidated building not with relief but with gratitude, lighter by a few drops of blood. He had faced the demon. His fear that had been a companion for nigh on thirty years. It was like a visit to the doctor, but not at all like it as well. Both could mean bad news, but. Murder. In the old days, even in the forties, a conviction could mean death for you. Dev had had two IRA men dispatched by none other than Pierrepoint during the war. Execution by hanging. Taken from this place and hanged by the neck until dead. What a thing, to hear such words in a tumultuous courtroom. Your body burned through by shock. Knowing you had done the deed and that it was all well deserved, and no one to question it or save you. A moment of utter loneliness and horror, he did not doubt. Thou Shalt Not Kill. You shall not, boyo. Not at all, not even a little bit. But you cannot kill a little bit, killing is absolute. K-i-l-l. A tiny word for a deed as big as a planet. Who was there to say that the rebels he'd killed, at a distance of four hundred yards, lads with a gnawing in their bellies, lured by ordinary hunger to the villages, weren't good souls enough? His job was to dispatch them. Kill – ask questions later. He was a murderer, of course he was. He had killed many times. The butt of his rifle was notched with fifty-seven knife-marks. There nearly wasn't room for them all, and only the recall to England had put an end to it. These strange wars at the end of the long tale of Empire. Putting things right, putting things in their right places, before leaving for ever. Mopping up operations. Every problem in the country caused by your own army in the long-ago. A proud people and an overweening foreign army. The arrogance of his officers. Kill – ask questions later. They're only *Jakuns*, Tom. You've a great touch on that popgun. We'll have to send you to the Olympics.

Murder.

He was just entertaining this word, trying to dislodge it from his craw where it had proverbially stuck, when a man came tearing along behind him, like he was doing a Ronnie Delany there, beside one of the keepers' cottages in the Green. The wind of late spring that liked to sort through the buds and burgeoning greenery, also laden with vaguer memories, had blown open Tom's coat, and he was just adjusting it, and smoothing his lapels in an unconscious gesture, when this man quite forcibly put a hand on his right shoulder, so forcibly Tom in the first moment thought he was being assaulted. He was being assaulted to the strict letter of the law. It was actually illegal to put your hand on someone, unless— Well, it was no violent stranger, but Wilson, in a different suit than the previous encounter, this time a well-tailored job with a green sheen. Funny the things you noticed.

'Jaysus, Tom, I was only shouting after you.'

But the traffic was tearing along behind him, racing the lights there at the juncture of Harcourt Street and the southwest corner, as was its wont. Every so often a pedestrian was killed crossing there. Notorious.

'Sure I'm gone deaf,' said Tom, despite this kerfuffle pleased to see Wilson. This running after him was almost a gesture of friendship.

'Do you have two minutes, head?' said Wilson, indeed in a very chummy manner, although you might say that using this familiar matey word was not altogether respecting of their rank difference. But of course there was no rank difference now. 'Shall we plonk our arses down somewhere?' said Wilson, and not waiting for an answer seemed to steer them both towards one of the myriad wooden benches, green as letterboxes. It was at this moment that Tom had a sudden craving for a cigarillo, though he was not only formerly a detective but also a cigarillo man. He had a shocking sense of the cigarillo in his mouth, and the hot sharp tart taste filling it. Delicious. Calming. Like the bloody ad on the television. The man in a hole, and his smoke rising from it, was it? And some appropriate music.

'Fuck it, you know, Tom,' said Wilson, 'I'm getting too old for running like that.'

Indeed he was sweating like a navvy, he was nearly spewing up sweat from the pores of his skin. An extremely pretty young mother passed by with a double buggy, a twin, it looked like, in each seat. Wilson paused the necessary length of time to take her in, to idolise her, to imagine himself married to her, serving her, never letting her down—

'And merciful Jesus, it was my fortieth birthday yesterday, and I feel more like seventy.'

As Tom was sixty-six, he said nothing.

'I wanted to talk to you about this fucking priest.'

'Fleming was telling me,' said Tom. He was distressed now. Shaky. They were in St Stephen's Green, an important site in every Dubliner's childhood. He hadn't had a childhood as such himself, granted, but he had often observed as a grown man, as a serving officer as it were, the mothers and their kids at the lip of the large lake that lay many yards behind him. Crumbling the slices of white pan, and feeding the famous ducks. The eternal ducks. How long did a duck live? He had only found out recently that the robin, that best mate of birds, lived but two years on the earth. Then was gone. Better than the deal for the dragonfly with his measly one day, but still. In Mr Tomelty's graceful garden, when you sat in the healing bower of hedges, there was always a robin with you there, hoping you were going to do a bit of digging maybe. With his lovely red breast, or more brown than red in truth, if you looked closely. It was his job, or had been formerly, to look closely at things, even a robin's breast. Did he love the robin as much as he loved Winnie and Joe? Why not – was that not alright in the document that was God's plan? The famous unwritten unseen hidden document.

'He's only the most egregious fucker,' said Wilson. Tom didn't remember him cursing so much when he'd visited. Perhaps they were on cursing terms now, old mates, perhaps not. That was a big word, though, *egregious*, that was a word found only in books. So there was a mateyness in the cursing and a compliment in the use of the word. Maybe. *Maybe* was a good word to keep near Wilson. But you couldn't gainsay his odd charm. Tom felt he was really getting to know him. Very unexpected. A human person could only be revealed slowly, which was why multiple interviews were advised for suspects, not to mention victims, if they could stand it. The trauma and upset of victims was only a vague concern for some coppers. They forgot about it. But forget about it at your peril. It was the whole point of the entire enterprise. Healing the wounds.

'I know you had dealings with him, long ago. I know you talked to Fleming the other day, but if I could just pick your brains. You know what he said about you, of course?'

'No, no, yes, Fleming said . . .'

'Yeah, yeah, an almighty fucker of a man, with a big mouth on him. Spewing out all sorts. A priest, Tom, a fucking priest. Can't we have decent men as priests, no? Not allowed?'

'He's not a priest, really,' said Tom, and felt a powerful urge to expand on this, but swallowed the words he wished to say. He swallowed the words that rose mainly from his love for June, and maybe, he thought, and it was a new thought, his love for himself.

'These boys are hunters,' said Wilson. 'I agree, Tom. Me and O'Casey were over talking with him. He was as nice as you like. Made us tea, or his fucking housekeeper did. Tea, and Marietta biscuits. I hadn't had a Marietta in years.'

'You don't care for them?' said Tom, despite his sudden vow of silence.

'Fig rolls is me tipple,' said Wilson, and he laughed, that curious laugh he had, something a little out of character from his mostly tough-guy manner, a little high and brittle, feminine even. Just by chance there were two nuns of the old style passing as he offered this odd human music to the air, who glanced down at him with an incurious and unreadable blankness.

Wilson raised his hand to an imaginary hat and raised it though it didn't exist, and said, by way of respectful greeting, 'Sisters.'

The nuns made no response. The older one was wearing on her head what looked to Tom like some of the body parts of a swan. Another bird that loved the Green. Cantankerous, lovely birds, like those wonderful bitchy actresses in the Shelbourne years ago, when he was on guard detail there for famous visitors to Dublin. Two weeks of interesting hell.

Wilson seemed to fall into a long contemplation now. There was something tender in this man, thought Tom, and he was glad again he'd had the privilege of the night together, the three of them, in a Dalkey storm.

'I was going to try for the priesthood years ago,' said Wilson, solemnly, as if solemnity was all that had survived of this old ambition. 'I went down to Maynooth on the Athlone bus, you know. I was only seventeen. I was still at school. Christian Brothers. Bate the living Jaysus out of us all. But still I thought . . . felt something . . . You know they call it, what's it, a vocation. A voice calling you to service. I heard that voice, Tom.'

'That's – that's amazing,' said Tom. 'Really.'

And it really was. This veritable wodge of a man, Wilson, with his nefarious activities up north, possibly, and his curious roughness, his ruddy face, possibly – lots of possiblys – a nice pretty wife, possibly a brace of kids, his taste in decent suits, his necktie with the blue sheen of a blackbird, the few hairs under his jawline that he had missed with his razor that morning – well, at least he had shaved – had once had a thought, a deep thought, in the very centre, the powerhouse of his soul, to go and be a cleric.

'You know it was the fucking architecture put me off,' said Wilson, laughing again. 'Can you believe that?'

'In Maynooth, like?'

'Yeah, yeah – those fucking institutional buildings. Looked like prisons, or loony bins . . .'

And Tom laughed agreeably now, yes, yes, he understood. Wilson had not been able to insert himself into one of those buildings, let alone one of those dreary suits of clothes that priests were condemned to don.

'Anyway, this Byrne lad, if you can give me a heads-up, brother, I'll be grateful. The things he's saying. He knows he's fucked. We have him over the handlebars, bang to rights, no debate. There's actually fifteen boys will testify. Some of them wild boys, look it, some of them nice gentle boys from round where he lives. Would you believe it?'

Nice gentle boys, what a strange phrase.

'I never met him, you know,' said Tom. 'It was the other man I knew. I mean, I never met him either as such. Father Thaddeus. I never knew him, but I knew of him.'

'You knew of him, before the thing with the photographs?'

'I had heard tell of him, yes, I was aware he was a person not to be trusted, as such, I suppose. It's so long ago that—'

'Yeah, long ago.' And Wilson sighed as if there were a tragedy just in the very phrase. Long ago. The passing of time. Millennia. Human suffering. The dubious parade of history. Wars, oppressions, empires. And it was a question of empires, the empire of the Irish priesthood, with its princes and its armies. Those big men oftentimes of considerable girth – not McQuaid, he kept trim as a greyhound, and as sleek – whose ring you were being asked to kiss when you met them. Go down on one knee, a bloody policeman, and take the paw of such a man, offered to you with a strange gesture, like an eighteenth-century dandy, and put your lips on the big ruby or garnet, hoping your mouth was dry enough in that moment, and you wouldn't slobber over it. 'But this shit's not long ago. This shit is now.'

'We talked of this before, no?' said Tom. How could he tell him of June's troubles? It would be not just like a betrayal, but a betrayal. Words spoken in a marital privacy. There was no greater confessional. Not from penitent to priest, but from the beloved right into the heart of the lover.

'Do you know, we never really did,' said Wilson. 'That's the amazing thing. I am thinking back to all that we talked about, and I'm getting nothing from it.'

This was said not entirely without rancour, just a soupçon of it. It was the first time Tom had heard such a tone in Wilson. He thought he would do well to be troubled by it.

'I understand,' he said, not at all understanding.

'He's making allegations,' said Wilson, with a sudden air of helplessness. 'I am obliged to ask you. I am so fucking sorry that I am obliged to ask you. It's not very fucking dignified.'

This was a new thought for Tom. Oh, he thought. Wilson is embarrassed. Or if not embarrassed, well, respectful. Maybe deeply so. Astonishing. It gave Tom a sudden surge of delight. Courtesy!

'If I advance this investigation, it's going to be messy. So fucking messy.'

'You have to advance it,' said Tom, abruptly and passionately. He didn't care, at the core of the thing, he didn't care a jot for himself. His ancient burden of 'a sense of justice', a heavy bloody thing that would break a civilian's back, he knew, was not a burden he could ever put down, even now. Even now, as something gnawed at his own safety, his peace, like a monstrous rat, that was the tune that rose first of all things to his lips. Find out the truth and penetrate the crime. Bring the guilty to justice.

'I don't want to—' began Wilson, and paused, and stared straight ahead. There was something he didn't want to do alright. Tom thought he knew what. He didn't want to *fuck him over* in his retirement, was perhaps the phrase Wilson might use. Drag him out of his lair and shine that piercing judicial light on him, an old policeman. An old policeman with the Scott Medal! He supposed Wilson knew that too. Just the bronze, but even so. Took a bullet from a madman in '72. Well, a poor crazy boy with a great storm and muddle in his head. Crazy with the pain of life maybe. Was going to shoot his wife, but Tom stepped in between them, took the bullet in his shoulder. A moment's bravery, God knew. Had no idea why he did it, except, he did. He was interested in why, but he didn't know. Recklessness. A feeling of deep deep chaos in his soul after the Father Thaddeus affair. There had been times when he simply didn't care about himself anymore. He used to be tempted to drive through red lights in his little car, which was truly stupid, and truly murderous when he thought about it. Just now and then. And when that young man, what was his name, Purcell, something Purcell, Tim maybe, waved his army-issue gun around – he was a mechanic in logistics in the army, so why did he have a gun? – Tom didn't feel anything remotely like fear. He just thought: You had best not shoot your wife.

Shoot me instead. So they gave him a medal for that. It was called the Walter Scott Medal, but it had nothing to do with *Ivanhoe*. It was some boyo in the states, a Colonel Scott, set it up for the honour of the guards. *Valor*, with no *u*, Yankee spelling. He knew where the medal was, of course, but it wasn't something he thought about much, or his supposed 'valor', anyhow. He was thinking about it now, and Wilson hadn't mentioned it. But if Tom had been put to the pin of his collar to say what Wilson thought of him, he might be of the opinion that Wilson respected him, in his young-man way. Or middle-aged, he should say. Forty! He didn't want to be forty again himself. He didn't want to be sixty-six. Holy Jesus.

Wilson was still staring straight ahead. Tom didn't have a full view of his face, but it looked serious enough, the section he could see. The eyes, brown and moist, fixed on that curious place, the middle distance. The cars of Dublin beyond his gaze roared along the perimeter road. In older days you used to hear the nice clop-clop of carters' horses, going about their tasks. Hmm. Now it was just the leonine growls of the combustion engine. A gang of impish sparrows spread suddenly on the tar path in front of them, like big dice thrown from a hand. They were after some crumbs there, some reckless insects, minute things that would please a sparrow. Small wants.

Wilson nodded his head, as if coming to some conclusion in his private mind, not something he wished to share with Tom.

'I'll let you go,' he said, rather incongruously since it was he who got up, brushed a hand across his backside to restore order to his trousers, and nodded again, this time with an accompanying smile. He was letting himself go. He was a handsome geezer when he smiled, as he probably knew, Tom thought. But Tom was grateful for the smile all the same. 'I'll be seeing you,' said Wilson. 'Good luck.' And off he went, into whatever else lay in store for Wilson that day.

He shook himself as if rising out of a reverie. Or that feeling he used to have in the cinema at the end of a film, finding himself sunken into himself, a waking dreamer, the landscapes of the Old West being replaced again by the musty seat coverings and the stirring audience, like disturbed woodlice. Having to shake that off in order to be able to enter the 'real' world again. The real world. That world that so sorely lacked reality. The fecking real world, with all its random hecticality, its welcome pools of quiet, of beauty even. Aye. Like this park of marauding sparrows, and the road of roaring cars. There was a border between them maybe, but what policed that? Mysteries. Where did the world end and space begin? Where did the Milky Way end and some other great galaxy begin? If he was composed of atoms, as he believed he was, and there were those vast distances between his blessed atoms, where did he end and the park begin? Perhaps he had to shed a few atoms even to get up, as he was doing now? His friend in forensics could come down after him here, and make a sweep of this bench, and know very well, for an absolute fact, presentable in court, and leading to a conviction, that he and Wilson had sat here, deep in conversation. Or could you say shallowly in conversation? Lightly? Playfully? Dangerously?

What was it now to be old? How would he be seen now,

by these mothers and babies? And down by the duck pond he knew there would be students from Trinity ranged on the benches, if it wasn't too cold for them, and foreign types looking in their guidebooks, staring unknowingly at the complicated buildings of Dublin. Traitor's Gate, and the empty space at the centre of everything that once offered King George II to the mockery of the passers-by, blown up when Tom was seven. Even in his doomed incarceration, far away in Connemara, the Brothers had talked about that. Tourists and students would know nothing about those matters, nor all the matters that he, with his policeman's eyes, remembered at every corner, and coming into every street saw again in his inner mind, crimes, outrages, assaults, chases, questionings. It was not just because he was old, and looked old to them, but because he was a pensioned ghost from the strange past, a pointless survivor, an old soldier of forgotten wars. A remnant, with a torn gansey for a soul.

Nevertheless as he passed along Nassau Street, heading for the train, he bought himself a 99, with two Flakes, raspberry sauce and sprinkles. He had been surprised to find ice cream for sale, and supposed this was the true herald of summer. It was very delightful. A very nice girl made it for him out of her chrome-covered machine. 'Twas like a sausage maker in the butcher's. The 99 lasted him all the way to Booterstown, and as the train passed between the bird sanctuary and the widening strand he bit the end of the cone in immortal style, and sucked the last bit of ice cream till the cone was hollow, and then mercilessly ate the cone.

This was all very well. But as he wended his way along the old granite pavement of upper Coliemore Road, all the dwellings of Auld Dacency quizzing him with their dark windows, who goes there, friend of wealth or foe, noticing how the great lid of cloud had been raised, as if all that country and sea beneath had now been properly slow-cooked, and how the veins of struggling sunlight dropped from the upper cloud now like leaking waterfalls, as if light itself were a celestial flood and couldn't but fall under the rules of gravity, like all created things, he knew there were rats in the roof of himself. His belfry. His bloody belfry. He knew he was invaded and rightly. It was a pleasant evening. Surely this was weather to be happy in. To be not thinking of anything but the beneficent view. But perhaps he had been excused such happiness now, as a master excuses a child his lessons for an evening. What had been so easy, so unexpected, during those quiet nine months, was his no more. Of course he knew that. He accepted it now. But there was another stage after acceptance. He was a brave man for a bullet but not so brave for an arrow – this little floating arrow arcing high in the sky of things now, so high you would be forgiven for thinking it was heading away from you. But it wasn't. Soon its own weight would check its upward path, and slowly, slowly, like the arrow of old archers of ancient wars, it would begin its journey downward. An arc still but one searching for his heart. Fleming and Wilson and O'Casey and their friendly vice. His fingers were in it. The screw was being closed on them. Soon he thought he might well be screaming. In a plastic bag swinging tightly in his grip were a half-pound of sausages and a half-stone of spuds. This was in the interest of ongoing life. The arrow was going higher, higher. Soon it would catch its breath at the apex, halt gracefully, truly, and begin the fabled descent. Like an arrow of old. In the old stories. In the old wars. In time already lived, whose inhabitants were gone to their reward. Whose troubles were no more. Whose journeys were done.

Chapter Thirteen

Who will read the liturgy of the dead? God posts you your fate, the envelope is opened and the page is blank, but everything is written there. He supposed that was true. He had a sudden strong desire to tell his story to someone, as long as it was someone without ears. So he could speak but they wouldn't hear. Ah yes. Billy Drury had known the whole business, but only up to the point of his own death. All the rest was unrecounted. June knew the story up to her death too, of course. Though Billy and June would have different versions. They were sort of uncompleted chapters, and even when he put them together in his own mind it was hard for him to find where they joined. Even to believe half of it. But he was obliged to believe it. Because in the first instance a witness should be believed. A lot of mischief and mischance had arisen from not believing witnesses. Rejecting out of hand. Poor soul standing in front of you, spilling the dreadful beans, and it not sounding likely. But oftentimes the unlikely was the truth, as you might find out, in the end, when it was too late. He felt he should believe – believe himself.

He was thinking all this, just readying to turn into the gates of the castle, looking forward by habit to the refuge of the wicker chair, a decent fry-up in his lap, when the cellist next door caught sight of him, and hailed him with what was almost a glad shout. Almost. Or else an involuntary cry.

Or was it directed at someone else? Tom looked about him but there was no one. His neighbour's smart little house was Victorian, but the balcony was of course new, or newish. The salt sea was slowly stripping away the varnish off the wooden rail. He had his Remington on its tripod but also his cello propped between his legs. As an assist to his cry, he had raised the bow aloft, and given it a shake, to try and attract Tom's gaze. Tom didn't know what to do. Was this an invitation? He had promised himself after the visit of Wilson and O'Casey that he would engage more fruitfully with other souls. And from what he knew of him, he did like this diminutive fellow with the long locks. He was tempted to raise a hand himself, and just call a greeting, and push on home. But that was simply cowardice. Tom believed himself to be fairly well educated, but a cellist — this was a rarefied profession, surely. Lots of arcane technical knowledge. Strange music, strange composers. Beyond Bach, Tom was an ignoramus. This might be soon found out. But maybe — this thought came unbidden, as if under its own steam — the cellist liked *him*. When they had spoken before, Tom had noted the English accent, and the nice sardonic way the man had of talking even about the weather. As if the Irish weather were his adversary. Which it was, in its way, the Irish weather, which would so rarely play ball with the plans of citizens. All public holidays were guaranteed to be rainswept, stem to stern. It was a given of Irish life. A trip to the beach, begun in blazing sunshine, would inevitably end in shivering tears, in sudden storms, in lids of cloud. How often the Irish person, of whatever age or sex, had lain on his or her towel, on any beach in Ireland, body stiffening with the assault of the cold, waiting for the cloud cover to pass away, and the gladsome sun to pour down again. Soon the shivering passes to convulsions, to an epilepsy of exposure. The victim quails, squints up at the sky with one eye, because there is a glare even in the cloud, trying to make a judgement. Should I stay or should I go? Is there any point in lying here, as gradually death seems a desirable thing?

But now the cellist leaned his instrument carefully against the chair, which he had just vacated, and walked over to the edge of his balcony at the spot nearest to Tom.

'What a beautiful evening,' he said.

'It's just lovely,' said Tom.

'You'd nearly chance a swim,' said the man. Now Tom was struggling to remember if he knew his name, if his name had ever been mentioned or verified, but he struggled in vain.

'Come up and have a glass of something,' said the cellist.

Tom of course hesitated. He had enjoyed Wilson and O'Casey's company, but that didn't mean he was a convert to sociability just yet. He was sorely tempted. The casual, easy-going air of the man. After all, his neighbour. He might be living here a long time yet. How long did the body survive after retirement? Unknown. And Tom had been so heavy with his thoughts all along the Coliemore Road. He was suddenly willing to be trusting, to let go of that copper-like tendency to keep back from the community, just in case. Just in case of what? That someday he might be arresting the cellist? Come on, Tom. Unlikely. But the unlikely . . .

'Jesus, I will,' said Tom, 'thank you,' he said, surprising himself, his legs surprising him too by carrying him as if of their own accord up the little flight of new concrete steps to the right of the cottage. There was a moment of panic when he couldn't somehow bear to arrive burdened by his shopping. Embarrassed him. He had a wild thought to throw it down into the gap between the properties, but he didn't. The little fancy gate banged behind him, nearly giving him a fright. Terra incognita. Incipient friendship. Suddenly his mind was full of thoughts of future harvest, this small moment leading to a litany of lovely things, long nights in the winter dark drinking whiskey with the cellist and maybe playing chess – he couldn't really play chess, but still – talking over old matters, even listening to music, expanding his info beyond Johann Sebastian. Was this the earless man he might tell his sad tale to? Probably not. Anyway, he had ears, he had to have ears, for the cello playing.

When he got up onto the balcony, which was quite spacious, maybe even the square footage of the cottage itself repeated, he realised he had only seen a fragment of it from the road. From his window he could see just the front edge of it, where the gun was mounted, and always when he heard the shots, and he would peer out, he could only view the head and chest of the cellist, and never the steadying legs, though he had imagined them. He had imagined them and therefore in a way had seen them. He had talked once to the man at his ornate gate, or he thought he had. He had certainly gained an impression of niceness, somehow, even if the details were under a sort of frosted glass. But actually the man seemed entirely different in the round. As if he had been into Brown Thomas's and bought himself a new self. Tom knew an expensive shirt when he saw it, because he would never purchase such a thing. In not having good clothes, he was an expert. He was used throughout his career to 'reading' a person, and he was reading the little cellist now. Silk, if he was not mistaken. And a pair of wavy trousers, how else could he describe them, wavy, made of some thin material, and lots of it, like the old Turkish trousers, the dress trousers of one of the French regiments, he couldn't remember the name. No – Zouave! He could remember it. Bingo. He felt shabby beside this resplendent gear, in his old suit and the ill-considered coat. But the cellist veritably grasped his free right hand, actually plucked it up from Tom's side where he had left it, abandoned it as it were, forgetting to offer it, stupidly, and with both his own hands, the man squeezed it and shook it. The shopping was gracefully ignored. The lid of Tom's head lifted and puttered, indeed like a pot of potatoes just coming to the boil. What was his name, what was his name?

'Ronnie,' the cellist said, rescuing him. 'Ronnie McGillicuddy.'

'Oh,' said Tom, 'of the Reeks.'

'The very same.'

'Tom Kettle.'

'Yes,' he said, and gave the hand a last little workout, and dropped it softly. He had ever so slightly crushed it. He would have great strength in his fingers from the cello playing, Tom supposed.

'I thought you were . . .' Tom said, and then didn't want to say the word *English*, in case this Ronnie McGillicuddy would take offence. Take it as a reference to miserable Irish history. The old story. The crushing grip of the Sassenach.

But then he said it anyway. It was the pause, the discretion of the pause, that allowed it. '... English, somehow.'

'No, no, my lot have been there a thousand years. More. On the Reeks.'

'It's a beautiful part of the country.'

'It is.'

'But you live here?'

'This was my wife's place.'

'Oh.'

'I kept it on, you know.'

'Ah, sorry to hear that.'

'What?'

'She's not . . . ?'

'Separated. She was sectioned, actually. Hmm.' And he shook his head, the hair shrugging, as if forbidding further questions.

'Ah.'

'Are you married, Tom?'

'Was. Widower now.'

'Ah.'

So they had got this far. He wondered if Ronnie was regretting calling him up, or possibly even enjoying it. You only had to stand near a fellow like this to feel a bit rough. He didn't believe he *was* so rough, yet . . . out of his league? But then, he wasn't going to be his girlfriend. That's what they used to say, himself and Billy, when they saw a goddess, a goddess in the street. Out of our league, Tom. But then, he had actually married a goddess. So out of his league he was still astonished she had married him. Astonished.

Maybe all this was written on his face, or even broadcast

by it, because Ronnie said:

'I can see you miss her, Tom, and I'm sorry to hear of your loss.'

'It was a great fucking loss,' he said, 'right enough', regretting the F-word, but all the same, it had bounded out, heartfelt and intimate.

The cellist laughed. 'I know exactly what you mean. My wife's still *overground* but I miss her.'

Then the cellist beckoned Tom to sit on one of the two metal chairs. Actually, he thought, this was quite enjoyable. They had gently communicated the core truths of each other in five seconds, remarkable. As Tom went past the tripod to reach the chair, he said: 'Remington.'

'Absolutely. You know your guns. Well, I suppose you would.'

'Aye. What distance is that, from here to the cormorants?'

'Three hundred yards, thereabouts.'

'I often hear the firing.'

'Oh,' said Ronnie, smoothing out the creases of his voluminous trousers, and catching something in Tom's tone. 'Oh – you don't approve?'

'Ah, no bother. I don't not approve. You know.'

'Will you take something? Coffee? Whiskey?'

'Sure I'd love a whiskey.'

'Straight, water?'

'Sure throw a drip of water into it.'

'A drip?'

'A drop – a drop, I meant to say. Ah yes.'

No human person could argue with an evening like this. There was just that bit of lengthening in the days that suggested the coming of the bounteous daylight term of summer. Dark at eleven. Not that yet, but if you were to ask him what kept him in Ireland, the long length of a summer's day might be cited as one reason anyhow. Americans marvelled at such things. He had heard them in O'Connell Street, when the light lingered almost preposterously towards midnight, as if they were at the North Pole. And if those drawn-out days were graced by decent heat – nothing could compare to the gift of it, anywhere. Weather and peaceful hours to make a saint of a gangster. There were no robberies or assaults on a late summer's evening, in his admittedly wonky memory.

Two whiskies were brought in nicely engraved glasses and the cellist returned himself to a smiling contemplation of the sea, the lambent island, the cormorants, and now and then, with darting eyes, his new friend.

'Three hundred yards,' said Tom, and nodded his head, and said no more for a full minute.

When the minute was up, Ronnie McGillicuddy said: 'Three hundred.'

'No bother with that gun,' said Tom.

'You want a go, Tom?' said Ronnie. 'She's loaded.'

Tom looked in surprise at Ronnie, as if this had never entered his mind. Well, it had not. The smallest imaginable pieces of gold and silver light were rioting tinily everywhere. For a moment he couldn't remember if the sun should be in front of them – if so, the cosmos had swallowed it whole – or behind them. The sun knew for itself and was going down behind the glassy house and the hill, all out of view the other side of the castle. But the light was piercing through the flowerless leaves of a passion flower that Ronnie had captive in a big pot. The climbing plant was held upright by a skinny trellis stuck in the soil. The tripod was another upright thing, and another was a music stand with sheet music on it, close by Ronnie's chair, and the deep crimson-brown of the cello. Tom thought that yoke must be worth a few bob. The title of the sheet music was *Kol Nidrei*, in clear black letters, a phrase that might have bamboozled him, might have bamboozled anyone, but it struck a chord in him. A memory from long long ago. Now the silver and gold light seemed to have got into his eyes, and it went in there, and was dancing there, he was nearly blinded. *Kol Nidrei*. Even as he rose to the gun, with Ronnie closely watching him, sipping his whiskey – Tom hadn't touched a drop, as he did not of course drink, but he had been happy to receive the glass and hold it, in the interests of courtesy – he was asking his old head what the phrase was. When he was seventeen, only a few months in the army, he'd been told he was being sent to Palestine. Yes, he remembered now. Those bloody booklets. They were still somewhere in the sacred boxes. Would he ever unpack them? He couldn't say. His sergeant had given him a booklet about Arab feast days and holy days, and Jewish feast days and holy days, so he wouldn't cause offence to the inhabitants. As if his gun wouldn't do that all on its own. And booklets about diet and customs and history and whatnot. And a book of handy phrases in Arabic and Hebrew. And how to talk to Jewish women and Arab women, and Jewish girls and Arab girls, and how not in any way to think he could ask a girl of any description to go out with him. Is this the way to the station? Can I have the key for my room? How many sisters and brothers do you have? And he had studied the backsides off of the booklets, because he was seventeen and wanted to get on in the army. He had finally been let go from the orphanage and he was never going back, and if he had to learn a thousand booklets off by heart he would do it, gladly. Then the British left Palestine at the end of the year, or was it shortly after, which anyway came as news to his sergeant for some reason, and all his learning was for nothing, and he was shipped off to Malaya instead, where the sins of empire were to continue. But yes, he had gathered a goodly amount of what in the end was to be of no use to him, except now, fifty years later, on this expensive terrace, with this curious man, and the phrase *Kol Nidrei*, which he knew, because the relevant booklet had told him, was sung on the eve of the Feast of Atonement. Atonement. A word that had meant little to him when he was seventeen, but meant a great deal to him now. All your oaths and promises made during the year, and that you had failed to keep, to be put aside and cancelled: *Kol Nidrei*. Something that also meant nothing to him fifty years ago, something he longed for now.

Ronnie made an adjustment to the bolts holding the gun steady, preparing it for Tom, Tom supposed.

'Who's that running around there, Tom?' he said, indicating with head and hand the garden of the Tomeltys. Tom glanced down.

'Oh, that's Miss McNulty's little boy.'

'I think that's a girl, Tom.'

'Oh, is it a girl?' He looked again. It wasn't just him, then, seeing her.

'I don't know,' he said slowly. 'I really don't.'

'Maybe it's a ghost,' said Ronnie lightly.

'The ghost of who, though?' said Tom, a little in dread of the answer.

'When they were digging there on the island, in the sixties, they found a child's bones thrown in a ditch. Not even buried. An ancient ditch, seemingly. An ancient child. Maybe that's her. Oh, she's gone.'

'Well,' said Tom.

'You don't believe in ghosts?'

'I do,' said Tom definitively.

'I've lined her up for you,' said Ronnie, meaning not the girl but the gun.

'This is a great scope, Ronnie,' Tom said, peering into it where it was fastened along the top of the rifle. 'I have an old Weaver on mine. Which is a good scope. But this is – this is . . .'

He really meant it. There must have been a revolution in rifle scopes when he wasn't paying attention. He hadn't been obliged to shoot his rifle for many many years. There seemed to be a component of light also in this scope that he couldn't see the origin of. There were the cormorants right in front of his nose, it seemed like, and the very barnacles on the black rocks, and the heavy skirts of dark-brown seaweed, shrugging in the late tide. It had an aspect cold and wild. The cormorants looked like they had been carved violently out of the dark rocks. He wondered what it would be like to pull the trigger softly, ease his index finger through the small arc of it, and peg a bullet into a breast, and watch the bird fall, far far off and yet so near. But he knew in his heart he would never pull the trigger.

When he stood back again, smiling at Ronnie, nodding his head, he thought a bit foolishly because maybe he had been expected to shoot, he saw the little man had taken his cello between his legs, and had lifted up the bow, and placed it on a string, very dancer-like, very elegantly.

'Do you mind if I play?' he said.

'No, no, I would love you to play. I hear you all the time. Bach. I know the Bach.'

'Do you know this? By Bruch?'

'By Bach?'

'No, no, Bruch, Bruch. *Kol Nidrei*. Bruch was a big old German Protestant but he wrote this beautiful piece of Jewish music.'

He was going to say, yes, I know about that, about the Day of Atonement, and the vows and oaths we all failed to keep, and the mercy of being freed from that, but he said nothing. Let Ronnie McGillicuddy think he was an ignoramus. He had no wish to talk about Palestine and about when he was seventeen and just months out of the orphanage. Anyway, Ronnie started to play the first long, single note before he could speak. Tom sat back down on his chair. Was this not one of the nicest things that had ever happened to him? A glass of whiskey – if never to be touched – and the last lights of a spring day, being played to by a man to whom it was obviously possible to say stupid things, and he would not mind. That was a good trait in a man. He sank into his chair, deeper and deeper, in his dark coat, and the cormorants three hundred yards off no doubt heard the music too, their lives extended by Tom's reticence, his love of things put in front of him to view, his confusion, even his old guilt, his head full of gold and silver light.

And likely the Tomeltys heard it, and the young mother, Miss McNulty, and her little boy eating his tomatoes and sausages. For it was still only teatime. When he thought of the boy's sausages, his own sausages seemed suddenly *companionable* at his feet.

Ronnie McGillicuddy didn't seem to hear the music himself exactly, his face had completely changed, had become serious, jumping with little expressive movements, his eyes shut tight, now and then throwing back his head, the locks stirring and swaying, not even looking at the music, and not so much listening as drawing the notes out of his very body.

Here was the man without ears Tom had needed. He sat there, sinking deeper and deeper, mollified, gentled, and into his mind, his own eyes closed, floated the beloved face of June. The loved, loved face. For the first time in a long time he could gaze on it without fear. Without dread. Like a soldier terrified who runs out to battle anyhow, and finds his courage has rinsed him clean of fear. The first face, when she was young, and all the other faces, as the years went by. June's face floating, carrying every day of her life. And after the demise of Father Thaddeus there had been many good days. He believed there had been. In the very aftermath, joy even. Elation. Something fell away from her – she was like a woman who had been covered in cobwebs. A sort of crazy version of Miss Havisham and the orphan Estella rolled into one. Not in her wedding dress maybe, but her communion robes, the strange marriage dress of a little Irish girl. Tom had been told a story that Miss Havisham was based on a real woman who'd lived in one of the big houses on St Stephen's Green. Janey, it was Attracta Geary herself, full of old stories, who'd told him that. In what context, he couldn't remember. And the babies were so small, there was so much to do for them, so much to marvel at. Maybe with Matthews gone she felt a cordon of safety had been created for her children. For their childhoods. As they grew, himself and June passed all the stations of parenthood. The first day at school, which so shocked Joseph. He came home after the long day and said to June: 'Well, Mammy, I will never have to do that again . . .' She almost hadn't the heart to tell him it was going to be every day. Those twenty years or so when the whole view, the only view, from the slit of your tank window, as a person might say, was their doings. Their shoes, the imperial sequences of shoes, the galloping sizes, the clothes, the clothes on their backs and the clothes on the sticks in the living room, on the line out the back, like the gallant flags of a medieval army in camp. And the marriage oftentimes like a game of jousting, not without its violent storms, the famous blazing rows that brought the children's eyes out on stalks of horror. Then rage subsiding, anger cooling, the little words that parents exchange in whatever provisional private space they can access. 'I'm sorry, June.' 'I'm sorry, Tom.' The bliss of reconciliation. The very key to peace in marriage, let alone Palestine, a thing he noted was still not achieved. Just to be still in yourself, like this stillness as the notes of *Kol Nidrei* pierced him like expertly handled needles, so there was no pain, the eternal nurse of all human experiences, sticking it in, voilà, voilà. Just to be still, and apologise. To recognise the essential trouble and unfairness of even the love he measured as great in his private mind, the great love he sincerely believed he had for June. And in their bedroom, her magical clothes, her 'things', her small box of jewels, the sapphire bracelet he'd bought for her in Brereton's in Capel Street for one of her birthdays, the ivory drop earrings ditto, all the bits and bobs of gold and silver gathered over those years, into a tiny harvest. As a woman without a mother, she was going to be herself a mother of mothers, start everything again, and she always said to Winnie, 'Sweetie, when you're grown, and your poor old mother is no more, all these bits of jewellery will be yours. And you'll give them to your daughter, and she . . .' And Winnie would cry, 'Mammy, Mammy, no, they won't, they won't, because you will never die.' 'That's right,' June would say, laughing, 'I will never die.' Every two years, having saved up like demons, they would all get on the ferry, you would catch it there on the banks of the Liffey, where warehouses and cranes bully-boyed the river, menacing, and sail to the Isle of Man, always staying in the same place, Gansey Cottage, run by the inestimable (June's word) Herbert Quirke, and always doing the same things, regulation buckets and spades on the windy beach, stupendous heaps of fish and chips, and a brace of evenings for Tom and June, the raucous dance hall, June's idea of heaven, twisting and churning to the hits of the day. An essential item that also came on holiday with them was June's little radio, and he remembered those holidays to a soundtrack of Radio Caroline, which she played from morning till night. Till teatime, anyhow. She brought it into the jacks with her, she had it on in the bedroom when they snatched their twenty minutes of love, praying the children would somehow remain contented in the cottage garden for the duration. As a little boy Joe's whole ambition as a human person was to be a mod. He loved their swank and glamour in the town, he stared with admiring eyes amid the racketing music of all the accents from Lanarkshire to Lancashire, the lads and lassies from Northern Ireland, released for a week from the dampers of their war. On the Isle of Man, Winnie experienced her first kiss, aged fourteen, from an English boy. He remembered the extraordinary heat of June's body in the dance hall, the clothy dampness of her as she danced and danced, and she had this sense of rhythm in her that he sorely lacked, but what matter, dancers in those times never touched, they created each and every one a little solo locus of fury and ecstasy, except for the slow dance, the longed-for (by Tom) slow dance, when she gathered him into her arms, all the sweaty loveliness of her, her face glowing, nearly red, 'Jesus, is my face gone red, Tom – don't tell me!', and her strong arms at that, and her soft flat belly, even after two kids, and her cushiony breast, oh the heat of her, yes, the furnace, the mad beauty of that, the wild enjoyment, better than any fairground attraction, better even than any vista of lonesome sea, that perfected woman, his ideal, rows and ruckus and contentions be damned, the beauty he measured all other beauties by, his rule, his template, the eternal shiningness of June.

The music pierced him, the music calmed him. Notes arranged by Mr Bach – no, Mr *Bruch* – held him still in the chair. His mind not jumping and running and raging. Like an unruly horse under the hand of a whisperer. The poem that was his wife floating clearly in front of his closed eyes. All that he had lost. Should he rage, or should he quietly mourn? He had the wild sense that, despite the tyranny of dates and time, she was there, not in memory but really, and he was careful not to open those eyes. He knew the second he did so she would be gone. But Ronnie McGillicuddy sawed his cello into sweetness, into a thousand sweetnesses, an old Jewish tune being *injected* into Tom, *injected* into Ronnie himself – swaying and even muttering, like a lunatic, a poor assailed person, you would think, away with the fairies. They were both away with the fairies and June was alive, she was alive, beautiful and wise, and she would always be there, bursting with life, calm as any old painted Madonna, as long as he did not open his eyes. He lifted both his hands and reached out to hold that longed-for face. To hold it, the soft cheeks, the dark skin, to hold it, to hold it.

Chapter Fourteen

Such was friendship, even a curious friendship lightly offered. It didn't surprise him, for some reason, and it pleased him hugely. This McGillicuddy next door, he was – well, what was he? The little god of music? Tom had survived the encounter, not bathed in humiliation and not blushing with stupidity. And the little girl, seen again. And the old story of the child in the ditch. The body at the bottom of the ravine. The knife wounds. The very bluster of savagery. Savage attack. Maelstrom. And June.

They had climbed the mountain path together, on the trail of the two priests. Easily said. But had they? His whole memory of this event he knew in his rational policeman's heart could not be true. Yet he saw it all in his mind's eye. Thus he remembered it, and in this way it was true. Not true enough, because that wouldn't serve anyone, but true. So true but not true. How could that be? It was the reason that, in lifting the weight from herself, she had put something else in its place. Much much lighter, much much deadlier. The seed of her eventual dissolution? The little spot of contagion, of poison. They had climbed the mountain path together. Absolutely together, like a bloody sandwich. Him the bread, she the slice of ham. She was in under his coat like a slice of ham, like a rat that had collapsed its bones to enter by a tiny crease-thin crack, and she lay on his back, on his backbone, as if she was almost not there, and perhaps wasn't. They had driven into the car park below as innocent as the most innocent citizens, as newborn babies. They had exited the gluaisteán, innocence still intact. To that point, innocent. Far ahead he had seen the dark back of what turned out to be Byrne, moving in the wake of his colleague, who had seemingly stormed ahead. But, Tom, don't go ahead of *yourself* here, said Tom to himself now, you didn't know at first it was Byrne. But there was no other car in the dusty, weedy car park except theirs and the comical bubble car. And they weren't but moments behind them. But he had thought: Boots, and thick socks, they'll be changing maybe, sitting on the thresholds of the bubble car, as may be, best linger in the leafy old lane and let them get away unseen. Unseen. And then he had driven in and then they had bounded from the car – she had definitively bounded – and then he had seen the two priests far ahead, surprisingly far ahead, because they were only moments behind them, so his copper's brain told him they hadn't changed into different shoes. What did it matter? Then he had scanned the track and the woods all lying above it, and seen a second track entering the trees, and for some reason, by some instinct, he'd thought they should get ahead of them, and maybe this other track looped away to the summit, he had adjudged, and they could lie in wait for them above. Lie in wait to do what? He didn't know. He was genuinely shocked when June took their humble bread knife from her gansey. She took it from her gansey, and then she went in under his coat like a bone-collapsing rat, trying to get in in a manner no human ever could. And she wriggled herself up onto his back, using his spine as a great brace, and she flattened herself like a huge plaster, not a human creature at all. He had clearly married a Trickster. And he entered into the woods by the other track, and since he was young and in his prime, God knew, he cantered up along it, ruts and all, leaping over the fallen timber when he needed, and up they went the way, him and his beloved, his precious June, now in rat form, no, now with all the abilities of a rat. And they must have passed Byrne, him on the lower track, panting along, with his soft belly, and the wrong shoes no doubt, and his horrible woollen jumper, his priestly black socks, all telling against him, and his progress. And passed his friend – was he ever a friend? – his accomplice, his co-conspirator, with their mutual hunger for the bodies of children, the souls of the children assailed by them, assaulted, soiled, threatened with ruin, and their whole lives altered by them, the underground stream of their lives diverted by that cataclysm, the wells of their happiness parched to dryness. And coming out on the summit at last, with all of Dublin thrown out on the plain below them, between the mountain and sea, and the sparkles off the fenders and polished paint of cars far far below, twenty miles maybe, flashing on the plain, was that possible? And beyond the summit the green little kingdoms of Wicklow, like a child's postage stamps arranged on a page, spreading joyfully, generously, to lift the walker's heart, if he had a heart still. And cutting back down through a cleared acre, they were suddenly walking towards Matthews, he was humming a tune to himself, making his sturdy legs power along, getting good exercise for himself, for a healthy heart, and a long life, and just as they passed him, at the high lip of the long ravine, with a great fall of sharp stones tumbling away into the abyss, like a ruined throat, June slipped from under his coat, slid, glassily, and issued forth, brandishing the old bread knife that they had bought the first week of their marriage. It had sliced every loaf of bread they'd ever owned. She was flashing with blue-and-green light like a kingfisher, it was flying out of her, spokes of it fleeting everywhere, her face bursting with light, the same stuff you saw in haloes, white and radiant, and she flew towards Matthews, he let out a confused cry, he drew back, did she stick the knife into him, at enormous speed, like a Japanese warrior, so fast her hand was a blur, ah, ah, ah, stabbing him, he didn't know, it was very quick, and she shouted out to him, something she needed to say to him before she killed him, Tom couldn't catch it, it was enormous, words the size of boulders, and Matthews opened his arms, he opened his arms, in supplication, in terror, in acceptance, Tom didn't know, they had taken the upper path, she had collapsed her bones, it couldn't be true, it couldn't have happened like that, there didn't seem to be a mark on him, where was the blood? Was he just a vampire after all? And then over Matthews went, like a piece of timber, over he went, losing the ground under his feet, only empty space under his soles, only the empty first inches of the ravine, it took him, the emptiness, he went down into it so fast, Tom never saw anything so fast, but all souls fall fast, down down, and Tom peered over the edge, and watched Matthews tumble and tumble, roaring out, bouncing on the terrible rocks, and June beside Tom, the light gone from her like an extinguished Tilley lamp, solitary, at his side, solitary, alone, with him, and she stared down at Matthews, who far below had strewed his own limbs on the broken ground, was Tom's thought, like a yardwoman throwing seeds for the hens, an arc of himself, tossed to the ground, and he was still, and it was done, and he gathered his wife, his lovely wife, his June, and they went back into the woods like wolves, like hares, like jays, like any animals not wishing to be seen, abhorring the company of men. Did he spy Byrne for a second, a vanishing glimpse?

This was the truth, if the truth were required. This was what had happened. According to Tom's brain. Now he searched around for an old tin of cigarillos in a drawer in his bedroom. He brought it into the kitchen and fetched the matches, those fiddly little jobs too small for his fingers. It was the day after McGillicuddy's magical playing, and since he was solitary again he could do no better than occupy his wicker chair. He could do no better than to itemise the view. If he wasn't mistaken it was late May, coming to June, so now he must credit all things he saw to summer. This was the Irish summer. There was a belligerent wind that galloped from right to left of the little strait. He could see the current surging in all the passion of high tide. Millions of gallons bullying their way in, between the rocks of the island and the rocks of the shore. He knew from chatting to the boatmen in the harbour that there was a whirlpool at the south tip of the island. He thought of the wild-headed water there, the rings and rings of turning power. What would it be like to be caught there, swimming? Winnie had swum from the rocks below the garden, but never more than ten feet out, for fear of that current. For fear of the whirlpool. The boatmen, who all used outboard engines on their boats. Sure oars would be no good to you. He had a sense of the thickness of the water somehow also in his own blood. Something was surging thickly through him also. He fumbled a match, struck it three or four times against the side of the box, got a flame, and ravenously lit the cigarillo. The blessed heat of it. The tasty smoke of it. Ah, ah. Filled his old lungs with it, breathed not for a moment, blasted it out in a great exhalation, like a hippy with a joint. Like June with a joint! Ah yes. Relief flooded through him. The medical sinner. The man without innocence. But if the sea was ravaged by wind, and the island looked marooned in a splashing chaos, there was heat in the day, he could feel it from the open window, that lovely fresh heat of summer, rinsed through by salt and frisking air. Planetary pleasures. Where he lived, this peculiar earth. Whose share of atoms he had merely borrowed. Till his own dissolution was decreed, and the mortgage paid back in full.

Happy for such a long time. Happy, he had thought. Vindicated? Justice served? But he was a copper. His brain would grind to a halt, his thoughts stop turning, whenever it touched the lip of the event in the mountains. The event in the mountains, what was he saying? Murder, first degree, would be given life in prison, probably, due to the grievous and unrepentant nature of it, without parole. Let us say he had murdered Matthews. Let us say, out of love for June, out of an overwhelmed respect for her, and horror at her childhood suffering, he had murdered Matthews. What would that be to a defence lawyer? Nothing? To a sombre judge? To one of those grave middle-class men and women looking down from the dais on the floundering mayhem of lesser souls? Life, without parole. Killing a priest, a man of the cloth? Was that still an utter crime? If the man was a murderer of children's hearts? A devourer of their happinesses? A plunderer of their beings? A raper of their physical natures? A filthy dark evil cold murderous vile creature with a penis for a soul? Was that still murder, on the statute books? Step up, O'Casey, and give me your view, your sober assessment of the relevant statute, your quiet word on it that would fly to the heart of the matter with a wondrous exactitude. Lovers of children? The worst crime of all? *Crimen pessimum*, the Church called it. A *crimen pessimum* had to be reported to Rome. Archbishop McQuaid wouldn't do it. But his auxiliary bishop had *told* him it was a *crimen pessimum*. The priest with the fucking camera. Byrne focusing his camera. Get the right angle. What about that, Your Excellency? Didn't want to cause scandal. The moment it all started. June's hell compounded in that moment, cemented in, the hell of thousands of girls and boys. The chief commissioner at the door of the palace. Brandishing the photographs. Over to you, Your Excellency. *Crimen pessimum*. That was correct. A crime for which the punishment cannot be too severe. You might cut off little bits from such a person, lingchi style, then roast his extremities, Spanish Inquisition style, then hang him to the limit of his breath, then draw out his entrails while he breathed, then saw into him slowly, to make four quarters of his vile body. Irish execution style. Robert Emmet's own fate. Then take the butcher's barrowload of the remains, and feed them to the lions in the zoo. Roman justice style. Extinguish, remove from the earth, maybe split every atom of him, so that those whole atoms could not go into other things. Into stars and rabbits and seawater and gold rings. Into any other part of God's precious creation. Suffer the little children to come unto me. No crime more dark, more fucking *pessimum*, more beyond human mercy. To do this with the mote of June in your eye, her essence floating on the Irish wind. All the children gravely assailed. All the children in filthy Irish history, with no bugle blowing to announce their rescue, no arms of love to envelop them, no hand of kindness to wash their wounds. Priests! The boyos themselves, peddling piety and goodness. As pious and good as – but there was no entity, no animal, no thing, to compare to them. A shark was vicious, but it was all beyond the shark.

Tom was bubbling in the chair like a cowboy's skillet of beans. He had invoked many evils. He felt run through by mysterious swords. His assailants unseen. In killing Matthews she had not gone free. It had looked like freedom. It had looked like a new time. Things starting anew. She had mothered like a maestro. She had lived like a best example of humanity. She had been an ordinary woman who had graced creation. A murdered person who had murdered in her turn. With an absolute sense of the justice of it. Not trusting in any way to judges and courts and prisons. Her own swift fleet justice. She had looked down upon Matthews and delivered her sentence on him. Be taken from this place. Thrown into a ravine until you are dead. She had spoken, definitively, and carried out the sentence without ruth or remorse. Because it was just before God. If not before man. No. Not before Wilson maybe, not before

O'Casey. Or was it? Poor Wilson sitting in the park, trying to do the right thing, absolutely shot through with worry about Tom. Yes. Disturb an old policeman in his retirement, at the word of a reprobate. A threat Byrne understood so well. Even to speak the lie, the power of it. The revenge of it. The possible effectiveness of it. Stuff Wilson and O'Casey with silence. Bring it on no further. *Crimen pessimum*. Scandal to the Church. Did nothing, McQuaid. Nothing. Did nothing, the chief commissioner. Little boys whose private parts were photographed. Scandal to the guards. Scandal to Tom. Possible court appearance. If the DPP thought there was evidence. What of the blood sample? Would that be enough? The word of an evil man, himself under scrutiny, judgement, sentence. But what did Tom care? He didn't. He had served the only soul he cared about, not his own soul, or the souls even of his children, but the girl he had met in the Wimpy café, who had laughed at Billy Drury's taste on the jukebox, and in laughing, with her bright face, fished out his deathless love.

Now he smoked more quietly, he was sunk more deeply in the wicker chair, he was lurking, he felt like a robber, a highwayman. He farted, and even in his mute distress he enjoyed the smell of it, as he always did.

For the last few minutes, moving through his thoughts, he had vaguely heard a half-familiar noise. It was something squeaking, squeaking. Now, as he surfaced, and finished the last quarter-inch of the cigarillo, and stubbed it out with professional expertise, he got up and looked down into the garden. The great cycle of the year was well under way, and there indeed was Mr Tomelty, with his wheelbarrow, making that squeak, ghav, ghav, ghav, like a dog barking in Greek. He was raking up an awkward pile of withered stalks that he had cut from a flower bed, to give the new growth a chance. Fresh green shoots, like time beginning all over again, or time perpetually present. Eternal Mr Tomelty. On more than a whim, Tom came away from the window and crossed his quiet room, now graced with the pleasant afterstink of the cigarillo, and opened his ever-complaining door – would he ever fix it, no – and went round the castle to have a word with Mr Tomelty. His friend, after all, one of his new brace of friends. He saw no sign of the splendid motorcar. Mr Tomelty had just put as many weeds onto the barrow as it would hold for one trip to his midden, and had stuck a long fork into it, laying the handle back along the handle of the barrow.

'How do, Mr Tomelty.'

'Mr Kettle!'

'Don't want to disturb you, but.'

He thought Mr Tomelty looked much more stooped than he had the other day. More elderly somehow. Maybe it was the rags, the weeds as you might call them, that he wore for his gardening. Trews so patched they were all patches, like a map of the broken-up districts of Yugoslavia. He wore a cardigan so threadbare he might have invited a spider to have it for its web. He wore wellington boots as if in homage to Mr McGregor. The rather scowling face was lined, creased, a roadmap someone had scrunched up and sat on. It truly seemed an incongruous change from the dapper creature he had spoken to in Dalkey, and who had driven him home.

'I didn't see the auld car,' said Tom.

'I got rid of that years ago,' said Mr Tomelty.

Some movement caught Tom's eye, and he looked up at the part of the castle occupied by the Tomeltys, and there was Mrs Tomelty standing at her picture window. The Irish authority on tea roses was smiling down at him. He was on the cusp of waving to her, but he didn't somehow.

'There was just something I wanted to ask you, something Mrs Tomelty said.'

'Mrs Tomelty? Margaret?'

'Yes.'

'Said when, said what when?'

Mr Tomelty now looked not just twenty years older but many degrees wearier.

'The other day,' said Tom.

'Mr Kettle, my wife died in '88.'

'Mr Tomelty, no.'

'Yes. There was a break-in. A gurrier knocked her down. Poor woman died in hospital.'

'I'm so sorry, Mr Tomelty.'

'That's why I got rid of the car. She loved that car. I couldn't get into it but that I expected to see her in the passenger seat. Smiling. I will never see her again. Unless what they say about heaven holds true.'

Mr Tomelty didn't seem so scornful, so frowning, now. He seemed gentled, gentled perhaps by the memory of his wife.

'I won't trouble you anymore, Mr Tomelty,' said Tom, not at all sure how to extricate himself. Of course he had been going to ask him about the little girl. How Mrs Tomelty had referred to the little girl as living. Well, that explained that. When he looked back up at the picture window, sure enough, there was no one there. There was no one but there had been someone. He was 100 per cent certain. He'd swear in court to it. He was dizzy with these discoveries.

'Sure,' said Mr Tomelty. Tom was just turning to go. To go back again to his flat with his crazy thoughts. '"The other day", you said, Mr Kettle. What did you mean?'

'Do you know, Mr Tomelty, I think I'm going soft in the head. I don't know what I was thinking. I'm very sorry. I – I get confused sometimes.'

Mr Tomelty seemed to withdraw a touch then, maybe as a person not much older than Tom unwilling to catch this contagion of confusion.

'Fair enough,' he said. 'Everything alright in the flat?'

'Tip-top, tip-top,' said Tom.

'Good, good.'

Put that in your cigarillo and smoke it. He returned to his flat, fluttering like a daffodil, and much more gingerly, much more tenderly, got back in his chair. Maybe the cigarillo had poisoned his brain. Oh, he didn't think so. He had a piercing sense anew of being alone, no more and no less. Now he heard the creak, creak again of the wheelbarrow. Ghav, ghav, creak, creak. Ashes to ashes, old flowers to the dunghill, throw the truth in there too, it was no good to anyone.

The doorbell rang. The sound was like a spray of bullets. He nearly took leave of life itself. Poor Mrs Tomelty. Gone in '88. Taking her leave, after sudden violence. But—

It was Miss McNulty, trembling. With fury? No. Fear,

more likely. Her state of mind had conferred on her an aspect of strange humility. Of supplication. Almost with bowed head she held out an envelope to him. It was a scraggy thing, with the castle's address in thick black ink.

'From?' he said.

'Him,' she said.

'Will I read it?'

'Read it, please.'

At the top of the single page there was the sender's partial address in London, and in the middle of the page were three dots, and that was all.

'What does it mean?'

'That he knows where we are and he is coming to do something to us.'

He thought she was reading a lot into three dots but he also thought she was likely correct. You don't send a letter to your wife with three dots on it. The important bit was the envelope, with the address.

'How did he find your address, I wonder?'

'He rang Daddy at work.'

'And your father told him?'

'I never told Daddy why I left. Not the whole story. Don't ask me why.'

'What do you think?'

'I think he is a dangerous person and I think he will come and do something very very bad to us.'

'Did you go to the guards in Dalkey village?'

'They said what you said, they can't do anything. They can't do anything till he does something. I can't get a barring order because he's not in this jurisdiction.'

'I wish he had threatened you in the letter. Three dots.'

And Tom shook his head with the exasperation of the policeman over unobliging criminals.

'What does he look like?' said Tom.

'He's my age, he's slim, lanky, and he has a red beard. Also round glasses, like John Lennon had.'

'Who wears a beard nowadays?'

'He does.'

'If you hear anything,' said Tom, 'see anything, even if you feel something is not right, come and get me, or phone me. Here, I'll write out the number.'

And he went in and wrote his number on a scrap of paper and brought it back out to her. Now suddenly the little boy was at her side, looking at him. Like a character materialising in *Star Trek*. Beam me up, Scotty. He had close-cropped hair and was as brown as an Italian. A very serious look to him. The boy peered down into the lens of the box camera that hung from his neck, and stopped breathing a few moments, and took a snap. Frowning, concentrating. Just took it, like an evidentiary forensic scientist.

'You got your camera, then?' said Tom.

The boy didn't know what he meant and he didn't say anything. He was winding on the hidden film inside, ready for the next picture. Tom laughed with a slight sound.

'Good man,' he said.

Chapter Fifteen

For the next few weeks most of what happened had to do with the weather. It was officially summer, so the denizens of Dalkey made their annual effort to believe in it, and as usual the weather played ducks and drakes with their belief. Actual birds away all winter and spring began to return, for their own mysterious reasons. The swallows and house martins fired about like arrowheads in the limitless air above Mr Tomelty's labours. Girls passed the castle shivering in their natty tops. Overcoats were seen no more even on the old, and when a storm blew along the Coliemore Road, tearing the new leaves off the trees in a premature slaughter, the wind cavorting amid the despair of the citizens, their assaulted faith, people prayed for better weather on the morrow. The Irish people. Poor stragglers stuck on the edge of Europe. Took a wrong turn on some ancient landscape. Could go no further and could not go back.

With something of the mystery of the migratory birds about them too, Wilson and O'Casey appeared again at his door. They were extremely solicitous. They were there to tell him that the blood sample did not match the blood on the clothes in the old evidence bag, but that Byrne, in an effort to escape his fate, was continuing to make his allegations. The DPP may or may not feel there was enough in it to charge Tom. It was extremely unlikely, but the press would love it anyhow, if they ever got wind of it. Getting wind of things, as Tom knew, was what made the world of Ireland go round. Phrases drawn from weather always prevailed. Tom sat with his new friends, knowing full well that if it served their purposes, for whatever reason, Wilson or O'Casey themselves would leak it, no matter what they said to his face. It was just the way of things. He had done it himself a dozen times. But he couldn't see why they would do that. Nevertheless he was experienced enough to know that in the realm of law, friendship was a disposable thing. You had to get the conviction, willy-nilly, by hook or by crook. Not his, perhaps, but Byrne's. They wanted Byrne in court, in disarray, and in prison. They wanted to be down in Neary's bar, drinking celebratory pints. They yearned for it. He could see it all written on their beaming, jocular faces.

Was he relieved? He didn't really know. He wasn't sure he cared what happened to him now. He cared what happened to other souls. He cared what might happen to the little boy and Miss McNulty. And he outlined that particular conundrum to Wilson and O'Casey, and they sang the same sad tune as the coppers in the village. What could they do? Put a watch on airports, harbours? No. This vexatious husband could go where he wished, arrive where he wished. It was the dispensation of the law, of statute law and common law. There was nothing on the books that could help the young actress. No matter how pretty she was, said O'Casey, beside the point. He was actually quite keen to see her in the flesh. Hadn't he seen her pretty mug splashed across the huge billboard on the Ambassador, he had, he had, he said. It was the age-old alertness for a wife in a wifeless policeman. But surely O'Casey was married, hadn't they run all that by him? But he couldn't remember. And he didn't like to demonstrate that he couldn't remember.

In the last while Tom felt he had more or less crept up on himself, and seen himself in a new light. In a very curious way he was no longer fearful. He was less confused even if he was confused. There was no cure for what ailed him. He desired simply the presence of his wife and children. He wished them to be with him – they were not. He couldn't get over it. He couldn't but yearn. But he was no longer as confused as he had been. He had told himself the story of himself, and he was beginning to think he knew new things about himself. He was beginning to stand back from himself, hover over himself, looking down, looking in, and see new things. He didn't like or dislike them. They were simply manifest. If he had always in his life felt like the youngest soul in the room, no matter what his age, now he felt the oldest. He was the oldest with Wilson and O'Casey. But there had been a time when he wouldn't have felt that, exactly.

Wilson and O'Casey took their leave. For some reason O'Casey was inspired to embrace Tom, just for a moment, in a manly way. It was very like a farewell, as if he was their father and they were saying goodbye. Wilson took his hand and shook it, and nodded mysteriously. Tom was wholly approving of them. They wished only the best outcome. Byrne was a villain beyond reprieve. If he had a soul it stewed in a pot of acid. The very way that Wilson had waved his hand when he talked betokened a ferocious desire to capture Byrne, to pull the fraudulent priest's hands around his back and put on the bracelets. To march him away to judgement and retribution. To the particular suffering that men did in prison cells, oftentimes subtle and unseen. The inexorable punishments of the private mind. Would that it would all be so.

He felt he was disappearing to that final dot of light on an old television screen. Flick the off-switch and retire to bed. He had nipped up to the village for a supply of cigarillos and was studiously smoking them, a dozen a day, in a sort of wartime atmosphere. All around him he felt the press of strangeness, of mysteries, that he not only couldn't penetrate but was beginning just to allow. To puzzle his life no longer. What was the point? The energy in June, the light, the loveliness, where was it? For ten long years he had been without her and it was almost as if he was without her now for the first time. He didn't feel it as he had, in all its original shock, the very kiln of adversity, but in a way he couldn't describe. He was like the falcon breaking from the spell of the falconer, going higher and higher, going away into the aether, breaking the non-existent thread that bound them. Custom and hunger. Needing neither now. He was *without*, he had been *taken from*, but also released, yes, like a bird. There was no diagnosis for what possessed him. No doctor or philosopher could light a lamp of understanding. He was beyond it, far up in the thinning air of the blue sky. Juneless, weightless, Winnie-less, Joe-less. There was a fire of freedom in it. There was a curious wash of something freely called happiness.

It was a story of atrocities, certainly. It was almost beyond description, and he had laboured for years not to describe it, to anyone else, and more importantly to himself. Never to allow the little sequence of horrors to play in his brain. Think everything else before he thought of those things. Think of things that did not exist, talk to the tumbleweeds of souls that did not exist. See ghosts before telling that story. Clamp his mind shut with heavy Victorian metal clamps. Now no more. It was no longer possible to be a citizen of grief, his passport to grief was cancelled, he couldn't enter there. Now he must be brave. Of course, unbeknownst to him, he had been brave all his life. That was true, but not true for him. The main drone of the pipes he had heard under everything for sixty years and more was alarm and confusion, like the very pith of battle. Now that was not so, so much. He wondered was there God involved? Had he been released from his ordeal? He didn't know. He could be suspicious of the brightness in him, in his limbs, in his almost ecstasy, as being something slipped into him by a medicinal god, like a needle with a vaccine in it. He didn't know. Something else knew. It might as well have phoned him on the telephone. Come in, come in, you can row that boat no more. The current was against you. Here is a little harbour. Rest up there.

   Because. After the years of seeming normality, June one day, while he was at work, took the bus into town alone. Joe was in sixth year at school, Winnie in college – both flying along, both seemingly happy kids, in the round. Their victory! Safety, the sanctuary of a decent childhood. Why that day, in the mid-eighties, nothing unusual about it, Winnie in digs at UCD, Joe away for the weekend with pals. The quiet house. She was forty-five years old. She took the one fifteen bus — he looked into all this later, taking statements, looking for witnesses, needing to know the details, forensically — and alighted in O'Connell Street. She went to Lenehans of Capel Street — the receipt survived in her thick leather purse, she had paid with a one-pound note, and the ten-bob-note change and some coins were neatly put into the little pockets. Then she brought her purchase back to O'Connell Street and probably walked up past Belvedere College, and Mountjoy Square, and crossed Dorset Street, heading for Phibsborough. At the corner garage there she filled her one-gallon canister, probably forgetting or not knowing there was a garage on Parkgate Street, which would have saved her the trouble of carrying the full canister all the way to the park, a walk of some two miles. The boy who sold the evening papers at Baker's Corner remembered her passing, because he noticed the woman carrying the green tin, it had just caught his eye. Soon she was in the park, and likely passed the children's playground to her left, and headed towards the main road that cut the great parkland in two. She crossed that road, and entered the area called the nineteen acres, a broad grassy field of deer and emptiness, and went to the other side, looking no doubt for seclusion and privacy. She reached a little dell among hundreds of low trees, thorns and hazels. Here in her nice summer dress she doused herself in the petrol and set it alight. No one saw her immediately. The black smoke brought three keepers in a four-by-four. When they arrived, the fire had burned itself out and the body was smoking. The meadow grass around her had burned to a radius of some twenty feet, and then stopped. It took a whole day to find out who she was, during which time Tom, separately, unknowing, searched the whole of Dunleary and Deansgrange and Monkstown, utterly in the wrong place. She had left a note that said she loved him and Winnie and Joseph. When Tom read in the *Evening Herald* about a body in the Phoenix Park he knew instantly. He just knew. By then she was in the morgue in Griffith Avenue. He didn't need to see a recognisable face to know it was her. He would have known her fingerbone, if that was all that had survived. Anyway, the little charred purse told its story. The groovy shoes she had bought just a week before in Penneys. The few blackened threads of the summer dress. The gold marriage band with their names engraved on the inside, *June♡Tom*, and her sapphire bracelet.

It was a queer dark thing to bury your wife in a cemetery that up to then had been three hundred safe yards from your house. Was it now to be part of your house? Fleming in dress uniform, just like the other day. Dozens of women she had befriended all over Deansgrange and that Tom had never met. A whole long line of them, shaking his hand, and one or two giving him a vigorous hug. Their soft warmth in their nice coats. Strangers comforting him. Winnie and Joe at each side, like the presidential guards, their eyes he noticed flickering here and there, forever expecting assassins. But Death had already done his work. They were his children, and the story of their mother and of himself had led them here. The odd frosty weather of a mid-summer day, the body in the awful casket – she would never have approved the design – the beautiful sombre faces of her friends, and Fleming breaking quietly into tears as Tom said a few words at the open grave. Benign presences. Mrs

Carr dead herself by then but he had been half expecting that not to deter her. The rooks returning to their rookery in rolling smudges of black just as the humanist pastor – it was Mr Grene from the grocery store at the roundabout – said true and lovely things about her, the rooks going ra-ra-ra-ra-ra in answer, surprised and not a little put out by this disturbance to the ground beneath their beech trees. Winnie not crying, as though tears were on the plus side of grief, and she was somewhere in the minuses, deep in them. She had been a fabulous mother, no doubt. And when the pastor said so, it was not by way of overgenerous homily. Winnie looked just like June twenty-five years before, as if June were a mourner at her own funeral. Joe stricken, but confused, like a man being told urgent and catastrophe-averting information in a foreign language. Simon, his friend from school, with an arm around Joe's shoulders. All of them shivering with grief. Trembling like frightened dogs. Like newborn foals, bare, trying to get their legs under them in a bewildering new world. The world where June was not to be found. Not so many years ago the parish priest would not have let her be buried in hallowed ground. Not any fucking more. No fucking priests allowed instead. The succession of eyes, that's what he remembered, her friends with their elegant, knowing souls, and the surprising staunchness of Winnie – this staunchness in the face of disaster like a silent prayer directed towards her mother. And then slow cruel days after when the brain had to take in what had happened. The news had finally to reach them. Their mother. His wife. The epic woman. Who had survived everything except survival. And Winnie not so much heartbroken as not in possession of her heart. Making the tea in the dark-green teapot back at the house and serving the funny little sandwiches that she had cut so small they were like things you would tempt a fussy eater of a child with. Little tiny triangles of ham. Like a sum reduced to its primal equation. The smallest sandwiches on earth. And the hot tea burning your lips. In the cups June had bought in Woolworth's in Dunleary circa 1968. Sort of fashionable pop-art sixties brightnesses. Stirred by the teaspoons she had bought in Totterdell's. On the plates she had bought in Arnotts – went all the way into town for them, and met him after work with the heavy box, at the corner of O'Connell Bridge and Bachelors Walk. He remembered worrying about slowing the traffic (policeman's anxiety), and her laying them in the boot of the car like a consignment of new-laid eggs. And the lorry driver behind beeping his horn and giving her a big smile. She giving him the hippy V-sign with her right hand. Peace. Everything good with the world. In the room in which every last thing, every colour, every stick of furniture, every picture on the wall, of Bette Davis, of Bob Dylan, their favourite beach on the Isle of Man, the old lighthouse at Dungeness where once they had experimented with a change of holiday destination, had all been chosen and put in place by her. In bed that night in the bed he always thought of as her bed. Her place of safety in the dark night. Where he was her watchdog, her Cúchulainn. In the time of the owls, in the time of the moon. Without her. The children in their childhood beds. Her in the summer-cold graveyard. Her remains in the execrable coffin. Her heart not beating. Her mind not thinking. Her face not brightening, darkening. No more her thousand different moods, her modes of mind, her enthusiasms, her hated things. And in the kitchen, on the breadboard, chill and dark, the sacred bread knife. Which in killing had not killed. In exacting punishment had not punished. In seeking to be the instrument of redemption had not redeemed.

Chapter Sixteen

Sad stations of memory but now he had the strength for it. It must have risen out of the deep Dalkey earth. A boon to him, a benefice. The dust offering him a gift. And now he was of a mind to take it. Something creeping into his old noggin, a type of wondering pride.

Winnie. Sad stations of Winnie. Their best girl. Cutting the sandwiches smaller and smaller, with the innocent knife. The challenges of her second year at college made infinitely greater.

She moved among the mourners with the teapot and the sandwiches and when that was not required she stood again by her father. She linked his arm in hers, bolstering him up, holding herself up. Every ten minutes she put herself into his arms and he put his arms around her. She repeated this like an Alzheimer's patient. Always as if for the first time. The next day she and Joe brought him out for dinner, to that Japanese place at the back of Blackrock. Joe just a schoolboy still but astute in the ways of sorrow. They were never so close as that day and they were always close. Nothing between them but good things. A few years later Joe was to go but it wasn't as if he had nothing to bring with him. It was just too much sadness at home for him to bear, to live in, and anyway, he had other things weighing him down. Winnie ordering off the menu like a ship's captain.

The year before she had come first in her year but this year she was going to come nearly last.

'Are you alright?' he asked her a million times, and 'God, I am, Daddy,' she would say. Never entered her mind to tell the truth. That her brain was boiled cabbage with grief. The horror of her mother's decision just couldn't lift from her. Then she was drinking, of all things, or he thought she might be, because over at her digs she didn't care to tidy away the bottles. It looked like her little living room was the site of a permanent and unhappy party, where no one met their future love, and the hangover preceded even the first drink. His policeman's brain was able to notice everything, the suspicious reefer ends in saucers, and most discomfiting of all, in the later days, a needle just left there in the overflowing pedal bin. A needle. She said it belonged to a diabetic friend. He was grateful to believe her then. He could notice and imagine, but he seemed to lack the words to unlock her suffering. He would go over to her dutifully and bring her a pound of sausages or the like, fresh bread from the baker. Simple fatherly things could be said: 'How are you, Winnie, love?' 'I'm grand, Daddy, grand.' It all happened so slowly. She did scrape through her finals, she did eat her legal dinners, she did finally qualify, she did, but all in the neighbourhood of this other music. He could see she wasn't well. To admire her so much, and to fear for her so much in the same breath . . . And late in the day she even had a boyfriend, a beautiful lad as it happened from the chi-chi part of Monkstown, with a strong dark face, as if he were her twin. Her accomplice? As desperate as she was? The hoped-for husband? With enormous nervousness she had brought the boy to meet him, just the once. He was like a panicky pony. Tom had liked him, really wished the best for them both, oh heavens, yes. Human love. They were nice together, they looked so well, going gratefully out the door.

'Bye, Daddy,' she said, her gentle face looking back, as if she were planning to be away for a long time. She had good work at the Four Courts, yes, she was a rising person. So much of himself again in her. Justice, the rights of the citizen. The pride he felt, the pride. But. Tom couldn't ever work out the hard sums of it. All the numbers in a mess on the floor. Tangled wool basket, fishing line in knots. The unabashed cruelty of the Fates.

Oh, but then he did take action, he did. Any fool or wise man would have. He went over to the good people in Stanhope Street, got some guidance from them. There was a little man there, 'a refugee from New York' he called himself, with a little moustache and a big idea. Tom wondered as he listened how many fathers and mothers of lads or lassies he had banged up in the Joy had come in here, as desperate as himself. 'She just does a bit of drinking,' Tom heard himself say, an utter fool. 'She's a heroin addict, Tom,' said the little Yankee. Intervention was the strategy. Tell Winnie he and Joe would never see her again unless she went into a treatment centre. The Rutland. Was every building in Dublin called after an English general? So he did that. Huge flaming row. Then her spirit as if crushed. In she went. After a month alone there, wrestling with her angels and her demons, she came good. Then he was able to see her again and talk to her, tell her he loved her, hug her tight, and cry private tears – in a sort of tentative exultation. One of her last days in residence she sat silently in front of him for an hour. Not a word spoken. The two them, heads bowed, as close as closest friends. He was nearly undone by the feeling of love he had for her. Nearly fainting. Then she was out, and some good months followed. 'This is all going to stand to me, Daddy. I'll be a better barrister for this, you'll see.' Magnificent Winnie. Months and months. Plans, the boyfriend, were babies in the offing? Would that save them? Surely it would. June's grandchildren. He was wild with such thinking, long, burning thinking in the nights. Something to be rescued from the flames. The heart and soul of his precious daughter. Then it was over. Suddenly. A relapse, in the manner of the addict. In the dark winter. She fell back in a stupor against her own radiator. Lay there for hours till she was found. It burned one whole side of her. 'She was already gone, Tom,' the attendant coroner said, his voice exceptionally gentle, exceptionally kind. Tom had forced himself over to her digs. Staring in distress. The young guards from Store Street talking quietly. When everything had duly been recorded, he brought her over to the funeral parlour at the Five Lamps, sitting with her in the police hearse.

Fleming then with his flame of friendship. All *her* legion of friends. At the graveside, tucking her – her ashes at least – in with her mother.

'Whatever we can do, we'll do,' said Fleming. What he could do, he did. But how could he bring her back from the dead? That's what Tom needed. And June back. In a way he understood what had happened to June far better than he did what had happened to Winnie. So he asked God to give Winnie back to him until he could understand. And God had given her back, more or less, but nothing seemed to lead to understanding. It was up to him now to know less about times and details and more about the moiling mysteries of the human heart. Things happened to people, and some people were required to lift great weights that crushed you if you faltered just for a moment. It was his job not to falter. But every day he faltered. Every day he was crushed, and rose again the following morn like a cartoon figure. Road Runner, Bugs Bunny – crushed, yet recomposed. Never the smell of death in a cartoon.

He suddenly saw the whole thing from Fleming's point of view, from Wilson and O'Casey's. For surely Fleming had told them everything, if they didn't know already. Then to have to countenance bringing such a man with such a fate into the further torment of a court case. An old retired man with his fecking Scott Medal. His nine months of peace. What an outrageous victory that had been. It couldn't be surprising to him that it'd had to end. And not end in the birth of a child, but in the birth of further troubles. Who were the pals of Job? Who were the friends of Jonah? Was this the belly of the whale, this dark summer's night? Was this his fate now, to lie in the blank night, and mistake the glow-worms in the whale's belly for stars? But there *were* stars, infinite numbers of them, hanging over the rough old island and the fraudulent castle. Democratic, kind, gentling starlight. Shining through limitless inky air. God's unhurried messages? The pennies pushed in at the funfair to make the pennies drop.

And then his Joe. Secretive, secretive Joe. What of him? Could he tell himself even that story? Oh, by twisting ways and under mossy trees. A ruined house of a tale. Though Joe's long letters home had been chapters in a flourishing story. If Tom looked back through them now he might notice little hints of unhappiness. But he couldn't bear to do that. The curiously childish writing, the letters never joined up. Like he was printing his words for an official document. And he had seen his son writing like that, at the kitchen table in the era of homework, as fast and fluid as any cursive script. Would have been quite handy in a station sergeant, whose scribbles could be as vexing as a doctor's. Billy Drury's beautiful hand, he remembered that. Good Billy Drury, with his mess of blond hair, everything done to the letter of the law, except when it came to friendship. He was more convincing when he was lying than when he was telling the truth. With his brambly Roscommon accent. His mouth all on one side like the town of Loughglynn. But Joe wrote like the kingfisher flies, straight, fast, his face bright, sparking with his cleverness. Doctor of medicine. His letters home could be twenty pages. Chronicles of Albuquerque, where he had his flat, and of Zuni, where he worked. People he met in the bars, the strange pristine boulevards of imperial America. All so clean, he wrote, like the pictures of England in the twenties. Except the little Native districts, clumps of displaced Pueblo people, there all was ragged and desolate. Otherwise everything just so, you might think eternally, but balancing on the edge of nothing. Consuming storms and tornadoes that rattled the ears of the citizens. You could expect twenty tornadoes a year. Tom had seen something of all that when he visited. In the long letters Tom always looked for news of someone special. He thought Joe needed that. Maybe he was wrong. Maybe he caught a hint once or twice? He dared not ask. He liked to think of Joe in love. Bamboozled, overwhelmed, put a dint in that serious face he had. Late starter. No steady girlfriends at school, then the little revelation. The boy who liked boys. But where were the boys, then? Was there a young man, out there in that desert country? None that he cared to communicate to his father, anyhow. Used he to tell his mother things like that? All the days he had spent with his son, in the nice Buick, driving about like friends, Joe had never mentioned love. Nor in all his letters. Beautiful letters, though, full of observations about places on the old trail down to Santa Fe. He would drive up on his days off and have a dekko. Trading posts, old caves where wayfarers had sheltered. The pueblos still holding on the desert plains. His own pueblo in particular, he learned everything he could about it, and the tribal brotherhoods, and the ancient orders of medicine. Well he knew that the people went first to their own doctors, and only came to him when all else failed. He was good to sew a wound, but not so good at driving out the plunging poisons of witches. He didn't mind. He loved his work. He had friends there among the Indians, what he called his Native buddies. After a while he was shown the ancient wall paintings and drawings, marked on the underhanging parts of cliffs, that no storm of rain had ever erased. And the snakes and other critters – and what to do, Daddy, if a rattler bites you. Make sure the bite's below the heart. Or was it above? And Tom had read the letters dutifully, sombrely, catching the strange sorrow in them sometimes and missing the jokes. To be so far away, on such business, important business no doubt. His wage not the wage of a proper city doctor, with a white patronage, but a wage that allowed him to live and breathe in America. Away from Ireland. From things beyond his endurance. Among the Zuni, where he did his work, he was inside something old. Far beyond an Irish person's sense of time. Two thousand years at least they had been there, in the village they called the Middle Place. Plenty of problems, drinking, drugs, but also overwhelming moments of pure beauty, when the ceremonial dancers came into the village in tottering costumes, as the Zuni dead returning. Long hours of dancing, singing. Sincere, believing. No Irish person had any notion what their lot was doing at the time of Christ. The Zuni knew – they were doing just this. And Joe said it was his privilege to serve them, best he could. Good-hearted, clever Joe.

Simple-minded Joe, maybe... Because it had killed him. Whatever he was, and however he thought, and however he presented himself, whatever his secrets were, it seemed to have killed him.

When Tom got the telegram, Fleming immediately gave him leave. They had been up to their oxters in a case, two heroin dealers, small-time boys, who had been found dead. Foul play suspected. Addicts themselves in Dolphin's Barn, causing havoc and heartbreak in their community by selling to youngsters. Cooking up new business at school gates. But Fleming said he would deal with it, no bother, Tom, you just get on the next plane. Tom was desperate to do just that, but when Fleming said it he was suddenly moved. In his deep sorrow, moved. Which was a strange thing. He noticed it. But he was so afraid of what he would find. Well, he knew what he would find. The body of his son, in a morgue no doubt. He didn't *want* to do that, but deepest instinct bade him go. Go quickly. If he didn't go, would the long letters still come? Slightly long-winded letters, in truth? That now he would long for, long for, always. Keep sending those letters, Joe, and please do not be dead.

Malaya was further away than Albuquerque but Tom had never travelled so far. Who were these people in all these similar airports? Too much to eat and their clothes far too new and clean. It unnerved him. He was already on edge as he boarded the first plane in Dublin. He kept thinking, over and over, of putting Joe and Winnie to bed when they were little. Over and over. Like a stuck reel in the cinema at Glasthule. *A Fistful of Dollars*, the floor-length curtains all around the walls burned with thousands of cigarette holes. Winnie and Joe. He had been their protector. The sacred task. He stopped over three times and at each stop he festered in a plastic chair, ate nothing, drank nothing, stared ahead at the departure boards. By the time he arrived in Albuquerque, blinking with jet lag and almost deaf and blind, he was out of love with America. But also everything else. With living. With breathing. The journey was so punishing he almost forgot why he had undertaken it. It was only when he woke the next day at 5 a.m. in his hotel, without any idea where he was, and then forced himself to drink the lousy orange juice, and eat some eggs and bacon, that sense and understanding slowly returned to him, and it wasn't a welcome return. His son, his son. He was so sunk in sadness he almost couldn't speak. He could taste nothing. Nothing seemed real. If he had been a rat with a belly full of blue poison he couldn't have felt worse. Somehow he had thought, after the tally of the first two deaths, that Joe being left to him was a sort of weird recompense. As if you could be paid with the money you already owned, your own gold put in your pocket as a wage. But now that was no longer true. He was not just saddened, he was also jaggedly angry. Angry with the desk clerk, angry with the nice waitress at breakfast. A big, bulking, sulky old man from Ireland. Nightmare. There's a fucking nightmare at table seven. As he got up to go back to his room, he apologised to both of them. 'My son . . .' he began, and then didn't say anything more.

He phoned the number he had been given and an appointment was made at the sheriff's office on the Zuni pueblo. Tom knew the drive from his visit to Joe. He thought he might half-remember it, anyhow. They'd sometimes laughed so much, he hadn't always been watching the road. Joe was one of the few people on God's earth that could make him laugh. He was the funniest boy, truly. He knew how to tickle Tom's rusty funny bone. The town was 150 miles from Albuquerque and ten miles from the riverbank where Joe had been found. They told him Joe had been killed in his apartment in the city. They had found blood there. But then his body had been brought out to a dry river, on Zuni land, and dumped. A dry river under a great cliff. With those ancient markings. So they reckoned. And had nothing else to tell him. 'The sheriff will fill you in, Mr Kettle. Please be respectful on the pueblo.'

Tom had hired a little car and now he drove out through those miles of deserted lands that indeed he only half-remembered, past entrances to other pueblos, oceans of scrubby grassland. Zuni was a scattering of newer houses, a fragmented main street, with older buildings at the heart of all, and the bulk of an ancient church. As he came in he passed the little dispensary. He thought he would like to talk to Sean, the other doctor, just to see how he was bearing up. He made a mental note to do it. Forgot almost immediately.

The sheriff's office was a smart little place, not old, with concrete walls and a still fan in the ceiling. The sheriff was in his swivel chair behind a metal desk. Under his arms were patches of sweat, but his uniform was crisp and dry-cleaned, and an air conditioner roared somewhere like a cage of tigers, but as if far away.

The sheriff was extremely polite. A weary sort of a man maybe. A serious face, but smiling. He had a gun in a holster but it was behind him on a filing cabinet. Did the tribal police have full powers? Tom didn't know. He was all at sea in New Mexico. He was all at sea everywhere. The sheriff looked Indian. Tom's head was full of all the things Joe had written in his letters about Native people. How he really admired and respected them, and their way of life. Tom had witnessed it himself when Joe had talked to Sean. You could hear the admiration in his voice. But some instinct stopped him telling the sheriff that. He didn't think the sheriff would be interested in clichés about Indians. There was a restraint in the air.

'Mr Kettle, good to meet you, sir. Sorry it's in these sad circumstances.'

'I know. Well, likewise,' said Tom, 'and, well, it's good of you to see me. I'm sure you're busy.'

'You're a detective at home, they tell me – in Ireland?'

'I am, I am.'

'Your son is in our little morgue. I have filled out all the papers. We can ship him tomorrow. You'll be wanting to bring him home.'

'I will.'

Ship him tomorrow? Would they not need his body for evidence? Who had killed his son? They had said he had been killed, shot twice in the back of the head, so who had killed him?

'You'll be wanting to know what happened to him,' the sheriff said, as if in answer.

The sheriff said they might never have found Joe, only that the killer came the very next morning and turned himself in. Oh yes, sir. Confessed. He would go to jail, 100 per cent. The sheriff said he was a man from the pueblo. A father just like Tom. Tom asked the sheriff why Joe had been killed by this man. The sheriff said it was going to be difficult to explain. And who was he? Just an ordinary guy, said the sheriff, like you or me. I've known him all my life. Tom sat there trying to think of a better question, trying to think like a policeman, the only sort of actual thought left to him. It was a terrible thing to be thinking at all. To be thinking in any shape or form about the murder of his own son felt like a self-inflicted torment.

It had been hot in the parking lot outside but this room was like a fridge. He could feel the sweat going chill inside his shirt. The little rental car outside looked like an abandoned thing. It was in his eyeline through the glass door. He wanted to bring Joe home. He would never bring him home. Not Joe himself.

'You come home with me, Mr Kettle, and we'll fix you some supper. Okay?' said the sheriff, getting up.

Tom was surprised. He could have been in Ireland, only fifty years ago. Courtesy.

'Come on, Mr Kettle,' said the sheriff, now holding open the door for him. The New Mexico heat hurried in. 'You come with me. And I'll try to explain. It ain't easy to say these things to a father.'

They drove in the sheriff's pick-up to one of the new houses, with its little handful of small trees. His wife was a young woman and she was cooking away in the kitchen. Soon the food was brought in and Tom sat at their plastic table, but the sheriff didn't seem to be hungry. He had a cigarette pack in one hand and he was turning it over and over. *Parliament*. There didn't seem to be any intention of taking one out and lighting it. Tom couldn't get enough of the beans. The hunger of the condemned man.

Afterwards they sat on at the table and the sheriff spoke softly.

'This man, that killed your son, was the father of a young boy himself. The child was very sick and great efforts were made to save him. His father thought a powerful witch had cursed his child. Your son didn't agree. He said it was acute anaemia and the child must go to the big hospital in Albuquerque. The boy was taken out of the care of the shaman. The father protested. He was very angry. And when the boy died in hospital, he blamed your son. I don't know if this makes any sense to you.'

'And that's why he killed him?' said Tom. His brain had flooded with a sort of unwanted understanding. It just fell through his head in a fiery flame. It was truly unwanted. He needed to hate this man. He deserved his hatred. If he saw him he thought he might try to kill him. In his mind he saw himself doing it, choking the man's neck, a man he had never seen.

'I reckon so. I'm sorry, Tom. He's just an ordinary guy. Known him all my life,' he said, repeating what he had said before. 'He's the picture of remorse. He'll get twenty years in federal prison.'

That night Tom slept on the sheriff's couch and in the morning they went over to the morgue. It had only two berths in it, in a bare room with an autopsy table crammed in.

The sheriff was deep in his own thoughts and was saying almost nothing. Tom couldn't imagine what he was thinking. There was a part of him that wanted to see the murderer, talk to him, but about what he could scarcely tell. Overnight, as he had brooded on the couch, he had contemplated what had driven this man to kill Joe. He knew that anger, the rage of Cúchulainn. Someone had to be blamed and he supposed it was easiest to blame the outsider. But he didn't know. There was a sort of innocence to a murder like that. A little boy had died. Such grief unmoors you. The sheriff wanted to show him his own son, thought it was the right thing to do, and anyway Tom needed to see him. Needed to, even if he was in a storm of sorrow. The sheriff pulled out the long tray and the long thin body was there, under a sheet. Tom took the sheet gingerly from the face. Joe, and not Joe, but Joe. It was terrible to see the wounds in the back of his head. The bullets must still be in him. Low-calibre maybe. Don't be thinking like a copper now. It was as if Tom had lost him somewhere, and now he was found. The face – eyes closed, as if Joe were holding them shut, pretending to be asleep, as he used to do as a child – was dark and queerly serene. Like a death mask. But this was the actual face of his son. Joe. He loved him. In his mind he was repeating over and over the Our Father, a reflex action, and when he put his two hands on the stiff shoulders he thought of their last farewell at Dublin Airport, when he had nearly kissed his forehead. Nearly. His heart felt too large for his own body and his son was dead. His son was dead and yet Tom still wanted to comfort him, to say everything would be alright, he wanted to say that, but of course he couldn't. There was no one there with him except the sheriff. The tears that fell on Joe's face made little blotches as they briefly thawed the icy skin. And then disappeared.

When he got the body back to Dublin, Fleming took over. He just couldn't have been kinder. The cremation. The little ceremony at the graveside. The Scott Medal put in with the ashes.

He struggled through his last few years of policing. In a way more meticulous, more inspired, than ever. Even the man highest up thought he should take early retirement, but something deep in him needed to go on to the end. Then the little party and the sombre words and the happy words. Then his niche in Queenstown Castle. His wicker chair, the characterful sea, and the stolid island. And then, those quiet nine months not only of new silence, but also – what could he call it? A sort of blossoming sense of relief maybe, that the wretched Fates had done with him. Had noticed his great happiness long ago, and emblem by emblem taken it away from him. Then the day that Wilson and O'Casey came to him like Mormons, with the old rhododendron aflame at their backs. The screeching of the door and the whole thing cranked up again, like a Model T Ford.

Chapter Seventeen

His story was told and he had told it to no one.

How lightened he was. He marvelled at it. He should by rights have been weighed down further. But no, there was something about these deep summer days that he found delightful. The sea seemed to shrug in the heat, and how much of it was burned into the air was anyone's guess. Mr Tomelty's garden prospered, his plants grew taller in their beds, and their flowers opened into an ideal world. Every night Mr Tomelty did his tour with the hose. You might think the sound was rain but there was no rain. This was a rare summer and Tom sat in it gratefully. If Fleming had put him on some sort of advisory wage, he never saw it in his bank account. Second thoughts, no doubt. Mature reflection. It was only his pension crept in there, week by week, in a pleasing accumulation. He noticed he ate less, and sparely drank, even water. There was his old face in the mirror as he shaved, but he didn't feel any age, really. He thought he could do some sparkling police work if he were called upon to do it. He knew that could not happen now but he was ready. Like a Boy Scout. Wilson and O'Casey left him alone, and in his official mind he knew they would be gathering their ammunition against Byrne. He hoped to God they would not hold back on his account. He was 99 per cent sure they wouldn't. Let each man pay for his crimes in due course. Each woman. The nature of things demanded it. He believed that.

He went into town some weeks later and asked Mr Prendergast if he knew a good carpenter.

'Well, you don't want a bad one, anyhow,' said Mr Prendergast, his wife as usual like a dim moon in the shadows. And recommended his brother-in-law, who duly came out to the castle and tore out the beauty board – regretfully, an antique now, he called it – and put up what he called a 'suite' of shelves. This was three days' work, Tom paid him, cleaned up after him, and at last opened the boxes of books and got them up on their new perches. As he tottered on the chair he felt a curious excitement, like he was twenty years old and had just moved in. He was an old man and he hadn't. But.

How was he properly to praise the resplendent paradise of the garden? Mr Tomelty had outdone himself and the weather had of course conspired with him, but to sit in it, to leave his little lean-to flat and sit in it, on the rickety metal seat, with the airships of the big bumblebees bursting into digitalis, lupins, summer phlox, and the smell of the sea making his senses fizz, and the sweet composure put on everything by the light – what simple joy. For some reason, he thought, the human person was designed for this. The summer's justice, the planet's mercy. There couldn't be anything greater. His yellow togs were much in use and he didn't bother with Killiney or White Rock, or even the Vico Rock, which was the closest swimming place, but delicately, inch by chill inch, dipped himself in the water below the house. Ten feet out you could see the water deepen and the movement of the current stiffen, like a vast muscle, flattened out by some unseen hammer. You could see the marks of the blows on the surface, pockmarks shining a moment and vanishing, sparkles burning for a millisecond and dying. Sure even strangers came out to be in Dalkey in the summer. There were cars moving all day along Coliemore Road. He didn't blame them. Himself, he *immersed* himself in it. The sense of the epic nature of the channel, and the heavy island to cap the view – he took so much pleasure from it that it made him laugh to himself. A big man, yes, a paunchy man, with strong arms, his bashed old face, his thinning mop, but in the privacy of swimming, the privacy, he could just as well have been Johnny Weissmuller.

Coming up from the garden on one of these special days, and passing along the front of the house – a little indelicately, he thought, and he hoped the late Mrs Tomelty wouldn't mind, as he only had a towel around his waist, and his 'summer' clothes over a damp arm – a person unknown came in the gate. He looked hesitant and forceful in the same instant. He was a tall enough fellow with dark hair and a beard. About six feet tall. Thirty, thirty-five. Tom's policeman's brain whirred. Now preternaturally youthful again, if only to himself, it whirred all the more efficiently. Feeling incommoded by his outfit, Tom let the man pass, but the man himself stopped, and seemed confused by there being two doors. Tom solved that puzzle for him somewhat by stepping into his flat, and the man went on to the second door.

The primary school in the village had closed for the summer and indeed Tom often saw the little boy wandering about the garden, absorbed in his own thoughts. He didn't seem to have any playmates. No one as far as Tom was aware ever visited Miss McNulty, but he couldn't be sure. When she was rehearsing she would be gone out the gate at eight and he supposed the little boy was under the care of his grandfather. He had not even set eyes on this man again – he seemed to have the gift of invisibility. A very few times he had seen his back going away up towards the village, even though he believed the man owned the white Mini that was parked on the road. He thought Miss McNulty had told him that her father was an engineer and often had work that took him away down the country, but he couldn't remember when she had told him that, or even where.

He changed his clothes as smartly as he could and didn't even bother to dry himself properly. He was anxious now and bothered. He was in a bit of a hurry and of course slowed himself considerably because of that. He managed to step awkwardly into a leg of his trousers and fell loudly onto the wooden floor. Cursing himself, he finished the job just sitting there, like an eejit, like a man who had never put on his own trousers before. A bloody baby. Then he opened his front door to keep some sort of lookout and went back into the sitting room, and looked down into the garden. There was nothing stirring. The plants were as still as painted things. There was a lovely glassy grey light on the water but he didn't have eyes for that now either. He thought, in fulfilling his commission from Miss McNulty, he should just go into the main house and check what was going on. He had no official standing, he was aware, but she had communicated to him her worries. That was a human matter if not a police matter. He realised in that moment that he had never even heard the boy speak, or not to him. He had often heard the boy singing as he played about the garden. 'Weela Weela Walya' was one of his songs, a savage old thing that Tom himself liked. *There was an old woman that lived in the woods, weela weela walya. She stuck her penknife in the babby's back, weela weela walya.* If he only heard scraps of it, sure he knew the words already.

But when he stuck his head in the front door there was only silence in the little hall, and the dead bluebottles on the sills. That was a sure sign that Mrs Tomelty *was* deceased, he thought. There were cobwebs on the ceiling, and last autumn's leaves still lay in a corner, dry as crinoline. A few disregarded envelopes on the floor. Really it was like a deserted house.

It was very frustrating. The old castle seemed to absorb people, entombing them in silences. Feeling a bit foolish, he trailed back to his flat. But just as he did so he heard a commotion, as Billy Drury might have written, on the road. Small cries of No, No, in the tinny tones of a boy whose voice has not broken, and a gruffer voice giving orders, and a car door slamming, and then another. By the time Tom reached the gate and looked out, a car was pulling away in a blind hurry. The little boy had resourcefully opened the tiny triangular side window, and although it was too small even for his head, Tom thought he heard the age-old word, with an age-old terror in it: *Help.*

'Stop, stop!' Tom shouted, the very picture of a policeman, heaving himself towards the car. And he saw the bearded man's head turn, and look at him a second, an expression of pure *depravity* on the handsome face. The passage between all the parked cars each side of the Coliemore Road was clear for about a hundred yards – Tom's brain calculating – and the man's path was only blocked at Coliemore Harbour, where there were plenty of people strolling around, and the road chock-a-block. So Tom set off at a run not very convenient to his body, but suddenly feeling a queer vivacity, like he was a young policeman. His legs seemed to thunder under him.

Now ahead of him the car was obliged to stop unless the driver wished to plough his way through a dozen vehicles. And here was Miss McNulty, it was quite clear it was herself even in the distance, on her way home from work as must be, flying down the further pavement with streaming black hair, and trying to tear open the car door. Good for her, he thought. Then not so good, as he saw the man drag the child from the car and, as Miss McNulty seemed to throw herself at him, strike her down to the tar with a vicious blow. The arm completely without restraint. This stupid man, such violence. Against his wife! Tom was very surprised, but why was he? On he ran, his chest heaving for breath despite his initial feeling of strength. His feet burned in their boots and the sun really made the air as thick as honey. His eyes were interfered with by the sweat springing up on his brow. Jesus Christ, he was an old wreck after all. But on he went. Maybe he would have a heart attack and just end in ignominy and absurdity.

The husband's inspiration now seemed to consist of leaving his wife where she lay and dragging the child down with him into the dell of Coliemore Harbour. The road was twenty feet higher than the water, so the little stone path between the fishermen's huts was steep, and ended at the harbour wall. Now Tom had reached the abandoned car at least, and went to Miss McNulty's aid. He didn't know if she was dead or alive. She was certainly out cold. He lifted her to a grassy bank at the other side of the road and laid her down, gently as he could. Two women rushed to assist him, and knelt to her. That was all he could do for the minute. He asked the ladies to phone for an ambulance in the Coliemore Hotel, said he was an off-duty policeman, though they hadn't asked as such, and hurried to the sea wall and looked down. Mrs Tomelty's unicorn was standing on the little beach. Pay it no heed. There was the man already in the little ferryman's boat, without any sign of the ferryman, and he was dragging on the starter rope to get the outboard going. The little boy sat on the bench behind him, crying and gripping the seat, as if that might help him. Now the engine growled into life, and at the sound the actual ferryman burst from his hut, looking about urgently, like a cattleman sensing a rustler, but it was too late. The little boat, no more than a rowing boat really, surged out of the harbour and into the open channel.

But where was the idiot going? What was he going to do? Kill his child in a rowing boat? Drown him? Fling him into the current? Could a father kill his own child? Of course he could, thought Tom. So how was he going to stop him? There was no other craft there ready, and nothing with an outboard motor. Now the little boat was halfway across to the island. Was he going there? Oh, he longed for helicopters, speedboats, coastguards, but there was only the clement peace of a summer's day in Dalkey.

On a desperate inspiration he went running back again towards home. Coliemore Road was on a mild incline and he had the seemingly gentle slope against him. It was a torment, a torture, his old body now was racked by pain. It seemed to take an age, moving with this hardship through the treacly air. This was real pain, dark pain, pain that sapped your strength. But he was indifferent, indifferent, let him suffer, why should he not suffer? After two minutes of this merciless Olympics, he gained the little cottage of McGillicuddy, and climbed the steps in a lather of misery to the balcony. Here it was almost a relief to stand at the gun and its tripod, and train the excellent sight on the man and little boy. They had reached the island and through the sight he could see the man trying to tie up the boat. The little boy was still in his place on the bench. Tom had to make a calculation. Often and often as a detective he had had to do it. This child in danger. Tom checked that McGillicuddy had loaded the rifle. He pulled back the bolt and a spent cartridge flew out like a hummingbird. The man had the boat moored, he was turning full face to fetch the boy. A clear shot. Three hundred yards. Steady yourself, Tom. You have one chance to fire. Calm now, like a ballerina on pointe. Move not. Say the marksman's prayer, breathe out, breathe not. And fire.

Oh, Thomas Kettle. He went back to his flat, sat in his chair, keeping his eye all the while on the island. After half an hour or so had passed, he watched the noble Dunleary lifeboat surge up the channel and take the little boy aboard. He would have expected to see the coastguard, or better still a police or emergency chopper. It might be a terrible thing now to be that little boy, with his own father killed in front of him. It might be a terrible thing. Tom considered that. While he considered, no one came to find him. Neither Miss McNulty nor anyone else. Nor the grandfather, nor McGillicuddy, nor his colleagues in the police. No one. He thought, I am myself in a sense no one. No one comes to no one. So be it. But he was absolutely certain they would come. Just not yet. The wicker chair seemed curiously soft under him. Fitted him to perfection. He lit his last cigarillo and smoked it almost playfully. The day burned on into evening and when the sun went down behind him, broad acres of dimmed light were created on the generous expanse before him. The lighthouse beyond the island looked like a little steamer forever setting out. Eternally going nowhere. The cormorants sat faithfully, trustingly, on their rocks. There was more commotion presently around the island, as a tender arrived, and no doubt the local police would call for assistance, maybe even Harcourt Street would be involved. Perhaps not. There were boys in Wexford, Wicklow, South Dublin could do just as good a job. Then they'd be looking for angles of fire, and someone would have a good eye, he did not doubt, and at some point they would get a line on McGillicuddy's terrace, and he sincerely hoped they wouldn't arrest him. It was a thing of doubtful wisdom to have a loaded gun there, untended. The little boy was alive. That had been his unspoken promise to Miss McNulty, that he would strive to preserve him from the danger posed to him. Not just as a point of official principle, but as a secret, private principle that all children must be guarded. They must have safety and if they could also have love, so much the better. To threaten a child, to bring hurt to a child, was the chief crime before God and man. It must never go unpunished. A child was a small matter by definition. Who will speak for the child? Who will act for him or her? It seemed to Tom, in the great dark of human affairs, that he could say he would. And he had done so. It was a clear moment. As clear as this sea and this island in sunlight. He had met his moment with a precise action. The boy was saved. And in that moment he knew there was contained the seed of his own salvation.

It was now 11 p.m. It should have surprised no one, and it didn't surprise him – he did it as if watching himself from above – that he went down to the concrete platform below Mr Tomelty's garden and entered the sea in his odd yellow togs. This time, and only this time, he struck out into the channel proper, leaving Winnie's ten-foot rule behind. The water was warm and fierce. The salt buoyed him up so he felt he was weirdly lying on the water and not in it. Like the very sea under him was an ancient lilo. Suddenly all the things he had loved about his life, as opposed to the things that had hurt and oppressed him, filled his heart. Filled his limbs with strength. He knew that the whirlpool lay south of the island and he knew he had to strike strongly across the current to get there. It would need determined and continuous swimming, he wouldn't be able to rest for a moment. All the things he had felt about June came into him like a boisterous crowd of messengers bearing happy news. He was filled with the noise and bustle of it. His love for Winnie, which had endured beyond death, and his love for Joe, put into his heart a sense of immense completion. He swam under the continuous glamour of the freshening moonlight. There wasn't a cloud in this late sky. All around him the water leaped with little silver flashes of moonlight. Like the sprat that would bring the mackerel in in August. And the boys with their rods on the pier. It would all go on, for ever, the little glories of life. His strokes were firm and unbroken. He felt no weariness whatsoever. He felt only a sense of pure purpose. And victory. Once he reached the whirlpool there would be no going back. He was seeking its mercy. All his life he had been bankrupt of something he could barely name. He had asked if he might have June and in doing so felt he had been stacking up a heavy debt. All his friendships, all the admiration he had felt for people, seemed to him to have been on certain calculable terms. He had suffered like all human persons, but he had also been given immeasurable happiness. Now was a moment of simple reckoning. He had borrowed from the whirlpool and he would give back what was owed.

When he reached the circling currents, he was surprised how gently they took him round and round, decreasing all the time in circumference as he was drawn to the centre. Then he was plucked down, deep down. Even under the water he was astonished that breathing was possible. His body felt bright, dolphin-like, adaptive. He was drawn down further and then he was rising again, rising, and then he was surfacing from sleep in his own bed.

It wasn't as if he was confused. One moment he was in the water, the next waking. Coming to, snapping to. Oh, had he dreamt the little boy in danger, had he dreamt that strong swimming? Could any man have crossed the channel like he had just done? Maybe it was not possible.

Kol Nidrei creeping in from next door . . . The shot with the rifle was more than possible, though, that was not in doubt. He was proud of that shot. Three hundred yards. Put him down like a cormorant! His room was dark, though he thought by the glints in the window that it must be early morning, the very first sparks of dawn, the sun waking on the far horizon, lifting its ancient crown. He was shaking his head at himself and his stupidity, picking the grainy sleep from his eyes, when he realised that there was a woman sitting on the chair beside the bed. She was sitting on the chair and looking at him. Well, he knew her. She had her hands on her legs in the old way she had had of sitting, there was no mistaking it. She was only three feet from him – why had he not seen her straight away? He felt he had no need to speak, or for her to speak. It all felt entirely natural, normal. He saw she had put on a suitable dress to honour the summer, the strange summer. It looked as fresh and nice as the day she had first worn it. As the room brightened slowly, over many minutes, her face came more clearly into view. The face whose contours and colours affected him more than any other face in creation. The absolute feeling of blithe happiness that it gave him. He had no words for it. He was so grateful. He praised everything in need of praise, among gods and man. As she was so close to him after all she only needed to lean six inches forward to put her hand on the coverlet. She was smiling with the old smile, oh mercy, and it was as if he was being infused with morphine. The hand was delicate and dark, and he wondered, if he extended his own left hand to meet it, would he be able to touch her? And if he could touch her, what did that mean? He was afraid to move in case it made her vanish but at the same time he was brave enough to risk it and he extended his arm the few inches and before he knew it he was touching her warm fingers. He wanted to say something to her now alright but in a way the touching of the hands said everything he needed to say. It was like he had just met her, that very same feeling of old in the vanished café, and yet of course in the very same moment he knew everything there was to know about her. The strange privilege of that. The lovely wildness of it.